LIGHTNING IN MAY

By the same author

The Darkness of the Morning
(Bachman & Turner, 1975)

LIGHTNING IN MAY

Gordon Parker

Foreword by
Ted Willis

Bachman & Turner: London

Bachman & Turner
45 Calthorpe Street
London WC1 0HH

ISBN 0 85974 037 4

First published 1976

Computer typeset by
Input Typesetting Ltd., London

Printed and bound by Chapel River Press, Andover, Hants.

For Ann, Kim, and Tracey

The characters portrayed in this book are entirely fictitious and bear no resemblance to any person living or dead. The story however was conceived and formed on certain factual events which occurred in and around an East Northumbrian mining community during the first half of the year 1926. Although the characters are imaginary, they are, I hope, representative of some of the people in the area at that time and show how certain happenings caused normal law-abiding citizens to perform a criminal act which almost resulted in the biggest mass murder in the history of the British Isles.

Foreword
Ted Willis

The years of my childhood were the Twenties, that strange decade which was simply the first half of an intermission between two world wars. It was a period which began in a slump and ended in a depression and which saw not only the General Strike but some of the bitterest labour struggles in our history.

Life in the back streets of North London where I grew up differed in many ways from the life in the mining community which Gordon Parker describes in this superb novel, and yet, what moved and stirred me most were the similarities. It is clear that poverty and struggle produce the same kind of people, the same kind of responses, whether the background is a mining village or a city street. I found that I knew and recognised the men and women of the village of Allington in which this story is set, my memory matched them character for character. I even knew a young doctor who could have been the twin brother of the Dr John Kinghorn who is such a powerful character in this novel.

It was a master stroke on the part of the author to show us the life of Allington through the eyes of this young man. He is the stranger who comes from the outside, from what is almost another world, and he is wrapped in all the old middle-class myths and prejudices about working-class people. To him, poverty is the fault of character, a flaw in the individual, not a condition created by society. In his journey through these pages those prejudices are torn painfully away as he comes to understand the jagged truth.

This is not a history of the General Strike or of the mid-twenties and yet because of its realism *Lightning in May* tells us more than any history book. It is a work of fiction that reflects truth.

Those who had the privilege of reading Gordon Parker's first novel *The Darkness of the Morning* will need no recommendation from me. They will accept the fine writing, vivid story-telling, and above all that perceptive yet compassionate eye which makes the characters live, and they will not be disappointed.

I believe that in Gordon Parker we have a bright new talent whose work is worthy to stand alongside that of the many distinguished authors whose books have illuminated the struggles of the British people.

1

The train was older than the one before. Older, dirtier and with the smell of countless stale cigarettes impregnated deeply into the wood and faded dusty upholstery. Dr John Kinghorn looked wearily across at the empty seat opposite him, up at the tattered netting that served as a luggage rack, then directly above him to where his two bulky suitcases were held at a distance from his upturned face by the same well-worn string. Uncertain of its reliability he shuffled reluctantly along the seat to a position near the window. He tried to relax. He yawned and rubbed his travel-weary eyes as a growing feeling of depression mixed with uneasiness squirmed inside him. He sighed and thrust his hands deep into his overcoat pockets, withdrew his neck into its collar and fought against the growing desire to get out and return on the next train to London. But it was already too late. A shrill whistle echoed along the platform. There was a blast of smoke and exhaust steam from the engine and the stopping train to Berwick jerked, hesitated, then rolled forward out of Newcastle Central Station on its journey North.

It was hard for him not to try to analyse his condition. He couldn't help himself. He was a doctor, a doctor with the ink hardly dry on his degree and the words of the Hippocratic Oath still almost complete in his mind. His profession was still a novelty to him and it was difficult for him not to couch his observations in some medical diagnosis or explanation. He had watched the slim, middle-aged woman who had sat opposite him in the train from London. He had glanced cautiously at her from behind his newspaper several times. He noted the coarseness of her skin and the prominent excited eyes. He saw the slight tremor of her hands and fingers. Like a practised detective he mentally assessed the clues for and against and became convinced the high buttoned collar of her blouse concealed a swollen thyroid. Did she know? Was she receiving treatment? He had been tempted to ask, just to satisfy himself that his diagnosis was correct. His mind opened the well-thumbed medical books and silently he recited to himself. "Thyroid gland. The thyroid gland belongs to the endocrine system or ductless glands of internal secretion. It is situated in the neck and consists of two lobes with a narrow isthmus connecting them.

Excessive secretion of the thyroid gland causes a disease known as exophthalmic goitre . . ." He smiled behind his paper as he realized that he could remember it all if he wanted to. But he had said enough. He was satisfied. The mental consultation of the woman opposite had been positive and productive.

Then there was the short, fat man who sat in the corner from Peterborough to York with his legs splayed open and his enormous belly almost resting, like his podgy hands, on his kness. He had been fidgeting and easing his weight from buttock to buttock, his red face twisting with an embarrassed flush. Ulcer perhaps? Acting up after a gutful of beer, the fumes of which he now liberally distributed around the carriage with every breath. Possible – but perhaps not. Perhaps only painful wind bubbling around in his enormous innards. It could have been a multitude of things in fact, but John Kinghorn settled for haemorrhoids. Distressing thing, haemorrhoids. Gave one not only pain but such a feeling of insecurity.

Insecurity – that particular feeling gnawed at him at that very moment and brought his thoughts back to his present predicament. He gazed out of the smutty window into the gathering gloom of a January evening, but he saw nothing of the moving backcloth of huddled, stifling buildings. His introspection enveloped all of his senses and his depression increased. He cursed his impulsiveness and the quick temper that had catapulted him away from the plushness of the upper class civilisation to this back-of-beyond corner of England. Yet a few days before, the prospect of putting a few hundred miles between himself and William Fitzgerald Kinghorn, ex colonel R.A.M.C. and now enjoying all the importance and ascendancy that Harley Street could bestow on a successful physician and surgeon, had seemed like moving from darkness into sunrise. But now it didn't. In the stark light of reality it was different. All his excitement and grandiose ideas had disintegrated with each clickety-clack of the wheels on the rails.

Why should he join the Army? Why should he! Just because his father and his father before him had done stirling work sewing up great holes in men that had been blown asunder defending a little piece of land or a nebulous political doctrine. It was enough that his eminent father had talked him into studying medicine at all. But now after all those years of forceful self discipline, he was damned if he was going to waste it practising butchery in reverse on ignorant soldiers that destroyed each other with relish, then perambulated their soulless bodies around in flea-ridden garrets with pox-ridden foreign tarts. His ideas on being a doctor were different. He felt a cut above that. Let his old man call him a shirker and a coward. He could scream till he was blue in the face that the Kaiser and those like him would try again. If that was the case, let them get on with it. Let them all do their shooting and devastating and let the doctors that fancied it piece together the slimy jigsaws that once were human beings. His patients would be proper patients who by life's mischance and no fault of their own needed his help. He had seen them – people in pain – ill and diseased wanting help, relief, a cure for their agony and torment. Doctors should have respect. They should be looked up to, revered for their skill and knowledge. They were much more than the common or garden working class. They held life and death in their hands. After all, weren't they the last resort before God? Hadn't he heard patients calling out for a doctor to relieve their suffering? And when the medicine could no longer help, they asked God. Always God in the last resort. The doctor, then God.

But it seemed that after his endless journey, he had travelled beyond the domain of even the Almighty. As the train sped smoothly across the flat neutral countryside of Yorkshire in winter, the fields clinging relentlessly to the faded colours of the previous year gave way to the raw, usurping symbols of industry. The city of Durham had been his last glimpse of beauty. He had looked down from the high, elevated station to the cramped conglomeration of quaint narrow streets, the meandering river and the steadfast decorum of the Cathedral and Castle. Ancient, steeped in history. A seat of learning and philosophy, snuggling away from the vulgar encroaching architecture that exploited nature like a malignancy. The train had moved on, passing great sombre spoil heaps, black and grey and streaked with rusty red. They loomed and faded, the wheels and struts of the pit heads that caused them dwarfed against their massiveness. Then came more fields, giving a comparative blast of colour, then more heaps and smoke-blackened buildings. Then more fields – ploughed this time, patiently awaiting the rejuvenating spring. But even the colour of the earth was different. It had darkened as though in sympathy with its surroundings. Gone was the rich red-brown of the South. Gone was the vibrant hubbub of London. And gone was his impetuous notion that he had acted wisely.

The Berwick train slowed then stopped. He rubbed at the window with his fist but there was little to see in the darkness. There were double tracks, polished from constant use and illuminated by the scant light thrown down from the carriages in front and behind him. Then an expanse of black nothingness and only in the distance the faint twinkling of lights that meant there were others alive besides him. He gazed at the speckles, picturing in his mind the people that lived or worked under them. They seemed so remote, alien, on another world perhaps. Then suddenly the lights were gone, hidden by the roaring giant that sped past. He had time to register only a blur of green, then a dazzle of illuminated carriages, then as quickly as it manifested itself it was gone. The express to Edinburgh had flashed through the night, leaving the scene darker and more silent than before. Away in the distance, the lights still twinkled. He sighed and fished in his pocket for matches. He pulled the little dangling chain on the lamp above the window. It hissed and then plopped into life. Yet in the feeble yellow glow his world seemed even stranger and unreal.

As his train began to move again he wondered what they would be like, really like, these miners. He knew his friend Smythe's outburst that they ate their young was exaggerated, but to what degree, he didn't know. He did know that he was heading into a cauldron of unrest. Industrial unrest – the newspapers had been full of it for months. The miners had been at odds with the coal owners and the Government for years in fact. Ever since the boom days of 1920 had deteriorated into depression there had been trouble with pitmen. Agitating, arguing, demanding more money. God, he thought, more money! They think it grows on trees, these fellows. They think there's nothing to do but keep a machine printing pound notes day and night until everyone's got their pockets full. And for what? There's not one of them had to cram his head full of chemistry or Latin or biology. No fourteen hour days for them. No skill. No learned judgement. No irrevocable decisions that could mean a cure or a coffin. He rubbed his eyes and yawned again. The whole world seemed to be seething with unrest. Baldwin had said that not only the miners but all workers would have to accept less money if Britain was to stand on her own two feet again. He smiled. Less money – that had caused one hell of a stir. But all the political and industrial shenanigans bored Dr John Kinghorn to tears. He had no time and little inclination to bother himself with the intricacies of labour disputes or the eulogising of politicians and their T.U.C. counterparts. There had been the so-called "Black Friday" back in '21 when a threatened general strike had fizzled out, the "Red Friday" just the summer before when the Government reluctantly agreed to set up a Royal Commission to investigate the problems of the coal industry and subsidise it temporarily. Other than that he knew of only an avalanche of threats, pleas and demands as recorded in the press. But that was in the days when he was miles away. Now he was there, among them. Their problems would inevitably spill out over the surgery table and envelope him.

He cursed himself again. He was like a fish out of water. Everything around was alien to him. The scenery, the people, their trades and ideas. How he wished he had joined Smythe at Bognor. He could have been comfortably reassuring rich old ladies with a minimum of fuss and maximum of adoration. But that wasn't really his style either. The train gathered speed in the wake of the Edinburgh express. Allington, Dr Robert Jenkins. How he wished he had never heard of the place or the man.

The night air was still and cold and held a thick dampness in suspension when the train stopped at the tiny station of Allington. It had been less than an hour since it left Newcastle, but for John Kinghorn it had felt as long as the journey from London. The grime of the carriage had made him feel dirty himself, and as he heaved his two suitcases down onto the wet platform, the freezing mist that enveloped him did nothing to alleviate his feelings. He looked along to where the engine panted impatiently. There was no-one. No fellow passengers, no porters, only a sparse row of gas lamps that whispered to themselves and gave a sickly form to the low station building that supported them.

He turned and slammed the carriage door and the sound magnified by the heavy air echoed, then was lost in the darkness. A figure appeared from a doorway, a thin figure, small and stooped. It glanced quickly towards him and hesitated for a second before the shrill whistle was blown. There was a hiss of vented steam and a blast of smoke that sent sparks billowing skyward and the train moved away into the night.

He watched it disappear, almost mesmerised by the failing image of the guardsvan. In a few seconds he had been transposed from the relative comfort and confines of a train to the frightening emptiness of a silent unknown station. He felt a strange sensation of nakedness as though he had been thrust into some vast arena and the crowd were hushed, their breath caught in wondering expectancy. But there was nothing – no crowds – only one pair of eyes and a tiny poorly lit station and the smell of sulphurous smoke from the departed train.

"D'ye want this station, mister?" The voice was hoarse, yet high pitched.

His weariness turned to anger. "This is Allington isn't it?" he snapped.

"Aye."

"Then if this is Allington, this is where I want to be. I'm not in the habit of getting out at the wrong station."

The stooped figure seemed to stoop even further for a second as though nodding an apology. "I'll take the cases," he whispered.

"Yes and get me a taxi, will you?"

The man gave a little laugh, softly with his tongue between his teeth. He picked up the cases. "Eeh there's nowt like that here, mister." He put the cases down again and scrutinised the stranger through screwed up eyes. "But I'll wheel them on me cart. That is, if you're not goin' far."

The doctor shrugged, more a gesture of despair as the porter scuffled away without waiting for an answer. He followed him under the canopy of the station office through the shadowy porch and found him under the brighter lamp of the street outside. The cases were again at his feet and as the doctor approached him his bloodless lips thinned into a smile.

"Y've come a long way," he said more as a question.

"Yes, I've come a long way," he answered impatiently.

The porter's features matched his slight figure. His hair was thin and flat and parted in the middle. His dry wrinkled face had an almost oriental look as it creased even further into a broad grin showing a set of brown crooked teeth. "From London ah'll bet?"

He exhaled noisily through his nose. "Yes from London. Now where's this damned cart."

"Y're young, younger than I thought y'd be, but man y're a sight for sore eyes. We've been waiting y'know – Tommy and me and the lads. He's a grand lad is Tommy. Me and him are marras. He'll go far with a bit of help, will Tommy. But we need to know the right way like. We've been waitin' to find out how you lads think we should go on."

John frowned. "Waiting? For me? And who the hell is Tommy?"

The porter took hold of his arm and shook it gently. "Y'know man Tommy Nesbitt – we've been waitin' for weeks."

The doctor's irritability surged upward. He pulled himself savagely away from the spindley fingers. "For Christ's sake, man," he hissed vehemently, "I don't know who you're talking about or who you think I am. I want Doctor Jenkins, Doctor Robert Jenkins. Now will you kindly produce this cart or just direct me and I'll find the damned house myself."

The porter's eyes widened and rounded for the first time and he stood for a second with his mouth stupidly agape before turning and propelling his stooped body back into the confines of the station. He muttered what sounded like an apology as he reappeared with a squeaking hand cart. He glanced at the stiff upright figure under the lamp, then heaved the cases onto it.

"Dr Jenkins lives up the road in the village, about five minutes walk," he growled through his whisper.

John thrust his hands deep into his coat pockets as he followed him along the path. "Look – I'm sorry," he said softly, "I've had a long day. I'm rather tired."

The porter nodded. "We don't get many strangers here," he said as though explaining his mistake.

John looked ahead of him through the glistening mist to where the road developed into a broader street of terraced yellow bricked houses. "Yes, I can imagine," he said dryly.

They walked steadily along, past dimly lit windows, the wheels of the cart squeaking gently in time with their steps. A flood of questions came into John's head, relevant questions about the place, the people and Dr Jenkins but his weary mind dismissed them. He was there, in Allington, for that night at least. That was the regrettable fact. He was cold and hungry and at that particular point in time the prospect of a warm bed wherever it might be was enough to pacify him.

It was the porter that broke the silence. "Aye – it's Dr Jenkins y'want. He's got the big house in the village there. Y've never been here before?" he added, the question coming as an unmistakable hint for the doctor to explain his presence in full.

"No, never."

The porter nodded knowingly. He thought for a second or two then turned a smiling face toward his companion. "Ye just visiting?" he sang.

"No."

He frowned, straining his mind for another ploy. "We don't get many strangers here 'specially from London," he said at last, forgetting he had already said it.

John took his eyes away from the relative brightness of the approaching village. He looked down at the stooped figure hunched over the handles of the cart with his elbows stuck out like the flippers on a penguin. "No, so you said, " he murmured gently, "but you were expecting one."

The porter's brow tightened and he gave a nervous cackle. "Oh aye, a friend of me mate's, that's all. He - er, he promised to come an' see us. He's a friend of Tommy Nesbitt, y'see. Tommy lives over by – at Bolam Colliery. Works in the drift there. What's your line o' business?"

"I'm nothing to do with the colliery."

The porter's high pitched whisper went flat. "No, no I thought not."

The cart creaked on. The row of houses petered out and gave way on the right to a shanty town of allotments, wooden huts and warped greenhouses. On the left there was only the pavement between them and the darkness of fields beyond. Ahead, the village of Allington seemed to snuggle around the square squat tower of the church. As they neared it John allowed himself a question. "Are there many people live in this area?"

The porter was quick with his answer, eager to rekindle the conversation. "Oh aye – a canny few – mebbe two or three hundred. But there's Bolam Colliery down the road y'know an' . . . "

John cut him short. "Are they all on Dr Jenkins' books?"

The porter hesitated. "Aye," he said cautiously, "all the village and Bolam and the big houses down t'other road."

"You'll be on his books then."

"Oh aye. Never been to see him, mind. Not for a canny while, not for medicine, that is. He's . . . "

"He's what?"

"Nowt," the porter snapped. "I'm as fit as I need t'be and so's the wife."

"Good. You'll not be needing me then."

"How's that?"

"I said you won't need me. I'm Dr Jenkins' new assistant."

The porter stopped. He studied his companion once more through screwed up eyes. "Ah, so you're a doctor, eh, I should've guessed," he said before continuing his journey. "Y'sound all educated like. Y'sound like a doctor." He laughed again with his tongue between his teeth. "A doctor or a vicar mebbe."

They entered the village. There wasn't much to see in the weak diffuse glow of the lamps. The church dominated the centre and at first glance it seemed like any of a thousand villages in the country with old stone built houses facing into the square adjacent to the church. There was a public house, some small windowed shops and a large red-bricked Co-op. The road they were on led in from the West and curved around the churchyard on its way East. There was one other road that led into the square from the South. Other than that there was little more to see.

"Dr Jenkins' house is here."

John Kinghorn fixed his gaze on what was to be his new home. The house was in keeping with the others around it, but back about twenty yards from the road. It was stone built with small Georgian windows. The garden was orderly for January and several leafless fruit trees stood dolefully dripping water. He inhaled deeply. So this was it. This was from where the advertisement had emanated and wrenched him so far away from his own kind.

The porter held the gate open with his back and pulled the cart in.

"Are you lodgin' here doctor?" he said as they neared the blue painted front door.

"Yes, I suppose so. Where's the surgery, do you know?"

"It's round the side there. Y'get in through a glass lean-to an' the waitin' room's in the hall at the bottom of the stairs."

John nodded. Still filled with apprehension he steeled himself before pulling the bell knob.

The porter placed the cases beside him and gave a quick humble salute with one finger to his brow.

"Here," said John and held out his hand.

The porter took the coin and held it up. He gave a low whistle. "Here – that's half a crown. My, that's kind of ye doctor. Thank you sir."

John waved away the gratitude. "Think nothing of it. Thanks for your help."

The porter trundled his cart down the garden path. He closed the gate behind him. "Best of luck, doctor sir," he shouted hoarsely.

"Thank you," came the bored, stiff reply.

The porter gripped the half-crown tightly in his left hand and pushed the lightened cart with the other. He began whistling an unrecognisable tune. His mind saw pint after pint being drawn at the Fat Ox later that night and then suddenly he laughed out loud and the laugh became a ridiculous giggle. He had just realised and laid bets with himself that Ethel Friar knew nothing about the new doctor and when she did there would be bedlam in that house for many a day to come.

2

Ethel Friar lifted her pinafore. She lifted it slowly, gathering it up with trembling nervous fingers. She raised it to her face which was red and hot, and wiped away a glistening sheen of sweat from her brown. Her underclothes stuck uncomfortably to her skin and her chest rose and fell as she heaved air into her lungs. She felt sick and dizzy as she let the pinafore drop and placed a hand against the wall for support as she turned to survey the stairs. Her eyes ran from the bottom to the top, mentally tracing the contours of each angular, carpet-covered step. Each time they seemed steeper, each time longer and more difficult to manage. Her top lip, smooth but with a down of fine hair, quivered as she fought against the tears that threatened. The stairs grew more difficult – the times more frequent. She glanced again to the top and listened. She nodded in grim satisfaction. He was still quiet. He was still asleep.

She smoothed her pinafore down over her grey ankle-length dress and as the nausea passed she struggled to regain her composure with a sniff and a defiant upward thrust of her chin. She walked haughtily past the dozen or so brown cane chairs arranged in two straight rows, deftly patting at the tight round bun gathered at the back of her head. She glanced at the mahogany grandfather clock that stood guard at the right of the surgery door. Its tick was loud and came with a measured, tantalising slowness. Twenty past five, it read. Her facade of regal aloofness sagged for a moment and she gave a deep shuddering sigh. Normally the hall-cum-waiting room would have been populated by wheezing chests, barking coughs and the screaming of children giving vent to their boredom. But today it was silent; the brown cane chairs, the paint worn thin by a thousand assorted backsides, were empty. Only the clock registered its mechanical presence. Tall, sturdy: the eternal sentinel. Unruffled, unhurried, impartial.

She had to give this doctor of hers one morsel of credit at least. He still had a spark of sense. He had had the good grace to drink himself into a stupor on his afternoon off. But then it wasn't only his afternoon off. It could have been Saturday or Sunday or Monday night or any night. He was erratic, unpredictable and the uncertainty of it all was beginning to show. She was barely forty-nine, but at times like this she felt sixty. It wasn't so long ago that her face had been fresh and youthful enough for her years and her body straight and firm. But now the imperceptible daily changes were beginning to show. Her face was lined and tired, her flesh flaccid, her hair coarse and an accelerating grey. She remembered with vivid clarity the early days, when her position as housekeeper to Dr Robert Jenkins had progressed to its inevitable end and he had taken her with fairy-tale gentleness and a quiet radiating passion to his bed. They had hurt no-one. There was no bitter-sweet stigma of adultery. He was a bachelor, she a widow, and their relationship became as normal as man and wife but with all the added excitement of a surreptitious tryst. Even after almost thirty years of conventionality, the fact that they were not legally joined kept a spark of novelty dancing between the opposing poles of their bodies. But the fact that they had never married had done something else to Ethel Friar. She had not been an easy conquest. Her experience of men before she came to Plessey House had been short and a nightmare of pleasure and pain. For that reason she had been cautious, suspicious – downright afraid. She took her time. She ignored (or pretended to) his subtle, suggestive chit-chat. But he gradually melted her ice-cold properness and when she finally allowed him to take her, she gave herself with a ferocious animal enjoyment that seemed to bond them for life. There are times, however, in any relationship, when the passion is gone and the heavy breathing bodies must relax and replenish the dulled senses of love. It was during these times that Ethel Friar took stock of her position. She somehow knew even then that marriage was irrelevant, unimportant. Yet the security it could bring was important to her now. She had moved from the drab regimented rows of pit cottages at Bolam to the relative plushness of a doctor's house. She was free from the cloth-capped rabble who drank and swore and paraded around in wooden clogs, with braces hanging free over their pants. She hated them, everyone of them at Bolam Colliery. They were ignorant peasants. Evil, cruel people. Even their daily intrusion into the waiting room set her nerves jangling and forced her to the farthest corner of Plessey House away from their noises and images. That was the prime reason why Ethel Friar had become so possessive. She had realised long ago that if she provoked the doctor's displeasure she could find herself back among the people outside the confines of Plessey House and that prospect terrified her. So with a premeditated exactness she looked to her lover's every wish. She moulded her very being to please him, to impress him and for almost thirty years, her subtle cunning controlled him and everything in Plessey House. It was her house and he was hers to do with as she pleased.

But for the last six months there had been a change. Dr Robert Jenkins began drinking. In his fifty-ninth year, after a lifetime of an elegant aperitif, a glass of Chablis or Burgundy followed by a savoured cognac, he had suddenly, for no apparent reason to her, began to wallow in gin and whisky or any other alcohol that was to hand. Not in her company, not as a pleasant fore-runner to nicer things as she had been used to, but in secret, alone; with no finesse or decorum but with all the pig-like qualities that she thought could only exist outside the walls of her domain. Yet she had come to terms with it. Her gentle but forceful advice had been ignored. So her agile, calculating mind had taken on another role – that of the sympathetic saint, the holier-than-thou, with the maximum of understanding and the minimum of moralising. But her playacting ability was now being stretched to the limit. The strain of years of it was beginning to tell. Yet she didn't hate him. She didn't have any feelings for him at all. He was there and he was necessary for her security and comfort. So with an impeccable air of tolerance she now regularly coaxed, guided and sometimes carried the bleary-eyed, slavering doctor from his study up the stairs to his bed.

It didn't take her long to clear up the mess. She picked up the bottle that had fallen from the table and mopped up the whisky that was slowly settling into the carpet. The room was oppressive with the smell of alcohol and stale tobacco smoke and she strutted quickly to the window, wafting away the stifling odours with quick irritated flicks of her hand. The cold night air that gushed in felt good on her face. She stood for a moment breathing the thin icy mist into her lungs, then let the curtain fall back and returned to her housekeeping. She poked at the fire that was piled high with roaring coal and shook her head, cursing herself for leaving him alone that afternoon and cursing him for the annoying defiant streak that was growing in him. He knew she didn't like the fire banked high. He knew she didn't like wasting the coal. He knew that. Countless times in the past she had told him – not as a chastisement, but gently, sweetly – in normal conversation. If she had been there that afternoon, she would have seen to the fire. She would have appeared just at the right time and placed just the right amount on the glowing, settling embers. She straightened up and gave a mirthless smile to the billowing yellow flames. She would tell him again, just as soon as he was able to understand. She would invent a little story to emphasise her point and at the same time mentally scream at him to hear and obey.

She raised her eyes to the mantelpiece but ignored the row of Doulton figurines that postured romantically in front of her. She gazed at her own image in the ornate mirror that hung above them. There was a wisp of hair hanging down over her left ear and her dark, sunken eyes were heavy lidded and tired. She bit gently at her thin, pale lips to bring some colour to them and moved her oval face from side to side as she examined it. Did the doctor see her as she saw herself? She hoped not. She was losing her beauty – that was an undisguisable fact. Time was gradually moulding her features into hard yet sagging lines, but she turned quickly from the mirror dismissing the thought from her mind. She would prove her doctor still needed her. Later when he was sober she would go to him. She would slip between the warm sheets and slide her body against his. She would whisper softly in his ear and let her hands stimulate him. Then he would have her, gently at first but accelerating his passion to an ecstatic frenzy of pleasure. Then when it was over she would lie and listen to him panting in the darkness and she would smile a smile of reassurance and peace of mind.

She turned at the door and ran her eyes quickly around the room. Everything seemed in order. She had folded the newspapers that he had left in a heap on the couch and put the lid back on the tobacco jar. It was a dull room with dark colours and staid neutral wallpaper. The walls on each side of the chimney breast were filled with books; dust collectors most of them. Volumes of encyclopaedias, never opened during Ethel Friar's reign; medical books, novels by Scott, Dickens, Lawrence; poetry by Burns, Byron and Wordsworth. A bulky edition of the *Complete Works of Shakespeare,* and a sky-blue volume entitled *The History of Freemasonry*. There was the couch and two accompanying armchairs, brown leather, shiny and old, but deep buttoned and comfortable. Against the far wall stood a pianola, a touch of Victoriana with its deep red wood and intricate inlaid entwining flowers. An occasional table and a couple of framed Hogarth prints of Old London just about completed the decor. It did not impress Ethel Friar. It was too masculine; it reflected too much of his potential independence, yet it was a good deal more tolerable to her than it once was. She had changed it over the years, gradually, with the same coaxing subtlety that she used in all things. Yet she had known when to stop. She knew when his grudging acceptance of her ideas would mature into a rebellious complaint, so she had left it when it was tolerable to her and still acceptable to him.

She reached over and turned out the gas lamp that protruded like a swan's neck out of the wall to the right of the door and the mantle shrank to a cherry red. The room was still filled with the dancing light from the fireplace and as she closed the door on it she remembered the still open window. Tutting loudly she gathered her skirt for another angry trek across the room. She swiped the curtain on one side and pulled at the sash cord window but her actions froze before she got it moving. There were shadowy figures coming down the path. There was a squeaking cart and the dull murmur of stunted conversation. Her face creased into a wondering frown as she shrank away, allowing the tan velvet curtain to obliterate her view. Her mind raced with reasons for the visitors. Surely not Tomlinson for his game of chess and distracting boring prattle about the rising cost of keeping the pit going. Not at this early hour! Or the young vicar with his well scrubbed virginal face, ever keen to glean information about his suffering flock. She flew to the kitchen removing her pinafore as she went. Damn the Village! Damn the Doctor! She knew it would happen sooner or later. Someone was sure to call or someone was certain to take a fit or a heart attack when he was only capable of staggering around in a worse state than the patient! She stood stiffly in the kitchen, checking the neck of her dress and smoothing its voluminous skirt while a dozen or more excuses for the doctor's incapacity tumbled through her brain. The bell jangled above her and she watched it as it danced at the end of the agitated spring. Finally it stopped and she breathed in deeply and slowly, straightening herself to her full regal arrogance. She forced a semblance of pleasantness to her face and walked, lightly holding her skirt, toward the door, silently cursing the outside world and praying that the noise of the bell hadn't disturbed her snoring companion upstairs.

John Kinghorn stood back from the blue painted door as the bell gave out its muffled signal from some distant mysterious point within. He looked up at the half-moon transom that was wet and clouded with the mist and eventually it became coloured with a dull yellow ochre. There was the sound of a bolt being withdrawn, a stiff reluctant bolt, then the door opened and the tall imposing figure of Ethel Friar gazed at him with an undisguisable look of puzzled distaste.

"Good evening," he said politely, trying to make the best of a bad job and bowing his head slightly in lieu of raising a hat which he seldom wore. "I'm Dr Kinghorn. I believe Dr Jenkins is expecting me."

She stood for a second, blinking in the information, her eyes travelling from his face down to the cases at each side of his legs; then she lifted her eyes again. Her nose was narrowed and a pained look crossed her face as she drew her shoulders together and held her arms rigidly under the ample swell of her breasts. She tried to speak with authority but the words came with a weak high pitched uncertainty.

"Dr Jenkins can see no one. He's – he's resting."

John's mouth formed an oval and he nodded knowingly. "I see. May I come in, I've been travelling all day."

Ethel's hand moved to her throat. Her face twisted as though it had come into contact with some vile stink, then she regained some of her composure and bent her features into a sickly smile.

"May I ask who you are?"

John bent down and picked up his cases. "I'm John Kinghorn, Dr Jenkins' new assistant. He's expecting me. Didn't you know I was coming?"

Ethel drew a quick sigh of breath as he stepped into the passage. She felt the strength drain away from her body and a searing withering rage take its place. Her hands trembled as she shut the door. It was impossible! It couldn't be true! The burbling drunken ranting that he had spouted before Christmas had been so much drivel! She had taken no notice of it. She had forgotten he had even said it. Yet he had meant it – the stupid sot had been telling the truth – and here was the proof. He had sent for this young fresh-faced stranger – without her knowing – secretly, sneakily; allowing an incongruous alien to invade their privacy.

"Yes," she whispered, as though in a dream, "oh yes, I knew you were coming." She wafted down the passage to where it expanded into an oblong lobby, her mind a turmoil of unreality. She beckoned him to follow her, her actions automatic, uncontrolled by her numbed mind.

"Are you Mrs Jenkins?" he asked.

She stopped in the lobby and turned to him. "No – no I am not Mrs Jenkins," she breathed. "Dr Jenkins is not married. I am his housekeeper. My name is Ethel Friar, Mrs Ethel Friar."

John put down the cases and held out his hand. She allowed him to take her cold, limp paw for a second but already he sensed that his presence was not welcomed.

She turned like some mechanical toy and opened the door to the lounge. "Have you travelled far?" she said in a voice that matched the weather outside.

"From London. Er, Dr Jenkins – he's not ill I hope?"

Her eyes clouded. "No, he isn' ill, Dr Kinghorn, he's tired that's all. He works very hard. Today is his day off. May I take your coat. Perhaps you will make yourself comfortable here. We usually dine at eight, until then perhaps some tea will suffice."

John nodded. "Fine. Will Dr Jenkins be down for dinner?"

She hesitated. "He may," she said, "but he was very tired."

John smiled. "Perhaps I can be of help there. He may find his work easier now that I've arrived."

Again she drew herself up and puffed out her chest like some austere workhouse matron. "You plan to stay long, may I ask?"

He shrugged. He didn't feel like admitting that he had already contemplated going home. "I don't really know. Perhaps a year. I shall see if I like the place and the place likes me."

Her lips thinned slightly. A year! Oh God no! Not in Plessey House. How could he have been so stupid. How could he do this to her after all she had done for him. "Excuse me, please," she whispered, "I'll make some tea and see to your room. You are staying with us, I take it."

John frowned. His depression surged back and his uncertainty was greater than before. "Look here, Mrs Friar, didn't Dr Jenkins inform you of our arrangement?"

She thought quickly. She felt like screaming at him to get out, to go back where he came from; that he was not wanted by her or her doctor. But she didn't get the chance.

"Of course I did – didn't I, Ethel?"

Two heads swivelled simultaneously toward the doorway. Dr Robert Jenkins stood with a hand on the door jamb, the other in the pocket of a plum coloured silk smoking jacket. He was a smallish man, but stocky and carrying a little too much weight at his middle. He had a shock of white wiry hair that at one time must have been a sandy colour. His round red face was flushed and his blue eyes deep set and watery, but he was smiling a tongue-in-cheek kind of smile that gave him an impish, childlike look. He moved forward and put a hand chumily on Ethel's left shoulder. His movement was slow and unsteady. Ethel looked at him as though he was a ghost.

"Didn't I, Ethel?" he said as a question that demanded an answer.

Her brow tightened and her face drained of colour. Her eyes flashed wildly and flicked a fraction each way as she stared into his. "You must have forgotten," she hissed.

He moved past her as John stood up. "Did I forget Ethel?" he sang in a gentle chiding voice. "Never mind." He held out his hand. The shake was firm and friendly and his watery eyes shone with a sort of sad satisfaction.

"Welcome to Plessey House. Pleased to see you, man," he whispered almost reverently. He turned toward his housekeeper and his face changed. "Ethel, will you make our guest some tea. We have lots to talk about."

Ethel forced another insincere smile to her face. "Of course, Dr Jenkins, I was just going to," she said, reverting to the formalities she had long ago discarded.

She closed the door behind her and stood for a second with her back resting against it, her fists clenched and her head toward the ceiling in some vain hope that the nightmare that had manifested itself would evaporate. But she knew it wouldn't. She knew it was real – very real. She strutted into the kitchen and put the kettle on the hob and as she spooned the tea into the big brown pot, she knew for the first time in thirty years that all her scheming and acting could be in vain. She could not accept this latest development. The stage was not big enough for another player. She looked into the pot where the tea leaves lay in a mound waiting their scalding bath and for the first time in thirty years she was tempted to spit among them or better still lace them with some poison.

3

As Edward Sneed climbed the final steps out of the Bolam drift he quickened his pace instead of allowing his fatigue to slow him down. There were four hundred steps from the bottom to the top; he knew that all too well. As a boy, when such facts were pertinent he had counted them just as his own sons had done. He had raced his young marras from the very bottom, bursting out at the surface and collapsing into a heap of laughing, panting vibrance that dispelled the effort expended and made the end of their shift an enjoyable trial of stamina. His sons had done the same with their marras and the older men would smile and gently reproach them as a fleeting nostalgia ran through their veins. Running the steps was a young lad's sport. Working underground soon stiffened the muscles and bent the bones into the characteristic bow legs and stooped backs. But on that particular day Edward Sneed hardly felt the strength-sapping incline. He was anxious to be out, to be home. He was a squat, heavily built man, normally slow in his movements and deep in his thinking. His ambling gait seemed timed to his words which were dull-toned and well rehearsed before he uttered them. It hadn't always been so. In a past that he could not forget, he had been different; but he had changed. Now there were too many memories, too much to do and too much worry.

He looked up the ascending tunnel to where its mouth, darkened with the winter evening, loomed closer. His breath billowed out with his exertion only to be snatched away, back into the abyss, by the downward draught that dried the sweat from his blackened brow, leaving it icy cold. He knew it was freezing at the surface. He could smell it long before he arrived there and saw the glistening sheen of frost that had stealthily covered the rough and tumble conglomeration of buildings at the pit head. There were trains of tubs piled high with coal, now sparkling with a dusting of white; crackling pools, ice covered in the cobbled pit yard and the freezing mist that transformed the scene into dreamlike unreality.

He was one of the first of the shift to appear from the drift. In his hurry he had left the rest of the men still stepping the four hundred steps at their usual work-tired pace. But he was anxious to be home that night. He had been on edge all day. All day he had worried about Nellie. He wondered if she had realised and had been fretting and if she had managed to keep the fire going. A surge of relief came over him as he handed in his tally and his lamp. Soon he would be home. Soon he would know that she was all right. He almost forgot it was pay day. Normally the thought would have given a touch of pleasant anticipation to the previous twenty-four hours but it had slipped his memory until he saw the queue beginning to form at the little window of the office. The extra minutes would be worth it. He could put the money in Nellie's hand as he always did, then when she had counted it help her put it in her purse. She enjoyed that. The feel of a little weight and bulkiness in her purse seemed to give her a short-lived weekly happiness that evaporated as quickly as the money which he took as needed and paid out the few shillings that enabled them to eat and exist.

It didn't take him long to draw his pay seeing that he was almost first out of the drift and soon the thin envelope containing two pound notes and a few coppers had been checked and nestled comfortably in his trouser pocket. He heard the exuberant pay-day yells of his work-mates as they emerged from the ground but he took no notice. There were other things on his mind. He turned at the gate of the pit yard and walked two sides of its perimeter to where the rough uneven track meandered across the field to the village of Bolam and No. 8 First Row. His mind tumbled with thoughts of his wife and his sons and the last ten years that seemed to have flown yet somehow dragged on for an eternity. Could it really be ten years? It seemed impossible that his frail wife could have malingered in her rickety wheelchair for so long. Or that he had cooked, washed, darned and knitted for all that time. Yet he didn't complain. Nellie was his wife and he could remember all the years when they had laughed and loved and raised their sons. She had given him twins; as alike as two peas in a pod and he had been doubly proud. Two fine boys that had grown straight and true and strong. It hadn't been easy though. Their struggle to feed and clothe them had also been doubled. Yet it had been well worth it. He remembered with vivid clarity the day he had led them to the pit, their imaginary emergence into manhood causing them to strut haughtily, their beaming faces held high as they joined the legion of workers. And Edward Sneed had glowed inwardly with a father's satisfaction that is complete and unique.

Maudy Fenwick's shop showed faintly through the mist. It was at the end of First Row which was made up of thirty or so stone built terraced cottages that stretched away in a line to be met at right-angles by Second Row. Together they made up the village of

Bolam. It was not a pretty village. The cottages were low and smokey and had sprang up without thought to house the miners of Bolam drift. They were there because the pit was there. The penumbral shadow of the mine. In the middle of a meadow, away from Allington. Stark and alone. Ripe for introspection. Only the railway ventured near. The gleaming track of the main line to Edinburgh knifed its way alongside them, the thunderous roar of the expresses shaking the foundations of their cottages day and night; or the gentle click-clack of the stopping trains and the screeching of shunting coal waggons. All the time, noise and activity surrounded Bolam. The regular to and fro of shift-bound miners, the mechanical din from the railway. The rigid religion of commerce enveloped them, yet passed them by. They worked six hard shifts a week and drew their pay which did not last a week. That fact had not passed them by.

Maudy Fenwick had a little shop with tiny windows and a dingy dimly-lit interior. Its fixtures were old and sagging and packed higgledy-piggledy with everything from sewing cotton to smoked bacon. The floor was littered with packing papers and cardboard boxes and the confectionery jars that lined the counter were cloudy from the inquisitive grubby fingers that had poked at them. He opened the door and a little bell shook out a fairy-like signal. He wanted a treat for Nellie seeing that it was pay-day and the tenth anniversary as well. If she had realised she would be in a state when he got home, of that he was sure. Something nice and tasty, he thought. She would enjoy a nice meat pie. Maudy always bought in a few Smart's meat pies on a pay-day. They were renowned in the area; round and with a glossy brown crust, full of meat and rich thick gravy. Nellie would like that.

Maudy appeared as if by magic out of the shadows at the back of the shop. She shuffled forward from somewhere below a Bisto sign that hung askew on the wall and looked warily up at her customer. She was a tiny, dumpy woman with a plain, flat face. She was a spinster of about fifty and looked every inch the part. Her skin was pale and almost transparent and she had a brown mole at the side of her chin that sprouted three or four long whispy hairs. Her eyes were dull and uninterested and her expressionless face sat firmly on top of a short, stiff neck. It was only the appearance of a man in her shop that caused her expression to change. She seemed to withdraw her neck deep into her shoulders, her eyes growing round with the look of uncertain anticipation as though all males had only rape on their minds and not bread or meat or backache pills.

The pies were straight from Maudy's oven where she kept them hot and the smell as he carried them home made the saliva swim in his mouth. Jackson's whippet also got the scent. It left its pastime of sniffing at the ash closets that stood like sentry boxes down the back lane and plodded along beside him with its thin worm-like tail curved down between its legs. He gave it a nudge with his foot and it veered off but it was back again by the time he reached his door. He shushed it away and it retreated, watching him sadly as he entered.

A musty warmth greeted him as he moved eagerly through the tiny darkened scullery that smelt of coarse soap and damp washing. He was pleased the cottage was warm. It meant that she had managed to keep the fire going and that was a blessing in the winter. The fire was her only comfort while he was out at the pit. He didn't wait to discard his cap and his bait bag; he opened the door into the silent room that was unlit except for the dull red glow from the dying fire. His wife was in her wheelchair as always, near the big black range with its round oven door, warped mantelpiece and brass fender.

"Nellie I'm home," he whispered anxiously. "Are y'all right?"

Nellie didn't move. She continued staring into the settling embers. She was hunched and pitifully thin. Her greying hair was straight and cut bluntly across her brow and at the nape of her neck. Her tiny gnarled hands gripped tightly at the arms of the wheelchair and her legs, almost as thin as the whippet's tail, were covered in darned green woollen stockings that clung with an ill-fitting bagginess to her wasted calves.

"Aye," she said at last, singing the word; dragging it out, making it sound like an agonized cry.

Edward smiled with relief and patted her boney shoulder. "Good lass," he said gently, "I see y've managed with the coal an' all. Y've kept warm hinny – that's the main thing."

He took off his cap and laid it with the pies and his bait bag on the bare wooden table. He took the empty coal bucket and knelt down at the hearth. He gathered up thirty or more bits of coal and smiled reassuringly into her face. He knew how difficult it was for her to feed the fire. She had to pick from the bucket and with her tiny strength aim it into the grate. He knew how hard she tried. Sometimes she managed it; sometimes she missed, but she deserved some praise for her efforts.

"You're gettin' better, you're gettin' to be a good shot," he said with a smile.

Nellie nodded slowly, her beady little eyes shining into his.

Thank God, he thought as he struggled to his feet, she can't have realised. He threw the gathered coal onto the fire and pulled her wheelchair a little closer. Gently he fastened the top button of her dowdy cardigan and stroked her fringe to one side. She watched him with an expression of satisfied pleasure as though she were watching some distant sunrise and he felt a wave of pity run through him. "Nellie – oh Nellie," he whispered as his craggy face twisted with emotion. But he couldn't let her see him upset. He had to put on a brave face. He forced his lips into a smile and moved to the table.

"Look what I've brought you Nellie – look here."

She swivelled her head. He unwrapped the pies gleefully, like a small boy.

"Smart's pies Nellie – nice and hot. We'll have them with some boiled tetties, eh?"

She nodded and her confirmation of his suggestion came as before.

He was pleased. She had an appetite and that was a good sign. He took a spill from a tin on the mantelpiece and lit the gaslamp from the fire. Nellie blinked with the light and it seemed to awaken her dulled mind. She pointed to the table.

"What? What is it hinny?"

"Pies – in the oven," she croaked, "keep warm."

He picked them up. "Of course, I was forgettin'," he said with a self-reproaching voice, opening the round door. "Now I'll just fill the bucket an' bank the fire an' we'll have our dinner all cosy like."

She nodded and smiled a toothless smile. Edward patted her hand.

"Right," he breathed excitedly, "I'll get crackin' – it'll not take long."

He picked up the empty bucket, then put it down again, a look of concern crossing his face. He was forgetting something else. His usual routine had been disrupted with all the things on his mind that day.

"Nellie – d'you want the netty?"

She nodded again. His lips thinned and he shook his head in a gesture of amazement. She never complained, this wife of his. She was a helpless babe, innocent and vulnerable, relying completely on his ability to see to her every simple need. Effortlessly he lifted her flyweight body out of the chair and walked across the room. He could feel her bony frame lying loosely in his arms. He held her close to him and carried her outside to the little sentry box across the lane.

Edward Sneed relaxed for the first time that day as he rocked slowly in his rocking chair and let the smoke from the bowl of his pipe drift lazily up to his nostrils. His mind tumbled with soft, sad thoughts about his sons and then his wife who was sleeping upstairs. He was relieved that she had not realised the significance of the day. Time, it seemed was gradually numbing her memory. She had watched him intently as he laid four places at the table. It was a stout table, its planked surface white and worn with years of scrubbing. He cut the two pies and placed half on each plate, together with a mound of mash, glancing sadly at her from time to time, knowing she was following his every move. He poured tea into four tin mugs and milked them with condensed milk. He pulled her wheelchair to the table and sat himself opposite.

"There now," he said with a satisfied smile. "Eat up, Nellie."

She looked across at the two empty places for a moment, her eyes flickering as though struggling to regain some recollection of the past, then slowly concentrated on her plate, spooning the food shakily into her mouth.

He exhaled silently. "Nice?" he asked.

"Aye – where's the lads?" She mumbled through a mouthful of food. "Dinner's gettin' cold."

His brow tightened. He knew the question was coming, just as it had done every night for ten years. He spoke softly, trying with all his might to reassure her.

"Why, they're working late Nellie – you know they always work late. They'll be in presently."

She thought for a moment, her mouth becoming still. "Aye," she said at last and continued eating.

He breathed again, knowing she would ask no more until the next night. The ruse with the two extra places had worked once more. When she finished eating and was back near the fire he gathered the dishes together and slipped the two halves of the pie into his bait bag for work the next day.

He rocked gently and smoked and pondered on his life. There was no feeling of frustration. No bitterness for ambitions unfulfilled, only a weariness and regret at the misfortunes that had caused their predicament. He had often wondered what they had done in life to deserve such an ordeal, but could think of no reason. He had always been a quiet retiring man who worked and lived his life and antagonised no-one. Yet fate had decreed that their existence should be burdened with unhappiness and that fact he regretted. It hadn't been so bad when he was ten years younger. The effort of working all day at the pit and all evening at home had been lost against the hope that his wife would recover. But that was not to be. She was still as she had been on the day the news came. If only she would allow the neighbours to help, he thought. How much easier it would be for him and for her. But she was so fiercely independent, this wife of his. Even with her dull shadowy mind, her pride would let no-one near except the doctor and Bennett the "clagger man". He smiled a rueful smile as he thought about Raymond Bennett the collector for Goldsteins credit stores in Newcastle. He of all people was one of her chosen few. He could walk in and out of her sanctum as he had for fifteen years.

Edward remembered well the first time he called, a mere lad of eighteen with a strangely smooth, oily skin. He was as thin as a willow, with an acned face, an ill-fitting bowler and badly pressed suit. He was as keen as mustard to be a success, rattling away about the bargains only to be had at Goldsteins while his long delicate fingers flicked through the pages of his tattered catalogue. He expounded the merits of sixpence a week for a new suit or coat or fourpence for a new dress or a pair of strides. The village got to know him and his cheeky, cheery ways and they got to like him. His ebullient manner appealed to them, as he breezed through the village on a Saturday morning taking the groans and good natured jibes of the people and answering with a smile and a slick assurance as he collected their ill-afforded money. He was understanding, though, and honest. For fifteen years he had grown older with them. He knew them all and their idiosyncrasies. They were his personal flock that he looked after and that gave him a certain smattering of satisfaction. Nellie trusted him. She knew his quick urgent knock. She managed a smile and waited for him to pat her hand and tell her she looked gorgeous and ask her to run off with him. He would take her purse and extract the one and threepence she paid weekly for Edward's Sunday suit and two blankets, then gave her it back, respecting her trust implicitly. He was about the same age as their own sons, Edward thought, perhaps that was why he was favoured.

Edward lifted himself slowly out of the rocking chair and walked stiff-legged to the old sideboard. The clock was lying face down because that was the only way it would work. He lifted it and tutted when he saw it was already nearly nine. He stood and sighed eyeing a roll of hessian in the corner, undecided whether to work on the making of the new mat or go to bed or perhaps a quick pint, seeing that it was payday. His hand was resting on the knob of the sideboard drawer. He gazed at its cheap utilitarian form, long since removed of any veneer. He slowly opened it and rummaged among the paraphernalia of years. He clasped the photograph in his hands and gazed down at the sepia coloured twin forms. His sons looked out at him, tall and proud; stiff-necked in the uniforms; the flash powder putting a spark in their eyes. He shook his head sadly. He remembered how they had rushed away to war, not thinking, not caring that their trade as coalminers would have kept them relatively safe at home. Twins; identical; the same ideas, the same thoughts. They had the same instant of conception. In January 1916 they had the same instant of death. They died valiantly, their Commanding Officer had said in his letter. Side by side when the howitzer shell terminated its trajectory on a bleak, ravaged field in France. In an instant of explosion they were no more. They died for King and Country, the letter said, for the freedom of the world. Ten years ago that very day their lives had been blotted out. And for what, he thought, a rare surge of anger rising within him. Their names appeared on the impersonal grey marble monument at Allington. That was the reward of the grateful country. A country in the throes of yet more turmoil; struggling in a war of economics. Poverty and hunger were rife. What good had it done being the victor and not the vanquished? What use was their so-called freedom grossly diluted by want and suffering? His sons had died in vain. His wife had been a helpless cripple ever since. Hysterical paralysis Dr Jenkins had called it. Nothing could be done, he added, except hope that time would release the mental lock and allow her legs to move.

Edward sighed then looked to the ceiling and listened. Nellie was fast asleep. He thrust the photograph back into the drawer then took a shilling from her purse. He knew he should be cutting up cloth and getting on with the making of the large mat that was taking so long to do, or perhaps letting his tired body replenish itself in sleep. But he had already decided that he needed a pint that night.

The Fat Ox stood away from the Rows and almost on the edge of the flat patch of meadow that the village used as a football field. It was the focal point for the scant social activities of the miners and on pay night it was busier than at any other time of the week. When Edward arrived the air in the bar was thick with tobacco smoke and the reek of beer. The bar top swam with spillings and raucous laughter vied for supremacy with coarse off-key singing. He threaded his way solemnly past little Willie Cox who was in the middle of a weird unaccompanied dance, his cap pulled jauntily down over his left eye, his arms outstretched and his legs lifting alternatively to some mental alcohol-induced rhythm.

He bought a pint and sat down beside Abe Jackson. For the second time that day he moved the whippet with his foot and stretched out his legs under the small, round table. He answered Abe's casual chatter but his conversation was clipped and punctuated with sighs. Suddenly Willie Cox took their attention. His gyrations had come to an abrupt halt when he tripped over his own feet and toppled like a felled tree among a foursome of domino players. The singing stopped and there was a moment's silence from the bar before the place erupted into laughter. Even Edward allowed himself a grim smile.

"You stupid effin' sod!"

The voice came loud and angrily over the diminishing jollity. Robert Fulthorpe extracted his fat body from the pandemonium around the domino board and brushed the spilled beer quickly from his bulging waistcoat before grabbing the wallowing slight figure of Willie Cox. Using every ounce of his cumbersome fifteen stone, he lifted him off the table and hurled him savagely away. He tripped again, bounced off the door and crumpled at the base of it. There was an immediate silence, but different from the last. It was a shocked, mute stillness. The eyes of the bar were on Fulthorpe as he brushed at his waistcoat and looked around him, a twinge of embarrassment flushing his already heavily coloured face. He was an ugly man with sagging pendulous cheeks. His thick-lipped mouth was constantly open showing a fat round tongue and his tiny eyes stared arrogantly from under untidy bushy eyebrows. His actions came as a surprise to no-one. His swearing and brash haughty manner were well known in the village. He was a rolleywayman at the pit, but his position in life rankled his conceited ego. His craving for importance and respect from his fellow men had twisted his character into the mould of Jekyll and Hyde. He was a sidesman at the church. He had fought tooth and nail to a seat on the County Council. He waddled down the aisle with sanctimonious glory on a Sunday morning. He gave forth at Council meetings with all the style and pompous assurance of a Chancellor and spouted quotations from the Bible to erring juniors. But he drank like a fish out of his mouselike wife's meagre housekeeping while his four young children went hungry and his own two pairs of underpants were held together with thread and will-power. He could turn from a passage in Luke or John and then interlace each word of a sentence with obscenities used by the best of them. Yet his mind, so filled with fragile, fleeting glimpses of power and glory, could not see that his hypocrisy had reduced his respect to zero. The people of the village tolerated him, however, and he had become the object of behind the hand scorn and amused, hidden ridicule.

"Well?" he asked in an immature petulant voice. "What're you all lookin' at? The stupid effin' sod's nowt but a nuisance."

A figure walked slowly along the length of the bar, past the row of stunned drinkers and stopped barely a yard in front of the sodden fat belly. The atmosphere resounded with anticipated action.

"Pick him up!" Tommy Nesbitt said in a voice that was barely a whisper but carried all the menace of a viper's hiss.

Fulthorpe blinked stupidly, his mouth even more agape. He glanced quickly at the groaning figure of Willie Cox then back into the dark eyes in front of him that were heavy-lidded with smoke and five pints.

"Why should I?" he blurted, looking around him for support.

There was none. He fingered his podgy hands nervously. He knew he was no match for the athletic figure that now stood with his feet planted firmly apart and fists clenched at his sides.

"Because I'm tellin' you to – that's why. Willie tripped. It was an accident."

There was a murmur of agreement from the bar.

Fulthorpe stood for a second longer, his mind streaming with mental pictures of Nesbitt being given his marching orders from the football field after uppercutting a centre half the size of a bull. That was two weeks ago. The lad from Wallsend was back at work – minus a half an inch from his tongue. Suddenly his face twisted into a scowl of condescension. He pulled Willie to his feet and propped him against the wall.

"Willie's pissed," he snarled, feeling he had earned the right to say his piece. "He gets a couple of bob in his pocket and can't control himself. Some toff gives him a nice fat tip and it burns a hole in his pocket. He thought it was that mate of yours from London. Some effin' hope. This big noise of yours'll never come. He's not interested in a tuppence-ha'penny place like this. Anyway I reckon it's a load of cock."

Tommy smiled sarcastically. "You callin' me a liar?"

Fulthorpe swallowed nervously, realising what he had just said. He often did that when he was excited. The words just came – automatically, without thought.

"No!" he snapped quickly. "I – I just mean he'll not come," then with a burst of inspiration, "I mean he never meant to come."

There was a murmur among the onlookers and Tommy knew that he was probably right. It was two months or more since he had met Tilmouth, a tall, strange, gaunt man at a Union rally at Chopwell. Will Lawther had been speaking that day of injustice among the downtrodden working class. But it was Tilmouth who had Tommy's attention for the rest of the day; his soft, almost hypnotic voice questioning, advising, counselling him about the miner's lot. He had made an impression on Tommy Nesbitt at that meeting. His dark burning eyes had filled him with a euphoric sense of justice to come, of utopia ousting the exploiters. Organise and be strong he had said. Unite in the common cause; and he had left him with a solemn promise to visit Bolam. But that was long weeks ago. Tommy had returned to the village and rallied his workmates. He had spouted phrases remembered from Lawther's speech and Tilmouth's quiet magnetic talk and the men of the village felt a surge in their blood. But the days melted into weeks and the fire in their bellies turned to the cold ash of doubt.

He swivelled around and faced their unemotional stares. His brow tightened. He was angry with himself for his over-enthusiasm and with them for their lack of faith.

"Listen!" he breathed passionately. "Tilmouth will come – a man like that doesn't say things lightly. He'll come, I know he will."

Again there was silence that meant disbelief. He took a pace forward and clenched his fist on the bar. He was a tall, wirey man with a rough but unblemished complexion. His jutting jaw radiated determination and his clear voice always carried a tone that demanded attention.

"He'll come!" he yelled. Then his voice dropped in volume. "My God, he's got to come. But if he doesn't, it doesn't matter. There's others who'll guide us – for, believe me lads, it's in the wind. It only took the Government two months after Red Friday to form their O.M.S." He sneered into the sea of cloth caps and long, wondering faces, the columns of tobacco smoke drifting lazily upward in the stillness.

"Organisation for the Maintenance of Supplies – for what? I'll tell you for what. Churchill said just last bliddy month that Red Friday was a put-off. Playin' for time! – that's what they're doin'! The sods are organising against us. They're just waitin' for the end of the nine month subsidy and then what'll happen?" He waved his hand over them. He had them again. He could tell. Every nerve in every body gasped for more while Fulthorpe burned with jealousy at the power he had to make them listen.

"The owners'll drop the wages, lads, just like they said before. It'll be longer hours and less money!" His eyes narrowed. "But they're not daft, Churchill and that mob down there – they know we'll fight. They know we'll suffer like we've done before. But the buggers are organising themselves so life in this lousy country can go on – while we starve!"

He slammed a fist down onto the bar and the spillings flew. He stood for a second and drank in the tiny collection of silent staring humanity in front of him.

"We must organise," he whispered at last. "Unite and organise ourselves – and we'll beat them."

Edward Sneed plodded slowly home through the thickening mist that swirled around him. Abe Johnson was at his side but they did not talk. It was a cold, freezing night, silent except for the far off moan of a foghorn and the faint quick-slow chatter of a shunting engine somewhere down the line. For all the cold Edward glowed inwardly.

His sombre thoughts of earlier had been dispelled. Tommy Nesbitt's words still rang in his ears and the sight of Robert Fulthorpe slinking out like a whipped dog gladdened his heart. He thought about Tommy Nesbitt, the young firebrand who often worked himself up into a frenzy of revolution. He remembered his habit of getting a few of them to one side, holding on to the lapels of their jackets, and giving forth with his mouth an inch from their ears as though they were as deaf as posts. He had the right idea, had Tommy. Working in the mine was something more than a job to him. He was one of the new generation that refused to be trodden underfoot. There was more to working underground than the drudgery that had been their heritage. Tommy Nesbitt had a pride in himself and his fellow beings that would not be quelled by the threats and intimidation of the owners. He was a light in the darkness, a champion of his kind, a staunch adversary of injustice. A young lion born in the village and weaned on the weak pap of indifference. Edward Sneed suddenly felt that his sons had not, after all, died in vain.

4

Dr John Kinghorn watched the chubby fingers hover with blatant uncertainty over the ornate ebony crown of the white queen, then tremble slightly before grabbing at it and sliding it diagonally to black king two as though it was a hot ember.

"Check," Dr Jenkins whispered, the tone of his voice raised and brittle, questioning his own statement.

John gave a quick amused glance toward the beaming features and glistening bloodshot eyes that observed him with a growing expression of childish exuberance. He was profoundly glad that he had at last made the move after ten full minutes of concentration punctuated with grunts, drumming of fingers on the table top and various noises from tight and slack lips. It was perfectly obvious play and he had been expecting it from the moment he moved his black rook up in a last desperate attack. He made another cursory study of the board, noted the prowling bishop at rook five silently guarding the white queen and the inability of his king to move out of check. He took his long dead pipe out of his mouth.

"And mate," he said, toppling the king with the bowl.

"Ha ha!" his opponent yelled, gleefully rubbing his hands. "Victory at last! God – I thought I was losing my touch. It's weeks since I walloped old Tomlinson. But you played well," he added with stern conviction, "you're better than Tomlinson. He's one of those damn' philistines who snatch the queen as quick as he can. But you brought a touch of class to the game. You brought out the best in me, eh?"

"You played a cunning game," John said condescendingly, remembering with a dry smile how his queen had been eagerly snaffled early on at the cost of a bishop and a hurried castling of the white king with his following move.

Dr Jenkins sat back and stretched with glowing enjoyment. He patted his chest and smacked his lips. "Well, young man, this calls for a drink. You'll have a scotch?"

John shrugged. He hated being called "young man"; he'd had enough of that from the withered, prim matron at the teaching hospital, but it was a little too early in their relationship to show dissension. "If you like," he said.

He watched Dr Jenkins move eagerly toward the decanter and glasses that stood on the pianola. He saw the quick furtive look over his shoulder as the study door opened and Ethel Friar moved hastily to the fire, her face stern and rigid and her hand flicking at the accumulation of tobacco smoke. She poked irritably at the fire and replenished it and was gone without a word or a sideways glance at either of them. Dr Jenkins continued his pouring with a visible sag of the shoulders.

John's newness and neutrality allowed him a measure of amusement at the aura of hostility that radiated from her and in his short time at Plessey House he was as yet unsure whether it was her true nature or whether her employer had perhaps committed some unforgivable sin. One thing he had already decided was that she was far more than her title implied and it was possible that his presence could well be the catalyst for her manner. That notion he accepted with a superior stubborn defiance. She was a servant of the house whatever else she may be. She was one of the outsiders who spoke an almost unintelligible form of King's English – like the porter at the station, like the pathetic bunch who had presented themselves at the surgery twice that day. Rough, uncouth, down-at-heel most of them. Great ham-fisted miners using the oldest trick in the book – "a bad back"; or wormy-looking kids with wide frightened eyes in need of circumcision or a poultice for a boil on their backsides. But she was different in a way. She gargled her deep gutteral *r*s like the rest of them but she had a supercilious aloofness; an air of secure self-assuredness that made him resolve to defeat her, to bring her into line, to make her treat him with the respect he deserved. He was there whether she liked it or not. Dr Jenkins had required an assistant and he had been greeted with a warm enough welcome by him. From their hasty preliminary discussions the night before it was obvious the practice needed some fresh young blood. Dr Jenkins had emphasised that and by the time he gratefully undressed for bed his mind had dispelled the foreboding and swirled with ideas how he would impress these northern pitmen with his knowledge of medicine and streamlined London efficiency. He had slept only fitfully, though, for all his tiredness. The muted but decidedly angry whispers filtered up into his room until far into the night accompanied by quick agitated steps and the occasional slamming of doors.

Then there was Jenkins himself. Already John had noted the undisguisable inferiority complex that he had at first attributed to Jenkins' amazement that he was the son of William Fitzgerald Kinghorn; the thought had crossed John's mind that Jenkins perhaps expected the son of so revered a surgeon to have surpassed the knowledge accumulated from thirty odd years of practice. But it wasn't just in matters concerning their profession. It was the game of chess and the way Jenkins' victory had been engineered with a desperate desire to win at all costs. It was the way he had gone into a eulogistic speech over a bottle of mediocre hock at the dinner table and a half hour session of pulling out rolls of classical music from the bulky piano stool and books from the shelves. Even in the surgery his florid features took on a look of child-like delight at John's agreement to the diagnoses. Petty things that a vet could have interpreted correctly. The ganglion on Ripley the postman's wrist. The adenoidal drone from the youngest son of Bill Jarvis the winding engineman at the colliery. John's nod of agreement had split Jenkins' face into a beam of satisfied pleasure. He was a man striving for reassurance, John resolved. Someone doubting his own ability. Someone sadly in need of encouragement. And for John Kinghorn that was perfect.

"Water?"

John looked up at the glass of amber liquid in front of him. "What? Oh yes, just a splash."

Dr Jenkins beamed. "That's what's in. Guessed right."

John took the glass.

His companion sat down. "Well," he said with a satisfied sigh, "here's to you John, and to a happy stay at Allington – and good health to all who sail in her."

John made to reply in much the same manner as to a similar comment prior to the mediocre hock, but thought better of it as Jenkins devoured his drink in three noisy gulps, then sat back and rubbed his eyes with a thumb and forefinger. He blinked them back into focus and looked at the dark handsome face in front of him that sipped gentlemanly at his drink and surveyed the room. He felt a sudden weariness yet he felt agitated, keyed up, as though his body ended at the nerve ends. The young man opposite looked too young to be a doctor, his face had the clear immaturity of a schoolboy. But he was so very glad he had arrived. At last after months of anguish and indecision he had done it. He had got himself an assistant. In spite of Ethel – because of her. Surely now she would see that he had a mind of his own, that he still had a glimmer of self-respect. It had been a remarkable feat of will-power. But what was more remarkable was that she was still there, still in Plessey House. Still fussing and finicky, huffed to death – but still with him. And for that he was thankful. He needed her – hated her – loved her, like the turmoil of morphinism.

He rose again and brought the whisky and the water jug to the table. He poured himself another, larger this time and tried to camouflage it with a nonchalant, "Well now John, what do you think?

Think you'll like it up here in the wild and woolly north?"

John's mind flashed with a vision of the village, drab in the white frost of morning, his sample of the populace and the musty old-fashionedness of Plessey House. He thought of his father still seething in far off London as he hacked at a blue-blooded appendix and his mother's frosty faced silence as he packed his cases; Smythe's derisive titter and then the mincing appreciation of Dr Jenkins at his being there. He did not want to appear too enthusiastic.

"I think so," he said with a quick shrug. "On first impressions – I think so."

"Good man," Dr Jenkins breathed, offering the decanter, "first impressions count, I always say." He gave a chesty little laugh and relaxed in the chair. He sipped at the whisky, savouring it this time. "Tell me John," he said at last, the alcohol flooding him with a sweet calmness and confidence. "I've been wondering – I don't want to pry – but you're a well-bred man with an important father. What in Heaven's name made you want to come so far out of the way?" He waved a casual hand at the room. "I mean, well – this isn't the Ritz and our clientele could hardly be called wealthy. Ninety-nine per cent are the old penny a week lot and your job gives you only two sixty a year . . ." He shook his head as his voice trailed off, not wanting above anything else to sow seeds of doubt.

John reached for his pipe. His lips thinned. He knew the question would come sooner or later. "It's a simple matter," he said dryly. "I have a father who thinks I should keep up a stupid family tradition and join the Army. I do not want to join the Army."

Dr Jenkins nodded. "Family friction – eh?"

"Precisely."

"What have you against the Army?"

John sighed. "If men choose to blow themselves into bits that's their business. I don't want the job of trying to pump life back into them. Wars are for the rabble. I've no time for the glory of self-sacrifice."

Dr Jenkins hummed a short neutral noise that could have meant anything. Then he refilled his glass, enjoying the rekindled sharpness of his mind. "Well, that's an unusual answer. I thought the student bodies were hotbeds of revolution. I thought all young minds imagined themselves as St George and the Establishment as the big bad dragon. It was in my day anyway," he added nicely.

John smiled his dry knowing smile. "But then you get some sense. You begin to see that radical ideas are just a lot of flatulence. Utopia is fine until you add the one unstable ingredient – the human animal. I realised that a long time ago. I have too much respect for the good things in life."

Dr Jenkins pursed his lips. He looked around the room. "You're probably right, John, but where would your good things in life be if the 'rabble', as you call them, hadn't fought in the war?"

"Wars are like disease. You need a donor and a host. One without the other and the problem doesn't arise."

Dr Jenkins hummed again. His mind was clouding with the alcohol; his reasoning becoming befuddled. He filled his glass again in an effort to clear it. He attempted to change the subject, while his companion watched in silent amusement knowing full well the whisky was having the expected detrimental effect.

"D'you like the house – it's not bad, is it," he said as a statement.

"It's nice."

"I've a car, you know. You can drive? If you can drive y'can use the car for the rounds."

"Super," John said with a touch of sarcasm, imagining a miniscule battered Austin or something similar.

Dr Jenkins sat forward and rested his head on an upturned palm. "As you can see, I live pretty comfortably here, but I've been lucky you know," he murmured with a loose nod of the head, trying with all of his might to keep his speech coherent and fighting off the dull twilight world that threatened to engulf him. He took another drink. "Don't think I've had it easy though. Oh no sir, all this lot didn't come from tending to the rabble out there. That was a golden idea that quickly became tarnished. You see, I had father trouble too. I was one of your rabble a long, long time ago. I went to school with my arse hanging out and bare feet. I had an old man that couldn't care less if I lived or died. It was an aunt who got me through college. Aunt Jessy, you know." He shook his head morosely. "I emerged into the great big challenging world and what I wasn't going to do for medicine was nobody's business. But it's not like that. The world's not like the picture book drawing of dingle dell, where the trees are green and the sky is blue. They never show you the rotting vegetation at the foot of the tree or the birds' droppings on the branches. But I was lucky. She bought me this practice. She had money, you see, and no-one to spend it on. I knew the way they lived out there and I didn't want to go back to it. But they're the salt of the Earth, John, you'll come to see that. They're poor, but man they've got hearts like lions. Proud, friendly people. You'll like them, John. That's why I've been here for thirty years. She gave me the best start a doctor could ask for – my own practice. And then, an' then . . ." His voice trailed away in a whine of self-pity.

The telephone rang. A harsh ring out in the lobby. John sat mesmerised by the man who had disintegrated in front of his very eyes. Then he stood up. The old doctor looked up at him, then held his brow. "Oh Christ," he mumbled.

John moved to the door. Ethel Friar was already lifting the earpiece.

"Yes – yes I'll tell him. Hold on please."

She turned her frosty stare toward John. "It's for Dr Jenkins," she said as though addressing a usurper.

"I'll take it," he said, holding out his hand for the receiver.

She pulled it closer to her shoulder. "It's for Dr Jenkins, I said," lashing the words out at him.

He felt an anger surge up and make his head pound. He snatched at the instrument and took it from her. Her eyes blinked and her lips trembled. But only for a second.

"It's a call out and they asked for Dr Jenkins," she hissed.

"I shall attend to it, Mrs Friar," he said with a soft menacing smile. "Dr Jenkins can't go. He isn't capable. You see, Dr Jenkins is drunk!"

Monday was one of those damp, grey January days when the sun is a limp red ball and struggles low across the sky, dulling the colours of the Earth into depressing conformity. For John Kinghorn, however, his first Monday in Allington was far from depressing. He was filled with a euphoric sense of power that nothing short of Armageddon could disrupt. He had greeted the watery dawn, wide awake and with a tingle of excitement that had resurrected itself from some distant Christmas Eve.

It was a pleasant change from the day before when he had moped around the dispensary in the quiet of a Sunday with the house still, Dr Jenkins strangely standoffish and Ethel Friar ignoring him completely. In a way he understood both their attitudes. Dr Jenkins was so obviously embarrassed at his Saturday night escapade and, as for Mrs Friar, her stony face was the one saving grace for an otherwise boring Sabbath punctuated only by the clang of church bells and the pious singing from across the square. John longed for the telephone to ring, for a repetition of Saturday night, just to break the monotony. But it never came. He toyed with the idea of visiting his Saturday night call-out but then thought better of it. It wasn't really necessary and besides he'd had enough the night before.

He had dashed out into the bitter night, swinging his glossy new bag and looking for No. 10 Nelson Road: not caring in the least that Dr Jenkins' grunted directions were scant. He was well pleased with himself – at his first minor victory over Ethel Friar, at Dr Jenkins' mixture of apology and gratitude that he was going and at the thrill of his first personal case as a doctor.

It had been the stationmaster on the 'phone. He gabbled an excited message, prompted in the background by a frantic Mrs Cox saying that Willie had collapsed, "Said he felt dizzy. Stood up, doctor, and just collapsed in a dead faint. No, he hadn't been drinking, might've been mind, a couple anyway if he'd not felt sick all day. Can you come doctor? Lizzie here thinks he's dying."

It was a ten minute walk to Nelson Road, a short row of terraced houses down near the station and No. 10 was different from the rest only by its number, roughly painted on the green blistered front door. He knocked and waited, mentally sprucing himself, holding himself erect and setting his face with a firm dignified thrust of his chin that was bound to hold them in awe. There was a hollow clank of boots on carpetless stairs, then the door opened slowly. John looked down and a six year old boy looked up. His hair was closely shorn except for a ridiculous tuft at the front, his face was jammy and his wide eyes stared, giving a sullen examination of the stranger in front of him.

"Mr Cox," John snapped, matter-of-factly.

"No, my name's Frankie. Da's in bed. The doctor's comin'."

John was not amused. "I am the doctor, child," he said commandingly.

The boy turned without a word and tramped back up the stairs. His baggy pants were patched and ended below his knees. They seemed to take all the movement of his legs that shot up and down inside them like two piston rods. John followed. There was a smell of boiled cabbage in the square room to the left of the landing where Lizzie Cox sat with a baby sucking noisily at her breast. The furniture was old and sparse but the room was clean and tidy. There was a sombre poverty to it all accentuated by the dull light, the smell of the cabbage and the natural act of a woman feeding her child. Frankie was already back on his stomach in front of the fire, his nose buried in some tattered comic oblivious to the stranger's presence.

"He's in there, doctor," Lizzie said in a loud squawking voice nodding toward a brown varnished door. "We got him into bed and I would've stayed with him, but the bairn started yellin' for a feed. He's not been well all day – Willie I mean – he got up like a ghost this mornin'. I told him, I said Willie, bide off work, but it's like talkin' to a brick wall. He's not strong, you know. He got a whiff of gas during the war an' he's never been right since. Frankie! Open the door for the doctor. I told him when he came to, I said Willie Cox, you daft bugger – now see what you've done. You'll be laid off for a week or more and us already three weeks behind with the clagger man. Frankie, did you hear me? Anyway he doesn't look so bad now, doctor. There's a bit more colour in his cheeks."

She took a breath and changed the baby to the other breast. Frankie was still immersed in his comic. John moved to the door. He had intended to ask all the right questions and in his mental rehearsal the answers had come with a soft exact precision. He had not expected the rambling nerve-jarring chatter that had flowed from this thin-faced woman who looked anything but feminine except for her milk swollen breasts.

"How long was he unconscious?" he asked, his voice annoyingly weak as he entered the bedroom.

"Oh not long, just a few minutes. Isn't that right Willie? Frankie! Didn't I tell you to open that door for the doctor. He looked like death warmed up when he dropped. What a fright I got, I can tell you. I told him, I said . . ."

John gratefully shut the door behind him.

It was a straightforward case. Willie was awake and chirpy and looked even tinier among the bulky washed out bedclothes. It didn't take long for him to recount the incident in the Fat Ox the previous night and after a quick examination of the bump on his head, John concluded that it was a slight delayed concussion.

"Three days in bed," he said, "and no alcohol."

Willie's face broke into a wide smile.

"And if you have a headache or feel dizzy when you get up, send for me."

Willie gave a soft little laugh with his tongue between his teeth.

"What's so amusing?"

"Nowt," he said with a knowing blink of his eyes, "just wondering how you were settlin' down."

John's voice was flat but he couldn't help it. "Fine thanks, just fine," he murmured with a sudden twinge of annoyance that his rehearsed bedside manner had been forgotten. He snapped his bag shut and made for the door. "And remember Mr Cox, three days in bed," he barked with renewed authority.

Willie smiled and nodded again. "Call me Willie, will you doctor. There's only the clagger man calls me mister 'cos I owes him money."

John's facade held only for a second. He didn't quite understand what he had meant but he somehow liked this man. He amused him. Willie had a natural unfettered friendliness that was refreshing. John smiled. "All right Willie," he said softly as he opened the door.

Lizzie had her mouth moving at the same instant as the door. 'Well doctor, what's he like. Doesn't he look awful? It's that gas – that damn' gas – he's never been right since the war. He lost three stone and never put it back, y'know. Frankie will you get off that bliddy floor! What d'you think, doctor? Will he be idle for long?"

John managed to squeeze in his verdict while she took a breath.

"Oh that's good news, that's good. Three days isn't bad. Bennett'll have to wait another week. You'll have a cup of tea, doctor. It's good of you to come out at this time of night. Frankie, get up and put the kettle on. Frankie! Frankie!"

Frankie read on. His mother's face twisted into an irate scowl. She forced the baby away from its anchor point and aimed her right breast toward her seemingly deaf son. With amazing accuracy she squeezed and a jet of warm milk arched across the room and sprayed onto the back of his neck. She cackled loudly as he sprang to his feet.

John fled, making a quick excuse and breathing a sigh of relief when he was at last in the street. He had a hollow feeling of despair as he walked back to Plessey House. He suddenly longed for his own kind; for the clatter of trams and the bright lights of the metropolis. For the chic girls and the elegant men and the rumbustious carefree life they led. Dinner suits and monocles and jazz; intimate smoky night clubs where the conversations were witty and fresh. He remembered it all as, alone, his footsteps echoed up the silent street. But then, the rebellious stubborn streak in him took control. He was damned if he would return! He could see their "I told you so" sneers. He could feel the suffocating back-slapping condolences and hear the snide comments like "Old Kinghorn decided to fizz off to the Colonies, but the natives were too much for him, eh? What? Ha ha ha." He took a deep breath and clenched his teeth. His pace quickened. So what if the garrulous Mrs Cox had thrown him with her banter and her raw uncouth ways. The next time it would be different. The next time he would be prepared for anything. He would show them – show them all. In London – in Allington. He would have the respect he deserved.

He was highly delighted with himself after the Monday morning surgery. On his own he had seen thirty or so patients and despatched them with a brusqueness that may have been slightly overdone but he had listened, examined and prescribed as laid down in the handbook. They had departed clutching their medicine, reassured and smiling brave smiles, like the magic ritual of the confessional. When at last no-one responded to the tinny hand bell, he surveyed the silent waiting room, picked up a dog-eared copy of *The Illustrated London News,* grinned, then belched into the face of the ticking grandfather clock.

There was a quick agitated *parp!* from a car horn, then another and another. John walked through the waiting room and into the glass lean-to that housed an aspidistra and a few pots of drooping greenery. He could hardly believe his eyes. He moved quickly to the door, thinking for a second that the glass was distorting his vision. But he hadn't been seeing things. Dr Jenkins sat with beaming red face and beckoning him behind the steering wheel of a beautiful Sunbeam open tourer. Its chrome fittings sparkled even in the weak winter light and its deep blue paint work was polished to a mirror finish. Its mechanical symmetry filled John with admiration.

"Aha!" Dr Jenkins yelled, "surprise, surprise. Come and look. I've been busting to tell you all weekend. What do you think of her? Grab your bag, we'll do the rounds in style."

John stood and drank in every inch of its unblemished form. He liked cars, loved them, he always had. He touched one of the enormous pod headlights reverently as one might touch the Pieta. "She's gorgeous," he breathed.

Dr Jenkins giggled with pleasure. "Not bad eh?" She's the '24 model you know. Got her second-hand from a farmer in Durham last year. Not a mark on her. Hell of a bargain at £150, eh?"

John looked hard into the watery, blinking eyes.

"Oh, I know what you're thinking, John," he said lightheartedly. "You're wondering how the hell a backwoodsman like me can afford a luxury like this. Well, I saved a bit you know and there was always Aunt Jessie." His face clouded for a moment. "I like the good things like you, John. You and I have a lot in common." His face clouded even further. "And besides, Ethel likes it. She never goes out you know – only in this. She likes a ride in this."

John nodded a silent understanding and smiled at the enigmatic doctor who looked like a peppery colonel on holiday. He was dressed in a heavy tweed suit with a deerstalker to match and thick diamond-patterned stockings showed below the legs of his plus-fours.

It had been the night before that Dr Jenkins had returned to his old self, as though Saturday had never existed. There had been a session of agitated pacing about and chummy shoulder patting before treating John to a performance on the pianola. "I'll play you my favourite piece," he had said with the enthusiasm of a sudden brainwave, "it's called 'Träumerei' by Schubert. Do you know it?"

John had grunted an amused yes as the roll was fitted. He had listened in respectful silence as Dr Jenkins pumped away on the pedals, his left hand wafting in time to the poetic notes. John hadn't the heart to tell him the music was composed by Schumann.

Then they had discussed how surgery duty and visits would be shared. It was agreed that they should alternate morning and evening surgeries on a weekly basis and visits the same, except for emergencies. For that particular Monday, however, Dr Jenkins had suggested they should visit together, thus acquainting him with the area as a whole.

Now John's pleasurable morning was further enhanced by the appearance of this gleaming beauty. He imagined himself driving it to the admiring stares of the populace as he roared past about his business. He could have hugged the old man, who sat watching him admire it. There was something tragic about the forced extraversion put on to counter his inferiority complex. But for John, bursting with sudden enthusiasm, that observation was now irrelevant.

"I'll get my bag," he said turning and running back to the house.

Upstairs Ethel Friar turned away from the curtain as the car moved off. She had a feeling in her that she suddenly managed to identify. She was jealous. Jealous of the intruder who had wrecked their close-knit existence and in a strange way jealous of his youthful years and handsome appearance. She stopped at the mirror on the landing wall. She ran a finger over her lips then patted at the tight round bun at the back of her head. Then her face broke into a wide arrogant smile. She knew what she must do. Dr Kinghorn was young, like her ageing doctor had been thirty years before. Dr Kinghorn was virile. Perhaps – just perhaps she had enough guile and enough subtle charm to entice him. And then ensnare him!

5

The handle on the big iron mangle moved a fraction and the warped wooden rollers groaned a reluctant acceptance to Ruth Nesbitt's intense effort. She pressed her bare feet down even harder on the horizontal bar near the base of the senile contraption in an attempt to stop it tipping over, at the same time heaving at the handle, her face twisted and teeth bared like an angry dog as she strained to press home her advantage. Slowly the heavy water-sodden blanket squeezed itself through the smiling gap in the rollers and with a satisfying splash of water on the scullery floor it curved out, flat and damp and ready for the line. She clung to the handle for a moment, her brow against her hands, gulping air into her lungs and willing the ache in her arms to subside. Finally with a mental effort that was as determined as her physical one, she dragged herself away, gathered up the blanket and staggered out into the morning of a still, dreary Monday.

She observed the ashen sky and the rows of motionless dripping washing through eyes that were heavy and as dull as the day itself. Her face, lined and old for her twenty years, flickered for a second with a mirthless smile before it twisted again as she threw the blanket over the line. She knew it was a waste of time; that there was no drying in the air that day. The Sneeds' washing was as wet as when she hung it out three hours earlier, but at least that lot was done and she would get her two shillings when Ted Sneed returned from the pit. She washed for the Sneeds every week. Old Ted, using one of his quiet little ruses, would pack their washing into a pillow case and leave it behind the scullery door. Nellie never suspected. Her mind, clouded with inner tortures, dismissed such trivialities as clean clothes. And Ruth, no matter how much the effort wracked her body, was glad of the extra money. But she could never guarantee its condition, other than its cleanliness. The Sneeds' kitchen would be draped with it that night, just as her own and all the others in the village. Normally on a Monday such as this she would have postponed the washing of blankets until a finer day, but she knew all too well that the smell of vomit got worse by the hour and to wash them immediately was the only answer. She had risen at six, the prospect of a Monday's wash enticing her to stay in the luxury of her warm bed, but the groans of her brother in the tiny bedroom opposite had spurred her on at the same time as it put a cold dread in her heart. She had changed his bed quietly with a soft sad understanding that she had felt so many times before, then with a forlorn urgency she had washed for the Sneeds, then for all five Nesbitts, then the blankets.

She shuffled back to the house. Her shoulders were drooped and her hair hung in a tattered mess but she was not aware of it. The job was done. That job at least, now she had food to prepare and water to heat for the men coming in from the fore-shift. They would be ravenous and noisy and black. Her head would pound from their banter. Her temper would rise when they trailed coal dust and mud into her kitchen and left handmarks on the furniture. But she would be so very glad they were safely home. Sometimes she wished that Alan could be just like them, that he would annoy her with the same hopeless manly traits that his father and brothers had. That in itself would alleviate most of her worry over him. But he was different. He was cut from a different cloth. He had never been meant for the pit; his premature frailty that had killed his mother had remained with him for seventeen years. Pitwork called for muscle and strength and a constitution that could withstand the rigours of a black, enclosed hell. But Alan was different. He was thin and delicate and his revulsion for the pit manifested itself in a malingering sickness that angered his father and embarrassed his brothers.

She continued her work, resigned to her duties and ignoring the tiredness that nagged at her body. She trailed heavy pails of water from the tap down the lane to fill the set pot at the side of the hearth so it would heat in preparation for their bath. She peeled potatoes and added them to the stew already bubbling on the hob. She swilled out the scullery and pushed the heavy mangle into the corner before dusting and tidying the kitchen. At last she was finished. The fire was banked high, the tin bath was ready beside it and the table was laid. Gratefully she sank into a rocking chair and closed her eyes for a few precious moments before they arrived. But her rest was short-lived. There was a knock at the back door. She sighed and forced herself to her feet, coaxing her weary legs to move. Her hand went to her throat when she opened the door and recognised Jimmy Alexander, the boy from the pit office. All the subliminal dread surged up inside her for a second. Then she realised her foolishness. There could have been no accident. The hooter would have blasted out its mournful signals long before, if there had been an accident. She breathed again.

"What is it Jimmy?", she asked, surprised at the coldness of her own voice.

"Mallory said for me to deliver this, missis," he chirped from a round, colourless face as he thrust a small brown envelope at her.

She took it from him, examining it as though it were some interesting curio, turning it over and over in her hands. "What's in?", she asked weakly, finally staring at the scrawled name of Alan Nesbitt.

"Dunno missis. Mallory came stalkin' out of his office and told me to deliver it straight away."

Ruth nodded dolefully, a sickening tightness gripping at her stomach. "Thanks Jimmy," she whispered.

The boy looked up at her. "You're welcome," he said flatly, knowing full well the doubt and wondering that clouded her face. He had seen it often enough with others.

She tried to smile. "Would you like some jam and bread, Jimmy?"

His face beamed like a new moon. He followed her into the kitchen and watched with shiny, beady eyes as she sawed out a wedge from a flat, round stotty, then layered it with raspberry jam. She saw him to the door, thanking him again with a false light-heartedness that disappeared as she closed it. The letter was on the table, lying there like some dormant lethal monstrosity, coaxing her near. She circled it, staring at the smooth brownness, afraid of it, afraid of even allowing Alan to open it for she knew there was bad news inside. But her curiosity overcame her dread and with a rush she tore the envelope open. The letter was short and blunt and brought gentle, warm tears to her eyes. It was an old piece of Company paper that looked as though it had lain on the office floor for weeks. There was a tea stain at the edge and the blue printed heading stating TOMLINSON COAL COMPANY had been intertwined with penned filigree and ink filled Os by some day-dreaming clerk. It was a pathetic piece of paper, crumpled, degenerate and it disgusted her even more than the written words.

to: Mr Alan Nesbitt,
10, First Row,
Bolam.

> This is to inform you that your employment
> at the above Company is herewith terminated
> for excessive absenteeism.
>
> J. C. Mallory
> Manager

She read it again and again, her mind seesawing with the implications of the brief statement. In a way it was a sweet relief for Alan. She knew that deep down inside him he would yell for joy. He was free from his torment and she was glad for him. But he would fake anger that he had been treated thus. He would join his father and brothers in their cursing of Mallory. Yet she remembered well all the times he had dragged himself to work, his thin pinched face and sad searching eyes reflecting his subdued abhorrence and fear. She had recognised it where the others, intent on preparing themselves for another shift, had not. Yes, she knew Alan would be happy. But how were they going to manage without the few shillings he received for his physical and mental torture? That consequence was the hardest to contemplate.

Her father and two other brothers worked hard and played hard with barely a thought for her and how she made ends meet. She heard them regularly rant on about their paltry wages but they accepted the fact that they were clothed and fed without questioning her thrift and industry. She knew full well that left to their own devices they would live on bread and beer and cigarettes and spend every penny with no thought for the future. They took her for granted: she accepted that for she had known no other since she was old enough to cook and clean and wash their clothes. Perhaps, she thought, being miners, the future was not worth caring about. She wondered if she could take in more washing. The idea crossed her mind but her body reacted by draining the remaining strength from her legs. She sagged into the rocking chair and the dreary piece of paper wafted down to the floor. She knew with a hopeless foreboding that she could do no more than she was doing. Softly she sobbed into her pinafore.

Ralph Nesbitt gave up the struggle to keep up with his sons. His pace slackened as he gulped air into lungs that rattled with each forced breath and finally he stopped as they ducked deftly under the multicoloured walls of washing and disappeared from view. He coughed a deep searching cough that seemed to bring something from far inside him and he spat a great mouthful of black phlegm onto the ground. He looked at the splatter of mucus from watering eyes, searching for something unusual – what? He didn't know, but he looked anyway, intrigued by the glob of filth that had only a few seconds before been part of him. He remained bent forward for a moment, hands on thighs and enjoying the air that now had a free passage and the diminishing sensation of suffocation. At last he straightened up and joined the stragglers of the fore-shift who were heading for home like a troup of ragged vaudeville coons, their eyes and mouths accentuated by the grimy blackness of their skin. Coming to Maudy Fenwick's shop and remembering he had no tobacco, he separated from the procession and went in. The shop was empty. Maudy, summoned by the bell, appeared as usual, her small being materialising from the musty shadows. She observed Ralph Nesbitt and her arms folded tightly under her shapeless chest as her head sunk into her shoulders. Ralph was amused by her actions as he always was, but he kept his smile to himself. He watched her eyes go wide and round and her face stretch to a taut uncertainty. He could almost sense the visions of mayhem and debauchery that her mind so vividly pictured for her. He moved closer to the counter and she swayed back a fraction.

"Yes, Mr Nesbitt," she whispered.

"Tuppeny chow," he said, forcing a dramatic flatness to his voice.

She placed a short ropelike length of tobacco on the counter, her eyes hardly leaving his blackened face. "The Coll'ry lad's been to your house," she said quickly.

Ralph's face darkened for a second, but he composed himself in an instant. The shop was the gossip exchange for most of the day and he knew she was burning for information. His mind raced. "Oh aye, " he said casually, "it'll be about our Tommy. He did it again last night."

There was a sudden twitch to her face and a sparkle in her eye. She was switched on for a revelation. "Did what?" she whispered.

Ralph shook his head in mock hopelessness. "I've warned him. But it's gone too far this time. In front of Tomlinson's wife as well."

He saw her brow tighten as she allowed herself to come a step closer. "What? What's your Tommy been doin'?" she breathed.

He looked to his left and then his right. He beckoned her even closer with an upward nod of his head. She took the bait. He bent forward to her ear and he could hear her excited breath coming in discreet bursts. "You'll keep this to yourself?"

There was a quick nod.

"Exposin' himself!"

There was no reaction for a second. Then it gelled in her brain. He could see from her bulging eyes as her head retreated anemone-like into her shoulders, the flesh that haunted her, the pride of phalli swirling in her mind like a vision through the multi-lensed eye of a fly. He laughed a great gurgling laugh and continued his journey home. But not with a smile on his face because he knew when the office boy called it meant only one thing and that was trouble.

He discovered he had been right the instant he opened the door and saw the silent stares of his two sons and Ruth's red-rimmed eyes. He slid his bait bag off his shoulder and let it drop onto the scullery floor. He turned his small hunched frame to each of them, spreading his thin toothless face into a stiff-lipped query that made his grey moustache bristle.

"Well?" he asked quietly, the tone of his voice already resigned to bad news.

Tommy and his brother Norman were already stripped to their rough cream-coloured combinations and stood with their backs to the fire. Ruth sat forward in her rocking chair and hung her head.

"Is it Alan?"

Tommy turned to face the fire. He spat vehemently over the pans and into it. "Yes, it's Alan," he snarled. "He's got the sack."

Ralph nodded a numb understanding. "I knew," he whispered, "I knew it would be Alan. I'm surprised Mallory's left him this long with the slump an' all."

"Mallory wants horse-whippin'!" Tommy growled.

Ralph nodded again. He turned and moved trance-like into the scullery. He started to strip.

Ruth jumped to her feet. "Is that all you've got to say the three of you," she yelled. "Are you not going to ask how he is. He's sick you know. Don't you realise that? He's not up there in bed for fun. He was sick all over the place after you lot went out. I've had to send for the doctor again."

There was silence as she stared at the unemotional faces of her brothers. She willed them to show some spark of concern. But there was none, only cold work-weary eyes blankly registering her agitation.

"Dr Jenkins'll say the same as he's said before," her father muttered from the scullery.

"And what's that?" she snapped.

"That he's work-shy."

Her brothers nodded solemnly.

Ruth's green eyes flashed with anger. "He's not!" she yelled. "You know that's not true. He's . . . he's delicate, that's all. Just the same as he's always been."

Ralph appeared from the scullery, stripped to the waist and holding up his sagging trousers with his hands. His dirty skin had the leathery look of age and his sunken chest heaved under sparse grey hairs.

Ruth turned to him. "And you should know that better than anybody. You and granny kept him wrapped up and molly-coddled for years. He could only go out when the sun was shining and the wind was in the right direction. Then all of a sudden you had to have him in the pit, didn't you. You had to have him down the hole for money. A few extra bob makes all the difference, you said. And because he can't swing a pick or kick a ball like these two here, you don't give a tinker's cuss for him. None of you!"

She looked at each of them in turn. She stopped at Tommy. Her voice revealed that she was on the brink of tears again. "Look at the chance you missed because of the pit – and him!" she said, pointing to her father but keeping her eyes riveted on her eldest brother. "A few extra bob would make all the difference. He said it again, didn't he? – When that bloke came for you for United. You could have been away and earning a fortune with those feet of yours. But no! He wanted the few bob from the blasted pit . . ."

Tommy's brow tightened. "That'll do Ruth," he growled quickly.

A sickly look came to Ralph's face. The three of them watched as he shuffled uncomfortably. He seemed to crumble in on himself and age visibly. Ruth turned to the fire and sniffed back tears as she stirred the stew.

Ralph cleared his throat and forced a smile to his face. He tied his braces like a belt around his waist. "Come on lads," he said with false joviality, "we'll eat dirty the day – eh? I'm bloody starvin'."

They sat down. Ralph slapped each of them heartily on the back. "Give the lads the meat, Ruth. Remember it's the semi-final on Saturday and I'm expecting a hat trick off the pair on them. What d'you say lads?"

They thawed slowly, then nodded, giving him a tight-lipped smile.

"That's the lads!" Ralph yelled with a chesty laugh. "Mebbe if we wash up Ruthy here'll lend us a couple of bob for the Fat Ox. What about it Ruth?"

She didn't answer. She kept her back to them, biting her lip and closing her eyes in an attempt to shut out their callous unconcern. And upstairs Alan Nesbitt, having heard all that was said, curled himself into a tight ball under the bedclothes and did the same.

John Kinghorn viewed the scene in front of him and could not disguise the distasteful look that creased his face. His eyes played for a second on the drab buildings of stone and brick that surrounded the Bolam drift, then ran the length of the long ridged spoil heap that was its offspring. He followed its dark barren form to where it petered out and revealed the low embankment of the railway line. He saw the rough humpy meadow and the Victorian ugliness that was the Fat Ox. And finally he came to the village itself that even the clean colours of the washing could not enhance. He looked around again. A train of wagons screeched slowly along the line, the engine that was pulling them belching out great plumes of smoke and steam. It disappeared behind the heap leaving only the choking exhaust billowing into the heavy sky.

Dr Jenkins walked around the car and stood beside him. He smiled, amused by his reaction to the view. "Well?" he said lightly. "The stranger's eyes see clearest, so they say. What do you think of it?"

John kept on looking. "God it's awful," he breathed.

His companion nodded. "I knew you'd say that – and you're right. It is awful. The houses are damp and overcrowded. The sanitation is medieval. Oh, it's not so bad at this time of the year but, man, in the summer the flies swarm like locusts."

John turned to him. "But how can people live like this?"

Dr Jenkins became serious. "Don't judge them by the looks of the place, John. You'll find most of them clean and tidy." He sighed. "They would like the good things in life as well, John, but they can afford nothing better. Tomlinson owns the property and pays the wages, but he's just a businessman."

"You mean he pays them what they're worth."

Dr Jenkins shrugged. "Perhaps not. What I mean is he's a man who offers employment to miners. If they accept his terms, what can anyone say? The fact that we, as doctors, may crow about unhealthy conditions doesn't enter into his ledger books. It's too intangible for him. It's the debit and credit columns that matter to him."

John nodded. "Seems to me they're a pretty rough bunch anyway. Hacking coal out of the ground calls for brawn and not brain. If they had a few they'd not be doing it."

Dr Jenkins smiled a knowing smile. "You've never been down a pit have you, John?"

"No sir! And not wanting to either."

"Let's hope you never have to," Dr Jenkins said with profundity. "Because if you have it'll probably be like something from a battlefield."

John sighed and shook his head in desperation. Up ahead near the beginning of the row three ragged children laughed as they pushed a friend in an ancient battered pram. A lop-eared mongrel with fur that matched the quality of its surroundings approached them, sniffed, then scratched itself nonchalantly before wandering away. How John envied Smythe at that moment.

"Despite everything," Dr Jenkins continued, "you'll find they're a fairly healthy bunch. We had only ten fatal tubercular cases last year and, other than usual diphtheria outbreaks and the like, we get little that'll have you thumbing through the books."

He gave John's arm a playful punch and his red face broke into a wide grin. "Steel yourself, lad," he said with a chuckle. "They'll not bite you."

John smiled grimly as they walked towards the washing. Perhaps it would be better if they did, he thought, and wake him from the nightmare he was sure he was having.

The gears rasped as the Sunbeam swung around the corner and back into Allington village. Suddenly Dr Jenkins applied the brakes and the pair of them lurched forward as the car came to an abrupt halt. John didn't have time to ask the reason why. It was answered for him as his companion waved a greeting to an approaching figure. The man accompanied by two lolloping cocker spaniels stopped by the side of the car. He was a tall well-built fellow nearing sixty with a heavy yellowed face that had an ample sprinkling of pock-marks. His eyes seemed small and were dark and gleamed ferret-like from under black bushy eyebrows. The small square of moustache that was neatly trimmed under his nose seemed somehow complementary to his homburg hat and his stiff butterfly collar. He placed a big meaty hand on the door and his broad, somewhat forced smile showed gold among the remnants of his unusually large teeth.

"Now then, Charles," Dr Jenkins said jovially as he sat back and crossed his arms, "we were just on our way to your house. I wanted John here to see Clarrie. How is she?"

The head cocked stiffly to observe him and the beady eyes were unblinking. "She's grand, just grand," came the reply in a flat husky voice. "Matter of fact I've just this minute been to your house. Ethel said you were on your rounds."

"Nearly finished, Charles. Clarrie was the last call. I wanted John's opinion."

"Ah," he said with a nod, "so this is your mysterious assistant that you kept such a big secret."

Dr Jenkins rolled a beaming head around to John, obviously enjoying his new acquisition and the flurry of gossip it had caused. "Oh I'm sorry," he said with his usual chuckle. "Charles, this is John Kinghorn. John meet Charles Tomlinson."

They shook hands. John knew that this was the man who owned Bolam Colliery. He had that air of prosperity about him, an aura of well-being and confidence that comes with success.

"Well now," Tomlinson said, "John here's the reason for my visit. Clarrie wants the pair of you to come to dinner tonight. You've kept this stranger undercover for long enough. And you can save yourselves a journey. I've already told Ethel, so you can see Clarrie tonight. She's burning with curiosity and so are the girls."

Jenkins beamed at his companion. "What say you John? Are you up to some warped sandwiches and conversation that'll bore you to death?"

"Oh come now, Bob," Tomlinson retorted, the forced smile returning. "Times are hard but we'll manage something for our guest. We can't have him think we eat our young up here – eh?"

He laughed a slow sickly laugh that was fabricated and not spontaneous and by then John had taken a dislike to him. There was a strange automation to his speech and facial expressions which lacked any hint of sincerity. But he was still pleased to accept. The rise and fall of his feelings since his arrival had him in a turmoil and he sensed perhaps this man who exuded the prosperity of his own kind could offer him a smattering of the life he had been used to; some sanctuary where his intellect could find some gratification and he could forget the depression that was Bolam.

They made four calls in the village. He had met Nellie Sneed whose agitation at the sight of a stranger had been curtailed by Dr Jenkins scolding her like a father would to a naughty daughter. Then they moved on to Robert Fulthorpe's house and checked on his youngest daughter who was recovering from mumps. In the two minutes it took to examine her, John was subjected to a bragging précis of his life. Then on to see Bella Scott and her phantom heart attack. It was a classic case. Her daughter Miriam who showed them up to the tiny bedroom was abjectly plain. Her very actions radiated her undeniable virginity: it was her soft voice and gentle movements and flat unblemished face. But her eyes carried a spark of happiness in them that overrode her obvious concern for her mother. She was to be married in March, after twenty years of ritual courtship to Sam Usher, a hewer in the pit. She had succumbed to his wooing and her mother had resorted to cardiac palpitations and other invented symptoms.

Finally they came to No. 10 First Row. Ralph opened the door. He was washed and wore a striped, collarless shirt.

"Eeh, Dr Jenkins," he said apologetically, "it's our Alan again. I'm sorry he's such a nuisance."

Jenkins took the remark with a casual wave of the arm. "Well," he said in a bored tone, "let's see what's wrong this time." He breezed in ignoring Norman in the bath and Tommy in the rocking chair. John followed, nodding a cold greeting to their embarrassed stares at the unannounced stranger.

"This is Dr Kinghorn," Jenkins said gruffly as he clattered up the carpetless stairs. "Let's see what he can make of him."

They entered the bedroom and Alan Nesbitt shrank down among the blankets. He was pale and thin and had sunken cheeks. His hair was brown and fine and his eyes were large, green and seemed to cry out for pity. There was a fineness to his skin, a delicate smoothness that seemed to accentuate his frailty. Ruth stood up when they entered and there was a moment of flurried hair smoothing when she observed the new doctor. She blushed and hung her head for an instant before she began to talk. Her voice was cracked, faltering and tearful.

"He's been sick again," she whispered.

Jenkins nodded and sat on the bed. "This is Dr Kinghorn, by the way," he said, looking at John and Ruth in turn by way of introduction. "He's my assistant. You'll be seeing him from time to time."

She smiled a weak smile then her face creased into worry again. John watched her as she watched the examination of her brother. He could tell her youth beneath her laboured features. He somehow knew the drudgery of her life. It was written into her face. And yet it was a pretty face. There seemed to be some inner quality to her; a kindness, an understanding, a calmness behind those green eyes.

"Come on now, Alan," Jenkins said reproachfully, "there's nothing wrong with you, man. You've just got to face up to things. Everybody's got to work."

"He can't work doctor," Ruth said coldly. "He's got the sack."

"When?"

" 'S mornin', Mallory's given him the sack." Her voice was dejected, unemotional, automatic.

"I'll get another job, Ruth, don't worry," Alan said suddenly in a voice as fragile as his features.

Jenkins sighed and snapped his bag shut. "Here John," he growled, "see what you can make of it. I've given him every test in the book. Can't find a thing. Pure aversion syndrome if you ask me. General malaise brought on by his dislike of work."

"The pit, doctor," Ruth said firmly. "It's the work underground he can't abide. But not work. He doesn't mind work."

Jenkins grunted and stood up. "I'll see Ralphy about him."

He made for the door and John took his place.

"Please, Doctor Jenkins," Ruth begged, "could you speak to Mr Mallory and get him set on to some light job. He'll listen to you. All he wants is a chance. He'll show you he's not lazy. Won't you, Alan?"

Alan, sitting up now, clasped his thin sensitive fingers in front of him and nodded.

Dr Jenkins shook his head. "It's no good Ruth. Mallory's fed up with him. I've spoken for him before. He'll have to make his own way now." He clumped his way heavily down the stairs.

John examined the patient. There was something pathetic about his limp, slight form. He smiled a reassuring smile at him but there was little response. Finally he pulled up the blankets and turned to his sister. "I can find nothing wrong," he said gently. "Let him get up when he wants to. You might find he'll be all right now."

Ruth's lined and tired face nodded slowly.

"It is Ruth isn't it?"

She nodded again.

He could almost feel the exhaustion that stooped her young body. There was some help he could be to her; of that he was sure. He rose and closed his bag. "Will you come to the surgery in the morning, Ruth?"

She looked startled. "For medicine? For Alan?"

"No – for you."

She made to protest, to tell him that there was nothing wrong with her. That she felt grand. But she stopped herself. She felt so weak, like a crumbling shell, like a shadow within her being, as though the whole world was pressing its great weight upon her. "If I've got time," she whispered.

There was a strange feeling inside him as they walked back to the car. Dr Jenkins was ranting on about Tommy Nesbitt and the great centre forward he was, but John barely heard him. His mind was once again preoccupied with self analysis. This time the symptoms were more subtle and yet they were positive enough to vie against his overriding gloom. As yet they were a jigsaw of fragmented thoughts, but the sensation was there. A will-o'-the-wisp of sympathy. A nebulous prickle of conscience. Disgusted with himself, he drove them from his mind.

The house of the Tomlinsons was a big ten-roomed edifice, stone built and ivy covered, standing aloofly back from the road at a distance from the eastern edge of Allington. Its red gravelled drive ran for fifty yards and soared outward near the elevated, pillared front door and encompassed the whole building. Tall leafless beeches lined the drive, populated with dark knots of rooks' nests and swaying with an eerie, brittle rustle as a cool breeze from the sea disturbed their slumber. The whole scene was in keeping with Charles Tomlinson. It had the same blatant grandeur, the same awesome importance. Yet the house had an intangible falseness, a frigidity that the softly lit windows could not dispel.

Tomlinson himself opened the door, He seemed incomplete without his hat, smaller, less dignified. His round head was almost bald except for a few strands of greying hair that were brushed and parted as they had been for years. Three women were close on his heels and Dr Jenkins greeted them with hugs and exuberant jollity. He chortled his way through the introductions, revelling in their cooing delight at the handsome stranger. Clarrie Tomlinson was everything Jenkins had said she was. Born and raised in India and still carrying the "head-back" and "eyes down" pomposity of an officer's daughter. She was an ageing chinless wonder with so much powder on her face that the fine hairs stood out, accentuating her advancing years. She was a slight woman, round shouldered but distinguished with immaculate white hair and a single string of pearls at her neck. She seemed to have recovered from her recent attack of malaria that his companion had been treating with quinine and plasmoquine. Perhaps she had recovered too much, John thought, for her piercing, affected voice grated on his nerves. Her daughters seemed no better. Two wilting spinsters obviously both over thirty, hen-faced and shapeless with short crimp-waved hair.

For John, the hour's preamble before dinner was a gruelling one. He was bombarded with questions and opinions and flirtatious chit-chat from Grace and Jane who caricatured their sophistication by drinking neat gin and smoking cigarettes as though they were conducting the death march. Tomlinson stood authoritatively with his back to the ornate walnut fireplace and spoke little, listening to the others and occasionally smiling a forced, quick smile which was obviously false by the amount of teeth he showed. John slowly began to enjoy himself. There was something ridiculously amusing about them all. He remembered an old lecturer telling him that the rhinoceros showed that nature had a sense of humour. The Tomlinsons added more evidence.

Dinner when they sat down to it stifled their chatter somewhat. John relished the game pâté, having to smile and nod reassuringly only once to the two females sitting opposite him. Then there was a delicious sole mornay washed down with a pleasant Chablis and by the time they tackled the jugged hare there was only the clatter of knives and forks and the odd irrelevance from the irrepressible Dr Jenkins. John glanced at him occasionally and smiled inwardly. He could tell his immense pleasure at being there by the hearty way he ate and his avid comments to anything the Tomlinsons said. Poor old Jenkins, he thought. This is it. This is living. This is the antithesis of your childhood. You're made. You've arrived. You've reached the pinnacle of the social scale.

Tomlinson himself was rather subdued during the meal. He smiled his automatic smiles but chatted formally holding himself erect and proper and ignoring the obvious attempts by his embarrassed wife to melt his starchy attitude. It wasn't until the tiny bow-legged maid had served coffee and brandy in the ornament-littered lounge that he began to talk with any conviction. His nose hovered over his brandy glass and he brought the giggling of his two daughters to an abrupt halt.

"I'm glad you young'uns can laugh," he said in a flat voice. "There'll be no laughing shortly, I fear. There's going to be trouble. I can feel it in my bones."

His face darkened and his brow tightened as though to say "There – I've said it!"

Clarrie looked alarmed and flustered. Almost in one action she smiled a watery smile toward John and shot a black look toward her husband that was a mixture of concern and anger. "Now, now Charles," she chided, "don't get excited again – not now."

"What's wrong, Charles?" Dr Jenkins said with mild astonishment.

He looked into his brandy glass. "Oh it's nothing really I suppose," he said with a false lightness. "Just this damned Samuel commission and whatnot. I've got one of his inspectors coming next week. He'll be prying all 'round the pit and in the books. God knows what he'll ask to see or what the final report will have to say." He sat back and sipped his brandy. "The whole damned business is getting me down. We're living on a subsidy, Bob, and that's like charity. What's worse, the charity stops after April."

Jenkins grunted. "Oh, come on now Charles, you'll see your way through if anyone can," he added nicely.

Clarrie, sensing her husband was now well and truly mounted on his hobby-horse politely excused herself and the girls and left the men to discuss the whole sordid business.

John was intrigued. The man had given no impression that he could have any strong emotions about anything. "What will happen then?" he asked.

Tomlinson raised his head and his bushy eyebrows lifted. "When?" he asked coldly.

"When the subsidy stops?"

Tomlinson turned to Jenkins, an almost arrogant amused smile on his face. "It seems we must educate our southern friend on the ways and wiles of the pit, eh Bob?"

Jenkins nodded stupidly, replenishing his brandy glass. John glowered at him.

"Let us pray that Samuel and Beveridge and Company will see sense. Their report must come down on the side of the owners. If we are to survive we must have greater output and at the same time cut the cost of extracting the damned stuff from the ground." Tomlinson rattled out the words with swarmy self-assurance, with rehearsed and over-emphasised clarity.

"How will you manage that?" John countered with lamb-like

innocence, well aware of the measures required, but already seething because of the patronising attitude of his host.

Tomlinson leaned forward. "Longer hours and less pay," he said hoarsely. "If they want me to keep the pit open and provide them with a job, they've got to sacrifice some time and some money."

John's mind raced with devilment. "And what if they refuse?" he said with a dramatic softness.

"Refuse?" Tomlinson whispered. "Refuse?" he said again, his voice gaining in strength. He gave a tight derisory laugh. "Then there'll be trouble, young man. The lock-out notices will go up. It'll be like '21 again only this time there'll be anarchy."

John remembered well the slump of late 1920 when unemployment rose to almost three quarters of a million. Coal exports to the continent declined because of cheaper American coal. There were one million miners locked out when they refused to accept pay cuts. There were troops at the coalfields; leave cancelled. Lloyd George called up the reservists, and armed camps appeared in London parks. All very serious and dramatic and foreboding.

Tomlinson had now coloured. His yellowed face was flushed with annoyance. "Dammit man, Bob here will tell you, I'm one of the fairest owners in the county – eh Bob?" Jenkins' closed eyes fluttered then settled again. Tomlinson ignored him. "Any of them can come to me, you know – personally, mark you, if they've a grievance. I'll listen. As God is my witness I listen. They wanted pit-head baths. What did I do?" He waved a casual hand toward the window. "They're being built now, at Bolam, and all they've got to pay is six measly pence a week. Damned unions! Damned bolsheviks! They're out to ruin the country, John. Mark my words." He seemed deflated now, worried, spent. "There's not a fairer man than me, John," he whispered.

John sat back and viewed his host with contempt. He looked at the splendour of the room and remembered the delectable food, then compared it with the houses of the Sneeds, Fulthorpes, Scotts and Nesbitts and what he had noticed bubbling on their respective hobs. The transformation had been too much for him. All this rubbing shoulders with all that he thought; like being plunged from an icy bath into a boiling one. The Nesbitts! Suddenly he remembered the plaintive cry of Ruth Nesbitt and the cold rebuff from Jenkins. He saw immediately how he could put this misplaced saint to the test and cause him to bite his tongue.

"You are a fair man, I've heard it said by quite a few," he said casually.

Tomlinson's dark eyes blinked. "Already?"

"Yes, some of the people at Bolam said so today."

"Why? Why?" he gasped, intensely interested.

"Well, there's a lad there called Alan Nesbitt. He's not a strong lad, premature born. Lucky to have lived really. But he's sickly. Working underground's too much for him. He gets bouts of vomiting. To cut a long story short, your manager Mallory sacked him because he's often off work. He needs a job. He needs to be working. All the rest of the family were going to write to you and ask if you could find him a light job on the surface. They said you were sure to help because you're such a fair man."

Tomlinson blinked, his befuddled mind straining to accept the story. Then it rejected it and John saw he had rejected it. For the first time since meeting him, Tomlinson's smile was genuine. And John smiled with him, more from relief that he had taken it in such good heart.

"Hah!" he yelled jovially, "you're a sharp one Dr Kinghorn, you are that. You had me almost believing . . . but the lad, is that true?"

John nodded, serious now. "He needs a job sir, anything that's not too heavy and is indoors."

Tomlinson took a fountain pen from inside his pocket and made a note of the name on a piece of folded paper discovered in his waistcoat. "Alan Nesbitt, you say? How old?"

"About seventeen."

"Hmm. There may be something in a while. I'll bear it in mind." He smiled again. "I asked for that, eh Bob?" He punched the sleeping doctor playfully on his round belly. Two bloodshot eyes appeared from the folds of florid, wrinkled skin. There was a grunt and a drowsy mumbled apology and Dr Jenkins roused himself.

It was bitterly cold when they said their goodbyes. The trees were still now and the stars radiated their presence in glittering, silent majesty. The two doctors crunched their way down the red gravelled drive, shoulders hunched and heads drawn down into the collars of their coats. They did not speak on their way to Plessey House. The strange, abject hush that has a noise all of its own and is peculiar to such nights had a sanctity, an absoluteness broken only by their footsteps and by the time they reached the gate John, with a warm glow of achievement to keep him company had decided to walk to Bolam. He didn't bother to question the motivation for his decision. It was natural that he should go and he made an excuse to his protesting companion. His voice was clear and determined in the sharp air and Dr Jenkins, finally at a loss as to why he needed yet more leg-stretching on such a night, shrugged and mumbled about not making a noise when he returned.

There was something about that night that exhilarated him. The smell of the frost on the grass, the sense of eternity in the stillness filled him with a euphoric awareness of himself as though the universe revolved around him. The fleeting sensation of an infinite soul in a finite body. He was at peace and the world was his for the asking.

It seemed like only a minute until he was walking up First Row. It was late, he realized that, but it didn't matter to him. He wanted to tell her the news, to see some of the great worry lifted from her youthful shoulders. The silence was gone now. A train had rattled slowly up the line as he approached the village and he had heard it shudder to a halt in Allington. An express had thundered through in the opposite direction, a low luminous ribbon in the darkness. Then there was the clank of the pit and the barking of dogs and the murmur of sleepy conversation from the houses.

The light was still on at No. 10 and he was glad. It didn't occur to him that Ralph or one of his sons might answer the door. But that possibility was academic. They were all in bed and asleep; only Ruth was still on her feet clearing up after them. When she opened the door her look of surprise could not disguise the misery that shrouded her slim, dejected figure.

"Dr Kinghorn. What's wrong?" she whispered.

He smiled, his vapourized breath billowing outward. "How is Alan, Ruth?"

Her surprise turned to puzzlement. "He's all right. He got up at tea-time. He's eatin' again, but he's asleep now. Should . . . ? "

He shook his head. "No don't wake him. I've just come from Tomlinson's house. I've got some good news for you. He's promised Alan a job, a light job."

Her green eyes cleared and she inhaled noisily. There was a smile on her face in an instant. She patted at her unkempt hair and smoothed her ragged pinafore in her excitement as her eyes filled. She was pleased, overjoyed, he could tell. His journey had been worthwhile.

"Goodnight Ruth, and don't forget the surgery tomorrow."

"But . . ."

"No buts. Goodnight."

He thrust his hands deep into the pockets of his overcoat and set off back to Plessey House. A strange satisfaction ran through him. A completely novel feeling, similar but not the same as when he gave his first injection and when he administered his first drugs and the patient responded. It was a feeling of power, refined power, precious power, and he was thankful for it. Then the thought strayed into his mind why he had bothered himself that night. He could have been warm and in bed by now. Perhaps a touch of guilt at the good food and luxury he had enjoyed so close to such poverty? Perhaps just the impulsiveness and unpredictability that had governed his life and was so much a part of his character? He didn't know and chose not to ponder on it further.

There was a figure at the bottom of the row and as he approached he could see it was a tall man wearing a heavy trench coat and a trilby hat.

"Excuse me," the man said softly as the doctor drew level.

"Yes?"

"Could you direct me to the Nesbitts' house? I'm looking for Tom Nesbitt."

John looked up at the gaunt features and into the deep dark eyes that gazed unblinking at him through the weak light from a window. "Oh, the Nesbitt's house. It's up there. No. 10."

The man thanked him and moved on. John continued his walk. He hadn't noticed the man was carrying a suitcase or even that his accent was not local. Poor Willie Cox, still bedridden, would have been hopping mad that he had missed him. He arrived at Allington on the last stopping train out of Newcastle that night. John had heard it but it had no significance for him. Yet the stranger he had chanced upon would be instrumental in shaping his whole future life. It was the long awaited visitor from London. A man called Kenneth Frederick Tilmouth.

6

Slowly he looked around the crowded bar, turning his head with deliberation, letting his cold, dark eyes examine each of the faces in turn. He made a mental note of some, allowing his past experience to judge the calibre of their beliefs, the strength of their convictions. They were all there; all hues of character, all the delineations of determination. Some stood out, others were faded shadows. Drones, he thought, only drones. Yet there was a common factor to them all. A desperate brooding that united their hunger for justice and had forged them into a symbiotic regiment. He studied their faces: the young, their spirit fresh and squirming bringing colour to their cheeks, a sparkle to their eyes; the old, drained of their strength, pallid, heaving air into dust-clogged lungs. Faces that could tell a thousand tales from withered lips, pulling the memories from features that were blue-scarred and ravaged by their toil. But it was not a new sight. He had seen it before. Everywhere they were the same; branded by the same want, by the same hardships. Excited by the same humble dreams.

The Fat Ox was crammed to capacity on that Friday night late in January when Kenneth Tilmouth chose to speak to the working men of Bolam. He had shown himself several times since his arrival the previous Monday. He had aroused some curiosity, stirred a little controversy, bought a few of the old men double rums and thus made a few instant friends. But his actions – unknown to the locals – were preset and sterile, well rehearsed and as coldly unemotional as the impulses of a robot.

He knew what he had to do. His task could be defined quite simply but its success only measured by future historians. But he was undaunted. His narrow, rigid ideals had been forged many years before by the sight of a horrid, greasy-faced undertaker prising his dead parents apart from their last pathetic embrace. It was January 1900 and they died in the bitter night in their rat infested slum. They froze to death, their blood thinned by hunger, their bodies wrapped together under the rags which were their bed.

And now he waited for their questions. He had talked for nearly an hour. He had let his quiet, steady voice, that had swayed so many before, creep around the room, penetrate their minds, stir their imaginations. He breathed noisily, sensing the revolution that was in them, waiting for the first self-conscious question and the avalanche that would follow.

It was Willie Cox who took a quick gulp at his beer then stood up first. He rocked back and forward on his heels a few times and fumbled in his pockets as he cleared his throat. His thin, oriental face smiled, only he wasn't smiling. "Well, Mr Tilmouth – eh, what I'd like to know like – eh, is who the hell's t'blame for the slump anyway?" He looked quickly around for any agreeing nods then nodded himself and sat down.

Tilmouth smiled to himself. He could have gone into chapter and verse about the Franco-Belgian occupation of the Ruhr in 1923 and explained the consequences but limited himself to the salient points which he hoped would do to emphasise his earlier talk. He stared with unblinking eyes toward Willie Cox. "The slump can be blamed on one man and one man alone!" he said positively. "That man is the Chancellor of the Exchequer. He is a Tory and an enemy of the working class. He is Winston Churchill. He and he alone is responsible for our plight. He returned this country to the Gold Standard. Why? You may ask. Because he wished us to be the hub of capitalism in the world. He decided that a handful of rich men should be made richer, while one million of you miners go poorer!"

There was a murmur among the crowd. An angry murmur. A blunt nail had been driven home.

"And so," he continued lethally, "the consequence of his actions you are feeling now and will continue to suffer until you are prepared to rise up and fight for your just rewards. Revaluation has made good British coal too expensive for the export market." His black penetrating eyes moved over them. "He has returned you to slavery. You must rise up as one and conquer him!"

There was a deep throaty yell of enthusiasm. A thin humourless smile came to Tilmouth's face. They were responding and he felt a pounding in his body.

Sam Usher stood next. He was a tall, well-built man and had a benign ageing face. There was a quiet but firm honesty to his voice, an unquestionable logic to his thinking. "What about the Royal Commission?" he asked. "Won't that come down on the side of the miners? Won't the Government force the coal owners to improve the position?"

Tilmouth shook his head. "Listen men – and think hard. Think of who is investigating the industry. Samuel, a liberal, a High Commissioner in Palestine. Beveridge, a liberal and civil servant and

Director of the London School of Economics. Lawrence and Lee, bankers." He held out his arms. "What do these men know about pits? What can they learn? Nothing men – nothing! They will read statistics from scraps of paper. They will listen to watered down reports and form opinions that will suit them and their capitalist friends. They cannot comprehend conditions where you have to work, eat and excrete in the same black, foul space. You are a necessary evil, my friends. Samuel and his men will give nothing but the barest minimum. The coal owners will be laughing. Mark my words and be ready!"

There was a shocked buzz of conversation and Tilmouth looked in turn at Tommy Nesbitt and his brother Norman where they sat at each side of him. There was no need to speak. Their grim faces met and conferred with a telepathy generated by the intense magnet of their like minds. There was a tightness in Tommy's throat, an overwhelming surge of emotion. This man was a prophet, a saviour and he, and he alone, had brought him to Bolam.

Fulthorpe returned the bar to silence. He slowly raised himself with rehearsed dignity, looping his thumbs into the armholes of his waistcoat, intent on giving an oration that would impress the stranger and his fellow workers. There was no doubt about his persuasion. He was an ordinary pitman at heart and his veneer of quality was desperately thin. He was aware of that. He recognised the subtle ridicule that came from his councillor colleagues and the hidden derision of the villagers. Nevertheless he continued with his facade; a curious quirk of his nature that fulfilled some deep-rooted longing.

"Ah!" thought Tilmouth, "one of the drones." He fixed his gaze on Fulthorpe's bloated face and waited for the platitudes. Their eyes met. Fulthorpe cleared his throat gruffly, then began to sweat. The words wouldn't come. Tilmouth's eyes seemed to lay bare his soul. There was a wicked magic to them, a searching dominance that deflated him completely.

"But what about Tomlinson," he managed to say at last, his voice hopelessly unsure. "How can we complain about him? He's buildin' the baths. He must think something of us."

There was a ripple of groans and mocking laughter.

Fulthorpe spun around. "Well he is, isn't he? What are we supposed to do – murder the bugger?"

Tilmouth chose his words well. He had already formed his opinion of the man. He knew his weakness. He also knew of his position in the County Council. He could be a useful tool.

"Don't laugh," he said solemnly. "Mr Fulthorpe has a point. You must learn to recognise the wiles of the owners. Any gesture that seems on the surface to be generous has an ulterior motive. It must have by the very nature of their position. These things are designed to impress you, to lull you into thinking that your welfare is their concern. You must also recognise and believe in your own power. It is you, all of you, who are his strength. You are the cause of his riches. He lives in a fine house. You live in hovels. Compare your rewards. It is your profit he takes. It is your world. You must take what is yours!"

Fulthorpe puffed out his chest and nodded around the room as they yelled their agreement.

Tilmouth held up his hands for silence and when it came he waited a moment so that his words would have the emphasis they required. His voice was deep and had a thick liquidity. "There was a man who you have all heard of. His name was Karl Marx. He said it is imperative to overthrow all conditions in which man is a humiliated, enslaved, despised and rejected being. He meant you comrades – he meant you!"

Tommy Nesbitt jumped to his feet. His face was flushed with excitement, his eyes shone with a glazed delight. "I told you, men – I told you the day was comin'." He turned to his mentor. His voice dropped to a hoarse, urgent whisper. "Tell us what we must do," he demanded.

Tilmouth again waved away their noisy enthusiasm. He looked around them once more as they held their breath. He could taste the latent energy that surged inside them and he knew his visit had not been in vain. He had read them the gospel and their conversion had begun. He remembered another statement from Marx. "As soon as the lightning of thought has struck deep into the virgin soil of the people, they will emancipate themselves and become men." But there was much more to do. Bolam was a tiny cog in the wheel. He looked to Tommy. Yes, Tommy was the one. Tilmouth's intuition told him so. Tommy was the vanguard. He would keep the lightning flashing into them. Tilmouth had a new disciple.

He stood up. "You must do nothing," he said flatly.

There was a wondering gaze from his audience.

"Not yet. You must wait until the Commission publishes its findings. You must wait until the end of the subsidy. But while you are waiting, while you are hacking out coal and struggling to feed your families, train your minds. Tell yourselves that you are the masters. Believe in yourselves and that the right to work is not a favour, a whim of some one man." He slammed a fist hard into the palm of his hand. "Believe it! Believe it! Believe it! And when the time comes for action you will know what to do and when – all of you, all of this great country of workers!"

The questions came and the answers were given until they degenerated into irrelevancy. The bar was a mist of blue tobacco smoke and beer fumes. Hot bodies, sweating from their mental action, queued to shake hands with Kenneth Tilmouth. And he did so with pleasure and a shrewd inward satisfaction.

There was one man, however, who did not shake his hand. He had sat at the back of the crowd listening intently to all that was said, quietly smoking his pipe and analysing to the best of his ability the words uttered by Tilmouth. There was a deep suspicion in him that made him uneasy. This was not one of the union men exhorting them to fight their legal fight for a just reward. This man was a fanatic. He had entranced them and twisted their reasoning; of that he was sure. And the Nesbitts were almost kissing his feet. He had to speak to Tommy – soon – before he got himself into trouble, serious trouble. With that settled in his mind, Edward Sneed rose stiffly from his chair and set off with his slow ponderous roll for home – not a nebulous castle in the sky – but home where Nellie was.

Alan Nesbitt sprawled on his bed, dressed only in a shirt and a pair of underpants, his left arm under his head and his eyes staring dreamily at the flaking whitewash on the sagging ceiling. He listened to the muffled resonant roar of the fire carried from downstairs and the wind moaning a slow variable pitch as it chased itself around the eaves of the house. Occasionally it brought the far-off sound of cheering and the oohs and aahs of a crowd wrapped in the thrills of a football match. There was something about the sounds that gave him a strange, gentle pleasure as though the rest of the world was remote and unreachable and he was in a womb of warmth and safety and peace. He was enjoying his solitude. It was a luxury after a week of rumbustious excitement as his father and brothers lived the drama that was now being enacted. They had discussed the game, analysing it with keenness and a never-ending fervour that he could not fully comprehend. Football was their religion. It entered every aspect of their lives and even the arrival of Tilmouth had not quelled it. It became an adjunct to their nightly deliberations about unions and working conditions and political dogma that went on until well after twelve. Sometimes there was laughter, sometimes the low whispers of plot and intrigue; but he was like his sister, unable to interest himself in such matters, and the pair of them had retreated each night upstairs, away from their chatter and the chilling, searching stares of Tilmouth. Yet even sleep was denied them. The room that he, thankfully, shared with his sister now accommodated the stranger and

Ruth was forced to sit and doze at the foot of her own bed until the men below had exhausted their debating. He felt so sorry for Ruth, for her shuffling forlorn weariness; for her broken spirit and the way she accepted her father's suggestion that Tilmouth should have her bed and she should sleep on the floor downstairs. She had shrugged and nodded a blank, unemotional affirmation. He had made to speak, to protest; he did not want this unannounced man to share the room with him - an unknown, a strange body in such close proximity. Yet he said nothing as an odd feeling germinated inside him; a mixture of fear and excitement that made his skin tingle.

He had woken to his heavy ominous knock on the Monday night and, sleepy-eyed and with a hesitant formality, joined his family downstairs as they fussed around Tilmouth. The man was tall and imposing and exuded a slow clinical exactness through his movements and speech that fascinated Alan. He had still been awake when Tilmouth finally came to bed. He had held his breath and forced his vision to penetrate the darkness. He had watched the shadowy form and listened to the rustle of discarded clothes, his heart pounding, flooding his mind and body with an exquisite, delicate enjoyment. Finally there was a creak of springs as Tilmouth had lowered himself into the small bed opposite. There was a sigh and then silence.

Alan had stared through the night for a long time, wild ideas running through his mind that the man might rise up like some fiendish ghoul and strangle him. Then the strangulation was altered and the face became soft and full and kind. Perhaps he would come over and talk softly to him, console him and stroke his brow with a gentle, timed motion. But there was nothing, no movement, no sound of breathing. The stranger was asleep. Sadly he had turned over and sunk into fitful, dream-ridden unconsciousness.

He turned his eyes from the ceiling and looked around the room, thankful that in normal circumstances he shared it with Ruth and not his brothers. There was something about the room that comforted him; its tidiness, its paltry array of feminine bric-a-brac: the pot-pourri on the tiny dresser that gave off a smell of roses, her precious powder jar and a small bottle of blue coloured scent standing on a hand mirror. All her cramped enclosed world that was so importantly different from the rest of the house filled him with a peace of mind that made the harsh frustrating realities of his life fade into the realms of fantasy. His brothers' room was different. It was rough and untidy and carried the dank odour of sweat. Yet they didn't seem to care. Their life was tuned to work and play with none of the inner conflict that he knew. Why? Why was he different? He would have dearly liked to be one of them, to conform to their way of life, to drink and swear and feel the exhilaration of football and their enthusiasm at the conquest of a female. He had heard them talking often enough and imagined himself being the same, but there was some mental barrier to his thoughts, some uncontrollable repugnance at their actions that he could not overcome.

He sighed and sat up, then moved fretfully to the door. He saw Tilmouth's grey suitcase under Ruth's bed and his striped flannel pyjamas folded neatly on the pillow. He wondered how long the man would stay; how long before they could return to normal. There was a sudden roar of the wind. A goal, he thought or a near miss. Bolam Blue Star would be locked in battle, the scent of victory drowning out everything but the oblong of sloping meadow and the yellow shirts of Bedlington Welfare. They would have one hand already on the Welfare Cup and when they finally had two everything in the world would be right and just – for a day or so anyway. Then the polish of their victory would tarnish and their lives degenerate into harsh reality. They would toil underground and sleep the deep sleep of exhaustion, then cling to the fleeting pleasures of life as though each day was their last. He gave a derisive scowl as he crossed his arms over his chest and held his shoulders. He padded barefoot down the stairs and into the kitchen expecting to find Ruth about her chores, wanting the haven of her proximity to shelter him from the unremitting insecurity that permeated his every thought. The kitchen was empty. The clock ticked on the mantle and the kettle wheezed out steam into the flames of the fire. He moved to the back door and poked his head around it.

"Ruth!" he yelled towards the ash closet.

There was no answer. He turned and slunk quickly back to the kitchen away from the array of pit clothes that hung in the scullery and carried a heavy clayey smell that conjoured instant visions of claustrophobic dripping seams and hours of dark terror. He stood with his back to the fire, surveying the dismal room that somehow seemed large and spacious after the crowd of the week. He looked for a moment at the photograph of his mother hanging near the stairs and smiled dully at the wallpaper where it was gradually lifting with the encroaching dampness of the winter.

Then he saw it on the floor near the table. A white handkerchief, a neat square of broderie anglaise, unused; its scalloped edges smooth and unruffled. He picked it up. It was Ruth's, that he knew. It was Ruth's nicest that she kept for best, for the rare times she managed to dress for an occasion. Where was she? Where had she gone? His mind raced with reasons and places but came to no conclusion. He examined the handkerchief, letting his eyes focus on the intricate needlework. He unfolded it and the sweetness of lavender came to him. He closed his eyes and breathed deeply, letting the perfume swamp his whole being. He gave a wan smile as an intangible pleasure coursed through him, blotting out the pit and the village and the incongruity of his feelings. Slowly he turned, his eyes dreamily guiding him back toward the stairs and his room. There was a fleeting sensation of guilt as he opened the drawer of Ruth's dresser, but the guilt was exciting and lent itself to his mood. He had experienced it on other occasions when the men were about their business and Ruth had gone to the shops and the house was as still and lonely as it was now. He didn't care that when it was over the guilt would still be there in its true form. That didn't matter. At that moment in time he was free. He was Alan Nesbitt. He was himself. He looked down at the pale blue satin slip, so little used, so fine and smooth and shiny. There should have been a white one there as well and he realised that she was indeed dressed that morning. Slowly he picked it up, cherishing its niceness, rubbing gently at its texture before laying it on the bed. It revealed more treasures underneath. A pair of white cotton knickers, a brassiere, a pair of silk stockings. He fondled them all, his thin delicate fingers drawing satisfaction into his body. He got to his feet and took the slip again and it fell silently out of its folds. He held it up, then against himself, shutting his eyes, letting its smoothness touch his legs and arms.

"Well now, Alan!"

The words came with a menacing softness, yet they hit him a sledge-hammer blow. He stood with bulging eyes, his jaw moving involuntarily, seeing yet not believing the long, gaunt features of Kenneth Tilmouth in the doorway of the bedroom. The face smiled; the eyes gleamed, two black, overpowering orbs. Alan let out a bleating cry and dropped the slip. His hands clawed at the air as they slumped to his sides, then with a groan that slowly rose in pitch he turned and threw himself on his bed, burying his head into the pillow and thumping his small fists into the bedclothes in an agony of realisation.

Tilmouth moved quickly to his side, his thin bloodless lips parted and his face carrying the gloating satisfaction of supremacy. His intuition had told him; his mental dissection of the boy had told him: and now here surely was proof. And how fortuitous. He revelled in flaws of character. Not only did they give him a smug gratification that he was above them, but they were so useful to his cause; they were levers for the heavy cemented blocks of thought that could sometimes crowd his path.

"There, there, Alan," he said gently, patting the boy's shoulder.

"Come now, why are you so upset?"

There was no response other than the muffled moaning from the pillow.

"Oh, Alan," he sang in a sickly, sugary voice, "we can't let you be unhappy. I'm your friend, you know that don't you? What's the matter, do you think you'll get into trouble?"

There was a hesitant nod.

"Well come on, nobody's going to know. Nobody'll find out. I wouldn't get you into trouble for the world."

Slowly Alan turned over, his face a mixture of doubt and unhappiness. He stared dolefully up at Tilmouth. "I . . . I just . . ."

Tilmouth pursed his lips and shook his head. "No, don't explain. Don't say anything." He smiled again patronizingly and ruffled Alan's fine hair. "Just fold the things neatly and put them back so Ruth won't know and once the drawer is shut we'll forget all about it, eh?"

Alan sniffed and stood up. He looked to the drawer then back at the expectant, cheerful face. He bit his lip as he felt himself coming under Tilmouth's stare. There were tears of apprehension and mistrust running warm and salty into his mouth.

"Quickly now!" Tilmouth whispered urgently, "before they come in. The football match was nearly over when I left."

Alan hesitated, then moved to the drawer. He picked up the slip and swallowed hard. To touch it again under the inquisitive gaze of this man jangled his nerves, made him feel suddenly filthy, made his stomach squirm.

"There now," Tilmouth breathed when Alan finally closed the drawer, "it's done, it's over with, it never happened." He put an arm around his frail shoulders. "We have a little secret, you and I. But friends don't tell secrets, do they now?"

Alan's mind swirled with the unreality of it all; with the shame and the shock of discovery. He managed to shake his head.

"Good man, now let's get downstairs and wait for your dad and Tommy and Norman. You can make a pot of tea while I gather my books and what not. I'm leaving today. I've got to get back to London."

A surge of relief suddenly lifted Alan's heart. He tried to stop it showing but he was uncertain that he did. At least Tilmouth appeared not to notice as he followed him down the stairs.

"But don't worry," Tilmouth said with a sudden frost on his voice, "we'll meet again, Alan. Soon I'm sure. Your brothers are good lads and they've got the rights of the working class as their cause in life. That's how it should be, you know. You'll help them if they need help, won't you?"

Alan turned at the foot of the stairs, anxious to please, willing to say anything lest this dominant, frightening man should breathe a hint of what happened to his family.

"Oh yes sir," he bleated, "oh yes, anything you say."

Tilmouth slowly stretched his lips. "That's fine Alan – that's just fine."

The surgery at Plessey House reeked of carbolic and John Kinghorn's ears still rang with the screams of Wilbur Fulthorpe. The lad had appeared with his mother, a slight, wiry woman with round eyes and a pointed nose that twitched rodent-like above her sunken toothless mouth. She had marched her stout, lamenting offspring in front of the doctor and pointed with an air of hopeless boredom to the bulge on the right buttock of her son.

John waited, expecting a word or two of explanation. "Well," he said at last. "What's wrong?"

Mrs Fulthorpe's lips thinned. "Climbin' again, doctor. That's what's wrong," she said in a high, fragile voice. "Fell off the netty roof an' cut his backside on a stone."

John beckoned to the boy, a ten year old replica of his father. His hard, red bulbous cheeks showed the meandering of dried tears and his nose was bunged with green mucus. After a nudge from his mother he approached warily. It was a nasty cut, dirty and fairly deep. The bleeding had been stemmed with a balled rag held in a position by his short trousers and when John removed it the blood flowed again and the screams started.

"It'll need a stitch or two, I think," he said to Wilbur's mother.

She folded her arms and nodded a bland acceptance, obviously well used to and heartily fed up with her son's misadventures.

"You'll be a brave lad now, won't you Wilbur? There's a penny for you if you are," John said kindly. The boy wailed louder. Quickly John bent him over the desk and beckoned his mother to hold his shoulder. He cleaned the wound with carbolic solution and when the stitching started it became a wrestling match with Wilbur finally defeated, the doctor sweating and Mrs Fulthorpe yelling abuse at her wayward son. John was glad to see them depart. He washed his hands and slumped back into his chair. It had been one of those mornings, dull yet difficult, as in fact had been most of his first week in Allington. He found himself yet again thinking of Smythe and what he would say if he could see the mediocrity of the practice. But perhaps old Jenkins was right after all. Perhaps the glamour and excitement and glory was confined to story books. Maybe there were no more earth-shattering cures to be found and doctors would always be huddled in the same old rut swapping the same exaggerated stories until they were old and senile and faded away from life and memory.

He recalled his first patient of the morning and couldn't help a smile. It was an old man, stooped and thin with the bright watery eyes of great age. He had staggered shakily into the surgery, his walking stick wobbling under his gnarled, freckled fist.

"Good morning," John had said pleasantly. "What can I do for you?"

The old man had stood nodding for a second, then took off his cap.

John had stood up and sat him in the chair near his desk. "Now what seems to be the trouble?"

The old man had looked up at him. "Eh?"

"I said, what seems to be the trouble?" John had repeated louder.

The old man had cupped a hand to his ear. "Eh?"

There was a quick tap on the surgery door and a grinning face had appeared around it. It was another ancient. "Y'll have t' speak up doctor, owl' Billy's as deaf as a piss-pot."

"I've just gathered that," John had snorted.

The face gave out a gummy smile and disappeared. It had taken ten minutes of shouting in the old man's ear before he finally despatched him with a bottle for incontinence.

He sat back and shook his head. This was life without the false gloss of his youth. This was the bare wood that propped up the country. He sighed and rang the bell hoping there would be no response. But there was. The door opened and Ruth Nesbitt entered. She walked quickly to his desk, her head bowed, her pale cheeks with a slight flush of embarrassment.

John sighed with satisfaction. "Well, you've come at last. I'm pleased. Please sit down."

He observed her for a second. She wore a brown coat, out of fashion but smart, and a plain cloche hat that hid her hair and seemed to accentuate her lifeless skin. Her very posture revealed the weariness of her body. Her green eyes were dull and tired and fixed blankly to some point on the desk.

"You didn't come on Tuesday," he said gently.

She shook her head and lifted it until their eyes met.

"Why? You promised."

She shrugged. "I don't know. I didn't think there was anything wrong with me."

He smiled softly. "But you've come now. Tell me Ruth, how do you feel?"

She gave a mirthless smile that lined her face. "Weak . . . no energy

. . . sorry for myself."

He nodded. "Do you get enough sleep and enough to eat?" He asked the question knowing the truth whatever the answer.

"I suppose so," she said in a flat voice.

John breathed out slowly, trying to picture in his mind the girl's routine, seeing her father and her brothers and somehow knowing the way she accepted her life without question. Yet, in a way she epitomized the whole village. There was an undisguisable plea for help from her sorry features. She carried the silent dejection of the beaten and the defeated.

When he remembered on Tuesday night that she had not bothered to come he had been annoyed. After all he had bothered himself to speak for her brother and walk to Bolam to tell her. He had made it his business to try to help her and she had chosen to ignore it. So much for the friendly approach, he thought. Yet here she was after all, a shadow of the girl she should be for her years. He thought of his own sister Sarah, about the same age. Full of life, happy, finding her feet in a world where the new day was greeted with the champagne of the night before. Cosseted by wealth, hidden from the realities of life by the shallow padding of affluence.

He stood up and put his stethoscope in his ears. "Take your coat off Ruth, I'll examine you."

She unbuttoned the coat slowly, her embarrassment succumbing to her overwhelming malaise. He gave her a thorough check. There seemed nothing amiss. Her weight was down but not a lot. There was a paleness to the inside of her lips and her eyelids that was a clue to her condition but little else that could lead him to a final conclusion. Tuberculosis readily came to mind, a wicked disease that sometimes creeps insidiously into the lungs crippling them with abnormal masses of tissue and reducing the patient to a sunken, pallid shell before death casts its black net.

"Have you been coughing Ruth, or had chest pains?"

She shook her head.

"No night-sweating or difficulty in breathing?"

"No."

"How about colds. Have you had many this winter?"

"I had a head cold last month, that's all."

"Hmm. Periods normal?"

She looked to the floor and nodded.

"Good," he said with a smile, sitting back in his chair. "I think you're just run down Ruth, possibly a touch of anaemia which isn't helping matters. I'm going to give you some pills – an iron tonic which will help, I think. But what you need most of all is rest and fresh air and good food. Can't you take a holiday Ruth? Have you any relations in the country somewhere?"

"No, no-one." She gave a soft, sad smile. "And besides there's Alan and the rest of them to look after. They're not very good at looking after themselves."

"So I gather," John said dryly. "It's about time you gave some thought to yourself. You're run down Ruth, and consumption's a coward, you know. It catches the weakest first. If you can't get away, promise me you'll look after yourself a little more."

She sighed and stood up, fastening her coat and giving a wistful little smile towards the window. "I'll try."

John went to the dispensary and counted out 130 Blaud's pills, an old and reliable tonic and placed them in a box. "How's Alan by the way," he shouted to her. "Any news from the pit?"

She seemed amused. "No, nothing. He's fine now, but there's no news."

He came back into the surgery and handed her the box. She looked up at him. Her green eyes shone now with a luminous magic. "Thank you, doctor, and thank you for speaking for Alan."

"My pleasure. These pills will last you three weeks. Come back then. You should be feeling a lot better and perhaps Alan will be back at work."

He led the way to the door. The waiting room was empty. He showed her through the glass lean-to and on to the path outside.

"See you in three weeks," he said as she walked away.

She stopped and turned. "Three weeks doctor – yes, thank you."

He closed the door and watched her through the glass. There was a gentle femininity to her for all her work-worn hands and tired face. She radiated a subtle sexuality that made the back of his neck prickle. He rubbed it and turned toward the waiting room. Ethel Friar stood as immobile as the grandfather clock, her face with a stern frown of disapproval. But the instant he turned, it changed to an ingratiating smile.

"Surgery over, Dr Kinghorn? Doctor Jenkins is still at the football match. I've made a nice pot of tea."

There were sounds of great excitement as Ruth Nesbitt approached No. 10 First Row. There were whoops, yells and laughter and as she opened the door she saw the mud-covered football boots on the scullery floor and she knew they had won. Her father, dwarfed between her two elder brothers was recounting the match to Tilmouth who had seen most of it and Alan who sat hunched and white and uninterested at the far end of the kitchen. Ralph turned when he saw her and broke off his tale only to say: "Howay Ruth, where've you been. The lads here want a bath." He resumed his story, continuing the action exactly where he had left off. "So there we were leading two-one with only five minutes to go and that big rough bugger, Williams from Bedlington comes flyin' down the wing, dodges straight past this daft bugger here." He pointed a thumb at Norman. "So what does he do? Chops the legs from under him – right in the bliddy penalty area." He gave Norman a reproachful look. Norman smiled ruefully. Ralph continued, his face flushed with excitement, his small eyes bright and full of his imaginings. "Of course the ref. pointed straight to the spot. So what does this wonderful sportsman of a son go and do? Not content with giving away a penalty, he grabs the ball off the spot and takes off like a whippet over the heap somewhere. Had the game held up for ten minutes while they blew up another ball. Of course this daft sod doesn't show his face again. The ref. marks him down as bein' officially sent off, and now he'll be in trouble. He'll be barred from the final sure as hell." His voice went low and flat. "It's your own fault, Norm – one firey bugger on the team is enough, yet Tommy was as good as gold." Norman, a deep, quiet lad, nodded dolefully and turned away. His strip was caked with grime and his rolled-down stockings already revealed the bruises of a hard game. He had played well until then. They both had. Tommy had scored the first goal

"He just got himself excited, man," Tommy said casually.

Ralph's lips thinned. He patted Norman on the back. "Aye," he said. "Aye," again, with more conviction. "Anyway we still won – Wilkie saved the damn' penalty, didn't he." He gave a long, chesty chuckle. His eyes shone with pride. He hugged his two sons. "We'll win that cup now no matter what happens. Eh lads? Ruth? Howay lass, how's about some water for the bath?"

Ruth looked to Alan but for some reason he looked away. She unbuttoned her coat and walked slowly past the men and up the stairs.

"Where've you been Ruth, all in your Sunday best?" Ralph said, suddenly realising she was dressed. "You haven't been courtin' have you?" He laughed and her two brothers joined in.

She felt a surge of anger at the sarcasm of the remark especially in front of Tilmouth. She gripped the box of pills in her pocket and turned, observing them coldly. "No," she said, "I haven't," yet she had a fleeting sensation that perhaps in fact she had.

It was two o'clock in the afternoon when Kenneth Tilmouth took his leave of the Nesbitts. Ralph, Tommy and Norman insisted on a farewell pint at the Fat Ox and when it was time for him to go Ralph and Norman were thick in conversation and argument about the match. There was a strange, controlled excitement on Tilmouth's face as he said his ritual farewells to the men in the pub. He shook hands, breathing deeply, smiling his broad, tight smile. Finally he turned to Tommy. He gripped his arm. "Will you walk with me to the station? There's something I have to tell you."

Tommy readily agreed yet they were almost into Allington before Tilmouth spoke again. He seemed subdued, distant, deep in thought as they picked their way along the rough, mud-covered road and Tommy chose not to force him into conversation. It would have done no good. Tilmouth was an exact man, articulate, definite. He would speak when he was ready.

"Well, Tommy" he said at last, "I've spent a worthy week in Bolam. You and your comrades are good men. You are in the forefront of the exploited working class. When the time is right you will be in the forefront of their liberation. You know that, don't you?"

Tommy nodded. "We are ready to strike for a better life. We've done it before. Hardship can be endured if we can get some justice."

Tilmouth gave a brief, meaningless smile. "But do you believe that the struggle can go beyond a strike? Can you see a time when a few shillings extra pay will do nothing for you – that you will still be the cattle of the farm, that your share of the owner's profit is a mere fraction of what you deserve. You work, all of you. Why shouldn't the profits of your labour be yours and not this man Tomlinson's?"

Tommy shrugged. "It's a fair day's pay for a fair day's work that's all we want really."

Tilmouth stopped. His black eyes flashed. He put down his case and placed his hands on Tommy's shoulders.

"Tommy, Tommy – think man! Think of the power that is in us. We control our own destiny. I have chosen you because I know you to be strong, unshakeable. The villagers listen to you; they envy your skill on the football field. They point you out to their sons. Grasp the opportunity, Tommy. Shout it out from the rooftops that Communism is the truth, the way, the only way!"

"Communism!" Tommy gave a derisory laugh. "Eeh no, Mr Tilmouth, not me. I'm no Communist. They want to bugger the country. We want our just reward. No messin' about, just a livin' wage an' we'll be happy."

Tilmouth's hands slid slowly from his shoulders; he was shocked, numbed. His intuition had never let him down like this. He picked up his case and began to walk again.

"The name scares you doesn't it?" he snapped. "It scares you because those influential people who at present have the power have tarnished it with lies."

Tommy had cooled. The events of the week ran through his mind and he realised now that Tilmouth wanted only subversion; recruits for a cause as extreme and ruthless as Italy's Fascism. He set his face firmly as they entered Allington. "Yes it scares me, not for what it is, not for what it stands for; for the way it is engineered. The revolution we want doesn't entail taking over the country – just making them see the unfair system they use and withdrawing our labour until they do."

Tilmouth's voice was higher, on the verge of a whine. "Tommy! Use that brain of yours! All through history they've tried. With Communism you've got a positive goal. There's no woolly ideas to confuse the issue."

"I'm sorry Mr Tilmouth if I've disappointed you."

"Call me Ken, eh," he replied with a desperate smile, frantically trying to win a closer friendship. "Look, I'll tell you what, give it some thought. I'll come and see you again shortly. You'll be surprised if you knew just who believes in the cause. Big people, important educated people. They've seen the light. So might you."

They arrived at the station and waited more or less in silence. Willie Cox appeared and oblivious to the coolness between them, twittered on about the events of the night before. At last the train clanked slowly into the station, its wheels screeching and its chimney chaffing out smoke. Tilmouth turned to Tommy, his smile was forced, his eyes searched every pore of his face. They shook hands.

"Think Tommy," he whispered. "Accept the inevitability of it and cause it to happen with joy."

Tommy did not reply. Tilmouth entered a carriage and immediately lowered the window. Willie blew on his whistle and the engine's wheels spun on the track before they gripped and jerked the train forward.

"Goodbye Tommy," he said in a flat voice. "The future is ours. Think on it. I'll see you soon . . ."

The train rolled away into the distance and Tommy, hands in pockets, sauntered out of the station.

In the carriage, Tilmouth watched the black smoky pocket that was Bolam roll past. He stroked his chin slowly, deftly. And then he smiled. And then he gave a thin, watery laugh. Alan Nesbitt – of course! He couldn't wait to come back.

7

John listened, halting the tying of his tie for a second, cocking his head and at the same time smiling to himself as he strained his ears for some distinct word among the heated, raised but muffled dialogue that came along the landing. Strange, he thought, how their arguments had progressed from an exchange of low, drawn-out mumbles when he had first arrived to higher-pitched succinct vollies of words, obviously well chosen to cut deep and hurt with a minimum of effort. It had become clear, to him at least, that the deterioration of their relationship, while being sparked off by his arrival, had now become as a dog chasing its own tail. Ever since that Friday in January Ethel had slept in the spare bedroom and John was sure that his ardent employer had never since been allowed anything but the proper courtesies between servant and master. He had noticed the strained lovelorn looks he gave her; he had heard the whispered pleas at her bedroom door. But Ethel gave nothing and John revelled in the pantomime of turbulence between them. Dr Jenkins, however, took more and more to the consolation induced by whisky and the more he got drunk, the more she ignored him. Yet for some inexplicable reason he, John, who had been the prime cause of the disruption of their cosy little affair, was feted by both of them. Suddenly Ethel had changed her blatant show of antagonism to one of warm smiling acceptance. John was perplexed for a while and then concluded that she was making the best of an inevitable situation and at the same time exemplifying to Dr Jenkins the niceness she once had only for him.

He continued knotting his tie: their conversation terminated with the slamming of a door and heavy footsteps descending the stairs. Sometimes it was difficult to recognise the footsteps; the pace and weight were so often identical but he hoped that it was Ethel and that dinner would be on time. He was hungry and, whatever else, Ethel was an excellent cook. And such dishes! Recipes unheard of in the South. A suet pudding steamed with leeks and eaten with mince and gravy. A thick paste made from golden peas and delicious with ham and cold meats. Round, flattened bread called stotty cake that brought a new dimension to the taste buds. He enjoyed them all.

He reflected on his first weeks in Allington. February had spent its short grey days spreading sleet and snow, but it had not bothered him. He swamped himself with his work, fighting off home sickness and the sensation that his position was no more than a flippant facsimile of what he had dreamed it would be. He had written home – he couldn't help himself. He had been half-expecting a letter or a 'phone call from the day he arrived, but nothing came. So he wrote one night, a casual letter, a chummy letter as though to be in Allington had been a foregone conclusion on the day of his birth. He spoke highly of the place and of Dr Jenkins, exaggerating a little perhaps and giving them no hint of his mood. Then he wrote to Smythe at Bognor; it was a similar sort of letter, hopefully reassuring him that Allington was the place to be and that Bognor could not hope to match the North of England for interest and variety. He received a reply within a week. It was a quick, curt note from a Dr Kells, stating that Dr Smythe had authorised him to open any mail and inform the writer of Dr Smythe's extended stay in Austria and that he would communicate as soon as possible. Austria! John had frowned at that, wondering what he was doing there, then it occurred to him that he may be accompanying a patient who was taking the waters at one of the numerous spas. There was a twinge of jealousy for a second and then it was gone. He'd had some success of his own. Nellie Sneed, after three regular calls a week to see her, finally submitted to his obstinacy and allowed him near her. People began to wave or call out a greeting as he passed. He was becoming accepted in the area and it gave him a growing satisfaction. And now with early March, came the shy, hesitating flowers of spring and a feeling inside him that a metamorphosis had taken place during the dark weeks of winter. No longer was there a desire in him that people should kowtow to his superiority. There was no achievement in that. The achievement was in becoming one of them. He would have liked a letter from home, though, just a line that showed they were all still there or better still the rich, enthusiastic ebullience of his father yelling advice to him down the phone. But there was nothing and that left him a little sad. His father had written him off and that made him all the more determined to succeed.

"John! John!" The voice was that of Dr Jenkins. "Dammit – can you give me a hand here?"

John went to his room. The old man's face was almost purple with anger and the struggle to fasten his collar stud.

"Oh, John – thank Christ," he croaked. "Can you fix this stud, I've got to be out in five minutes. Tomlinson will be here to pick me up and he hates waiting."

John fiddled with the stud and the stiff, starched collar. "And where are you two off to in your finery?" he said through clenched teeth.

"What? Oh, just a club we're in. Meets once a month." He looked down his nose for any reaction. There was none. "I'll tell you about it sometime, ok?"

John smiled. "Ok."

Quickly the old doctor fixed his bow tie and pulled on his dinner jacket.

"Oh, it's a formal 'do' I see," John said with amusement.

"Yes, yes it is," Dr Jenkins gasped as he rummaged for a handkerchief. "It's sort of special, you know." He dashed for the door. "I'll be late. See you tomorrow."

He was halfway down the stairs before John yelled his name.

"Yes, John, what is it?" he answered irritably.

"You'll want this, I think." John held up a small, brown attaché case.

Jenkins slapped his forehead and ran back to the landing. There was the honk of a car horn outside. He grabbed the case, smiled a quick thank you and was gone.

Dinner was a quiet affair that night and John sat deep in thought through most of it, breaking his concentration only to thank Ethel or reply to her pleasantries as she served each course. He wandered into the lounge and glanced with a sort of listless boredom at a copy of the *Lancet* while he waited for coffee. There was an oppressive silence in the room and even the scrape of a match on the box as he lit his pipe seemed loud and irreverent. He looked to the pianola and toyed with the idea of playing it. He picked out the Träumerei roll and fitted it before sitting down and adjusting the timer. He began to pump the pedals and watched the keys magically depress themselves as the soft, romantic notes sounded around him. There was beauty there, sensitive, beautiful thoughts transposed into immortal music. He closed his eyes and let his mind melt among the sound. Suddenly he felt a hand on his shoulder and he jumped. Ethel smiled wanly at him, a mistiness in her eyes, a scent of wine on her breath.

"Oh, Doctor Kinghorn, I'm sorry," she said with sweet innocence, "I didn't mean to startle you. I just brought in your coffee and heard the music. It's so lovely. It's Dr Jenkins' favourite."

John spun round on the stool and observed her. She had discarded her pinafore and her hair was combed and tidy. She stood holding her hands at her lap, a light expectancy on her face. She pointed to the table. "I've taken the liberty of bringing two cups, doctor. I . . . I thought perhaps you might care for a little company . . . but of course if you'd rather be alone . . ." She broke off; the inflection of her voice almost demanding him to welcome her.

"No, no, sit down, Mrs Friar," John said quickly, intrigued by her approach, sensing some ulterior motive to her action.

He followed her to the couch and she positioned herself demurely on it.

"You have me worried, you know," she said as she poured the coffee. "You work hard yet you never seem to have a break. I'm afraid Allington is not a place where there's much for younger people to enjoy. You know what I mean – dance halls and picture houses."

John shrugged, amused by her interest. "It doesn't bother me, Mrs Friar. Or it hasn't yet."

She lifted her eyes from her cup. "My name is Ethel you know. Please call me that."

"Well . . . Ethel, what about you? You seem to be content with your seclusion," he countered. "You never leave the house."

There was a wistful look in her eyes and her brow tightened. "I am older, doctor, not young and . . . and vigorous like you. My pastimes are simple and confined to home. I have my wireless. That is all of the outside world I need."

John nodded thoughtfully. He was curious about her unnatural self-imposed confinement and anxious to probe further seeing that she was in a rare talkative mood.

"But you never go out at all. It's not healthy to be indoors so much."

She looked to the fire. Her face went cold and was impervious to the dancing, rosy glow. Her voice fell to a cracked whisper of nostalgia. "I go out . . . sometimes . . . with Dr Jenkins. That is all." She turned to face him once more. There was a pain of recollection over her now. "You see, doctor, I am a widow. Many years ago I lived with my husband in the village – in Bolam. But I lost my husband there and I fell out with the world."

"I'm sorry," John said with sincerity, "what caused his death?"

She sat back and fixed her gaze on some distant point across the room and sighed. Her words came in low, slow monotone as she gave life to the memories. "I was eighteen doctor – and pretty. There was this lad, George Friar. Oh, he was such a nice lad. I chased him and chased him until he fell for me. There was nothing I wouldn't do for him. I would have worshipped him before God, if that's what he wanted. But he wasn't like that. He was nice and gentle and quiet. We had such a time that summer before we were married. He worked hard at the pit and I was in service at one of the big houses at Gosforth. We saved every penny that summer, every penny. But it was worth it." She paused for a moment and swallowed hard. Her voice became stronger. "We were married in October . . . then there was the strike. But George would have none of it." She looked to John, her eyes bright with tears. "We owed money on the furniture, you see, and George hated debt. He couldn't abide the shame of not paying the instalments." She took a deep, trembling breath. "Each day he faced the pickets – took their calls and their blows, on the way in and on the way out. For thirteen days he did that, my George. And then the strike ended. But it wasn't over for George. The men ignored him, they spat at him and he would come home and cry in my lap. For a month he took it and then . . . and then he didn't come back one day. I went to the pit but nobody would answer me. Finally the Manager sent a couple of men down to look for him." Her voice became a hoarse whisper. "They found him in some disused workings . . . he had hung himself . . . with his belt!"

John grimaced. There was silence again. Then Ethel continued.

"So you see, doctor," she said, composed once more, "I have no love for the people outside. For thirty years I have never been rid of the sight of George's stretched, broken neck or the hatred I have for the people that caused it."

John hunted his mind for something to say, something apt that would confirm his regret, but nothing came.

She brightened in an instant. "But enough of the past, Dr Kinghorn. All that happened before you were born. You should go out more – enjoy yourself. Perhaps you have a girlfriend back home?"

John shook his head. There was a fleeting image in his mind of the nurse at the hospital and their quick, intense affair that sapped his strength and ruined his concentration for six weeks. "No," he said with a rueful smile.

Ethel blinked, a look of amused interest on her face. "But surely you've had girlfriends?"

He made to answer, but a rapid knock at the door stopped him. He had learned to recognise the worried call of emergency compared to the casual ringing of the bell or tap on the woodwork that signalled a social visitor. He jumped up. Ethel looked disappointed.

"Oh hell," he muttered, "I'll see to it."

With a sigh Ethel gathered up the cups.

It was just before midnight when he returned to Plessey House. He was weary and he was sad. Old Sam Watson had died; a veteran of eighty-nine, withered, shrunken, gasping precious air into lungs clogged with fibrosis. For sixty years he had worked in the pits, breathing the dust-filled atmosphere that cut into the delicate tissue of his lungs to such an extent that, ironically and tragically, the continual healing process finally left them almost solid with scar tissue. John had visited him twice before, examining him where he sat at his daughter's fireside. Time and the rigours of life had hunched his body and his mottled ancient skin was folded and pale on his blue-scarred face. Yet he was amazingly bright for his age. His heart was strong for all its years of stress and there was a philanthropic wisdom in his few forced sentences. His eyes shivered constantly with nystagmus, another common complaint among miners; but there was something grand about him, something venerable in the way he nursed his decline.

He recognised John when he arrived. His old hand grasped John's arm and there was a silent plea for help as he fought to breathe. He struggled on for almost three hours; finally with a feeble surge of strength he beckoned the doctor to come closer. John bent over him and put his ear near the old man's mouth.

"What is it, Sammy?" he asked gently.

There was no answer for a moment, only shallow, fitful breathing. Then he managed the words. "Dying is such a lonely thing," he whispered hoarsely.

John looked down at him. There was a wonderment growing on his face. And then he died.

The house was in darkness when John let himself in. The grandfather clock ticked out its presence and there was a whirr from inside as it prepared to strike the change of day. John climbed the stairs, his mind full of the demise of Sam Watson and the lamenting of his relatives. There had been something indestructible about him, his great age and his personification of a breed of men that were the very essence of every patriotic song ever written. Now he was no more.

The clock was still chiming when John got to his room. He had noticed the slit of light under Ethel's door and wondered as he passed the other whether Dr Jenkins was still out or asleep. He didn't ponder on it further, he was tired and his ordeal had left him with a feeling of frustration at the insignificance of man battling against the insuperable force of nature. He lit the gas lamp and slumped down on the bed, resting his head on his arms. There was a knock on his door and he pulled himself to a sitting position before answering. He didn't get a chance. The door opened and Ethel Friar stood looking at him. Her hair was down and brushed into a fine spray across her shoulders, her eyes had a wicked delight in them as she held up two glasses.

John couldn't believe it. "It's late Mrs Friar, I need some sleep," was all he could say.

She moved toward him, her nightdress of white silk whispering across the floor. "Brandy," she said softly, "it's to help you sleep, doctor."

He stood up and she stopped, a coy, seductive look on her face. She held out the glass to him and he took it, numbed by her forwardness and a sudden uncontrollable desire as her perfume tantalised his nostrils. She saw the slight sag of his shoulders that yelled victory to her and she smiled.

"Drink it up, doctor, you've had a hard day."

Her eyes never left him as they raised their glasses. He had the words formed in his mind to tell her to go; that her actions were wrong, that her presumption was a gross breach of properness; but somehow he could not. There was some inexplicable chemistry to her, a mature attractiveness as she stood before him. She seemed to devour his reasoning, swamp his senses until there was nothing in the world but her and her perfume and her sexuality. He watched, mesmerised by the disbelief of his own feelings as she took the glasses and put them on the table. She turned and took hold of his hands, placing the palms below each of her breasts.

"There, " she breathed, "you must enjoy yourself, doctor. You are so young and so healthy."

His breathing deepened and quickened as his mind wrestled with the excitement that swirled through him. "You are a witch," he said feebly.

Her face broke into a hard determined smile. Slowly she moved his hands upward, over the smooth silk that covered her heavy breasts, across the hard, proud nipples and up until they came around her neck. She pulled him closer, moulding her body against his, opening her lips as their mouths came together.

Suddenly the sheer ridiculousness of the situation gelled in John's mind. For a split second he was detached from his being and observing the stupidity of his own behaviour and the crass, debased performance of a woman old enough to be his mother. He grabbed her shoulders and pushed her away.

"For Christ's sake get out," he snarled.

She was startled for a moment, then smiled and moved back towards him. "Don't be afraid of me," she whispered, "it'll be all right I promise you."

A hot surge of anger rose inside him. He gripped her arm and almost ran her to the door. "Get out – get out you damn' slut," he yelled as she stumbled into the passage. "Don't you dare . . . don't you dare try that again."

She stood erect, arrogant, burning with ire at the rejection but controlled and in command of her outward appearance. She stared at him for a moment then gave a little curtsey, an icy smile returning to her face. "Will that be all, sir?" she said with cold sarcasm. "Then I'll say goodnight, sir, and thank you, sir."

The door slammed in her face. She turned and went back to her room, a fury of failure boiling inside her, the consequences looming large in her mind. She turned out the lamp and got into bed, sitting up, knees under chin and frantically analysing the possible repercussions. There was the noise of a car. It stopped and the carefree banter of Dr Jenkins and Charles Tomlinson came to her ears. She heard them walk up the path and the rattle of the key in the lock. She held her breath, expecting the bedroom door opposite to fly open and a seething Dr Kinghorn to descend among them. But he didn't; there was silence, a relaxing relieving silence. She slid down in the bed and pulled the covers up to her chin, staring sightlessly through the darkness. Then she realised she had nothing to fear. Let the young man say what he liked. She could deny his improbable tale; she could even reverse the circumstances of it. Perhaps he would just depart as suddenly as he had arrived; after all, that had been the ultimate object of the exercise. If he didn't, nothing was lost; eventually she would sicken him and extricate him from their lives. Then and only then could she again feel the security that she had enjoyed for so long. As for Dr Jenkins she knew now after all his whining and fawning that the beckoning finger was all that was needed and he would come, taking heed of nothing else, like a moth to a lamp. Downstairs she could hear the chink of glasses and his rollicking, chesty laughter. She had already detected the change in him since the arrival of his assistant; the independent streak in him growing stronger, his self-confidence returning. He drank only to kill the desire in him. He had need of her body and her body was her trump card. With a glow of contentment she closed her eyes.

John brought the Sunbeam down into second gear ready to negotiate the rough bumpy road into Bolam. He did not see its squalor now, only the people that existed there, and he somehow welcomed the uninhibited friendliness that accompanies poverty. He was glad to be out again, free from Ethel Friar and the false, stifling attitudes that surrounded her. The atmosphere at Plessey House had reverted overnight to what it had been immediately after John's arrival. Ethel continued her duties with a brazen normality but any comments she was forced to make were short and sharp and left neither doctor in any doubt of her hostility. Dr Jenkins countered by a greater display of forced, amusing comments and chuminess, perplexed perhaps by the return of her silent wrath and anxious to dispel the miasma of antagonism that seemed to ooze from the very walls. As for John the incident gradually melted to a farcical memory. At first he had been prepared to demand her dismissal but the story he wanted to tell made ludicrous listening even in his own mind. He decided to bluff it out, ignore her, let her see his contempt for her. He had not succumbed; that very fact gave him the superiority of the victor. She could see him each day and squirm with the thoughts that she had shamed herself. Yet annoyingly, if she had any shame, it did not show. She was erect and proper and icily correct.

She was the same the night before when Tomlinson arrived. She threw open the lounge door and let him in, taking the opportunity to poke at the fire and feed it and ignore all three of them on the way out.

"Ah! Charles," Dr Jenkins said joyfully, "come on in, the board's all ready."

Tomlinson stood with his back to the fire. He seemed subdued, worried. "No, no, I don't think I'll play tonight, Bob, if you don't mind."

"Aha, you've got that feeling you're going to get whacked, eh? Well so have I – come on."

Tomlinson shook his head. "No Bob, as a matter of fact I only came over to see if you've heard anything in the village."

"Heard what?"

Tomlinson shrugged. "Whisperings about the pit and whatnot."

John dropped the newspaper from his face and began to take notice. "What sort of whisperings?" he asked.

Tomlinson tried to look unconcerned but he fidgeted as he stood and could not disguise the worry on his face. "Well," he said lightly, "you know – their mood, what they're saying about the Commission's report coming out next week. That sort of thing."

Dr Jenkins waved away his concern. "Bah! We've heard nothing, eh, John? They're working, aren't they?"

"Yes, but Mallory came up to the house today." His face coloured. "Some trouble-maker painted that damned slogan along the whole wall of the new baths. 'Not a minute on the day, not a penny off the pay.' You know, the same blasted carry-on we had last year."

"Oh, take no bloody notice of that, Charles. It's some fool with nothing better to do. You're not going to let a thing like that get you down."

Tomlinson grunted, he turned and squinted at the fire. "Bob," he whispered with gentle conviction, "mark my words, this country is going to the dogs. When damned agitators like Cook of the Miners' Federation can spout mutiny publicly with such passion that crowds wind up weeping . . ." He broke off and shook his head hopelessly.

"Paper talk!" Jenkins snapped as he puffed vigorously on his pipe.

"Anyway, wait until Samuel has his say before you fly off at a tangent. Baldwin will sort out things then."

Tomlinson turned. "You think so?"

Jenkins nodded.

"I hope so, Bob, because I'll not give in," Tomlinson said with a sudden stiff determination. "I sink my money into coal mining and it's my enterprise that created their jobs." His face twisted with anger. "Christ, man, they've got no idea of commerce. the rise and fall of the market means nothing to them. Don't they realise that it's better to have a job whatever the pay than no job at all?" He tapped his chest. "And it's not only the ungrateful lot at the pit that want to see me ruined. Even the Commission Inspector ticked me off. Bad maintenance, poor safety record, out-of-date machinery – that's all he could spout. And not one word about the new baths!" He stalked up the room and held out his arms. "I ask you – is it damn' well worth bothering? Sometimes I wish they would nationalise the whole shooting match and I'll bugger off with my pot and live happily ever after."

Jenkins rose and poured him a drink. He smiled as he passed it to him. "Calm down and relax man, you'll make yourself ill. Remember it's the final of the Welfare Cup on Saturday. If Bolam win it and you hand that nice shining trophy to them they'll be eating out of your hand."

"For how long?" John interjected, ridiculing the statement.

They both turned to face him.

"Surely a triviality like a local football match won't cure the trouble. Seems to me from what I've seen that you're lumbered with a situation where they want a living wage and they expect they've got to work longer for less money. It has all the ingredients for a rare old ding-dong."

Tomlinson's jaw sagged. He looked sick and John found pleasure in it.

"And what would you do to prevent it?" Tomlinson snapped.

John shrugged.

"I thought so. If I were you I'd stick to doctoring, young man, and don't listen to their exaggerated stories. You're young, impressionable. There's a whole history of trouble with pitmen."

John's brow tightened. Tomlinson's boring righteousness grated on his nerves, as did the insipid comments of Dr Jenkins who was solely interested in continued rapport with his important friend.

"I don't listen to their stories," he said, "I see with my own eyes. How long is it since you've been into Bolam – into your houses and seen the state of them?"

Tomlinson drew in his chin. His face flushed. "I don't need to go, I . . . I have men to do that," he spluttered. "God, man you sound like you're on their side."

John stood up. "I'm on no-one's side," he said dryly, "but I know right from wrong and you, Mr Tomlinson, are wrong!"

There was silence as Tomlinson's eyes grew bigger. Jenkins took a long drink then attempted to change the subject. "Come on now," he said, "it's useless arguing among ourselves. Forget about the pit, Charles, and let's have a game of chess."

Tomlinson ignored him for a moment, then exhaled a slow, noisy breath. "No, I'll be off now, Bob, Clarrie's upset about the whole damned business." He walked to the door, then turned and studied John. "You know something, son? What you've said is true. No matter how we try to shroud it with excuses – it's true. But in these hard times it's me or them and I'll do anything to make sure it's me. Law of the jungle and all that. Can you understand?"

"You're grossly outnumbered," John replied. "You realise that, don't you?" Tomlinson stood with a pensive frown on his face, then he nodded reluctantly and said goodnight.

John parked the car at the bottom of the row and walked to Nellie Sneed's. Her face brightened when he entered and called out a greeting. She smiled and nodded her approval as he placed the kettle that was filled and waiting on the hob.

"Well now, Nellie, we'll have that walk today – just me and you. We'll get you up and out of that chair and we'll walk across the field. Can you remember the field, Nellie? It's green and fresh and speckled with clover and dandelions. You'll like that, won't you now? – and Edward'll be so proud of you." He took hold of her hands. "Come on then," he whispered urgently, "up Nellie – up!"

Slowly her gnarled fingers feebly closed around his. Her brow knotted with the concentration and her withered mouth twitched. Her left leg began a spasm of shivering as she strained to lift herself.

"Good, Nellie, good girl," John encouraged. "You can do it. Come on, walk . . . walk!"

Her eyes shone unblinking in her determination. Her hands gripped harder as her bottom lifted off the chair, then disappointment clouded her face as she relaxed, defeated and weary.

"Excellent, Nellie," John said. "I'm proud of you. Every time you're better. By the summer we'll be sick of running around that field, won't we?"

Her face broke into a toothless, brave grin. "Aye," she croaked.

John patted her shoulder. "That's the stuff. Don't give up. You'll do it. Now, we'll have a cup of tea and have another try – ok?"

She nodded. John turned to look for the tea-caddy and noticed the roll of hessian, partly held in a wooden frame, lying across the table. It was almost finished, and he marvelled at the intricate pattern of flowers perfectly proportioned, the colours blended in subtle shades, all from random woollen rags cut and selected by Edward Sneed. It was a cheap and simple way of rug-making. The small clippings of rags were hand-woven into the hessian, but the patterns required some inbred skill that was far removed from coalmining and could have had the expertise of a trained artist.

"The rug's beautiful, Nellie. It's a grand piece of work. Do you like it?"

She turned her head. "Aye," she said in her cracked voice. "For the lads' room."

"Of course it is. They'll like that, won't they?"

"Aye," she said blankly.

And John smiled and made the tea.

Ruth Nesbitt was waiting for him when he left No. 8. He had contemplated calling to see her; to see how she was and, he told himself without a qualm, just to see her. The treatment he had prescribed seemed to be helping and when she had returned to the surgery two weeks before for more pills he could see an improvement. Her pale, tired face was going; the freshness of youth taking its place. There was still the burden of her drudgery, however. It seemed to envelope her slim body, as though her arms and legs were weighted and her eyes viewed nothing but despair. She was different that morning though. Her smile was broad and living and lit the green of her eyes, magnifying the simple beauty of her features. John rubbed the back of his neck.

"Dr Kinghorn, oh I'm pleased I've caught you. You'll never guess," she said with excitement.

He pursed his lips. "I give in," he said with a mock solemnity.

"The office boy's been from the pit. Alan's had to see Mallory. It's about a job," she became serious and the delightful hint of embarrassment came to her cheeks. "I just wanted to thank you again, for your help – for Alan and me."

"That's grand," John said, a wave of pleasure running through him that Tomlinson had remembered. "Good. I'm glad Ruth. You'll find he'll be a lot happier with something to occupy his mind."

Ruth frowned, "I hope so, doctor, he's been so moody these weeks."

"And how about you – still improving?"

She smiled again, but this time she disguised its lack of sincerity by looking down the lane. "Getting better every day. I laugh now at some of the stupid things that upset me. Oh! Here's the men – black and hungry. I'd better see to the water."

John followed her gaze. He waited while Ralph, Tommy and Norman dragged their grimy bodies towards him. He called out a greeting as they neared, tempted for a moment to ask them to help in lifting Ruth's burden but their silent, sour faces stopped him. Ralph stopped by the door and gasped for breath while his sons flung their bait bags savagely into the scullery.

"Something wrong?" John asked.

"Everything's wrong," Ralph growled. "We thought we'd got away with it, but it's our rotten luck." He nodded his head toward Norman. "After all these soddin' weeks of buggerin' about, they've banned him. They've banned him from the final for one stupid mistake."

John tutted his condolences.

"But that's not all," Ralph continued. "Tomlinson's jiggered it all together. His highness gets the game pulled forward from eleven to ten so's he can get to some meetin' in Newcastle."

"What's so bad about that?" John queried.

"We're at work, man," Ralph bleated. "Tommy'll have to take a shift off. Me and Norm here'll miss the first half. The whole team'll have to have a shift off. It's gonna be a pricey final. All season we wait for this. God! For a pinch a'snuff, we'd be doing the same."

Ruth appeared at the door. Her face was stern and positive. "You'll do no such thing. Money's more important than football. You should know that!"

Ralph looked to his daughter. His moustache twitched, then he looked to each of his sons for some smattering of support. There was none. He sagged and sighed and stalked angrily past them all into the house.

John said goodbye and turned to go but he stopped when he saw Alan running up the lane.

"Well?" he said. "Don't tell me – I'll guess that Mallory gave you a job."

Alan gave a sickly smile and nodded.

Ruth was anxious to know. "Come on then, Alan. What is it? What's the job?"

"Oh, it's a grand job," Alan answered in his thin delicate voice. "I'm an attendant at the new baths!"

Saturday dawned to high, grey cloud and a blustery breeze from the North. As the light of the new day crept over the village of Bolam the fore-shift miners had laboured underground for three hours, and Ralph Nesbitt gave vent to his anger on the seam of glistening coal whose abject indifference to his rage made him grit his teeth and curse it and football and Tomlinson and himself. He lay on his side in the three and a half foot slit, his body chilled by the black water that swirled with his movement and his eyes stinging with the fog of dust that hung in the seam, illuminated by the weak light of his lamp like some eerie emission from Hades. There was the rumble of a low tub behind him but he did not stop.

"Da-da!" Norman's voice, thickened with phlegm came to his ears. "Ease up man, y'll kill yersel."

Ralph ignored him, his pick flying back and forth, digging with a satisfying crunch into the coal that splintered and crumbled after eons of still, silent waiting.

"Da," Norman called again.

"Piss off will yer," Ralph yelled.

Norman gritted his teeth and sighed. He rolled over and grabbed the other tub that his father had filled in his absence and pushed it through the cloying water to the flat. He knew the disappointment that ate at him. He knew his every thought would be at the surface, for Tommy in his blue and white strip so carefully washed and ironed by his sister; for the team and for the exquisite thrill of seeing them charge toward their opponents' goal. He felt sick inside that he was not playing himself and that he would have no part in their possible victory, but he felt it most for his father. He was not a perfect father, he knew that, but he was a man who had worked hard all his life. His pleasures were few and simple and Norman knew well how his mistake of not letting Tommy go to United constantly haunted him.

It was more than two hours later that Ralph dropped his pick and yelled to his son as he heard another empty tub approach.

"Aye da – what is it?" Norman asked.

"What's the time?" Ralph gabbled breathlessly.

Norman thought for a second. "It was half-nine a bit back. Stop lettin' it eat at yer, man. We'll get to see the second half".

Ralph slithered backwards until he was level with his son. His eyes were white and large against his blackened sweating face. "We'll see the effin' lot. Come on, let's get t' bank. W'll louse sharp."

With their noses almost touching, Norman slowly smiled, his eyes lighting up as the idea got through to him. "Aye," he whispered "Aye," he said again with a chuckle, "come on!"

They crawled along the face to where Sam Usher scraped his shove through the wet coal and into the tub.

"Sam Sam!" Ralph whispered urgently. "Come on, boony lad, stuff this. We're away t'bank. W'll see the whole game."

Sam stopped shovelling and wiped at his brow. "Nay lads," he said gently. "We'll get sacked, man. A'll see the second half. Miriam – what? She'd set about me if I get the sack. Anyway even if we divvent, we'll get fined, an' we need money for the wedding."

Ralph tutted impatiently. "Lissen – Mallory'll never know. It'll be just us three. We'll sneak out as easy as pie."

Sam hesitated. He wiped his mouth with the back of his hand, his eyes distant, in deep thought. "T'hell – come on then," he said suddenly.

"What's up with you lot?" Edward Sneed crawled into their view.

"Shh," Ralph whispered, "we're pissin' off up top to see the game".

"Y'll get hung", Edward said urgently. "Besides, it's dangerous walkin' t'bank while they're haulin' tubs".

They ignored him. Their minds had only one thought now and that was the mystic angular meanderings of a brown leather ball.

They reached the main way. Robert Fulthorpe gazed inquisitively at them as they passed.

"Where's you lot going?"

"T'bank," Ralph said gleefully.

"For the match?"

"Aye."

"Effin' hell, I'll come with yers."

The four of them walked to the base of the drift. "Oh Lord, in thee we will have victory," Fulthorpe whispered as they began to climb the steps to the surface.

"Watch now," Norman barked at them, "there's a full set comin'."

The wire rope set mid-way between the tracks that guided the tubs up the centre of the tunnel lifted off its rollers and tightened as an echoing rumble gathered force behind them.

"Into the manholes, lads," Sam yelled.

They each found a narrow slot cut into the tunnel wall at intervals of a few yards and squeezed themselves in as the train of eight coal-filled tubs roared upward and past them.

Ralph let out a gurgle of pleasure. "Right," he yelled, "let's away."

There was another rumble a couple of minutes later. "Here's the empties," Fulthorpe warned. Again they took to the manholes as an empty set returned to the workings under the impetus of the incline and checked from accelerating too quickly by the slow, reversed action of the winding engine. They were half way up when the next full set started its journey. The wire rope lifted and tightened, then vibrated with its tension. "Here's another set," Fulthorpe squawked.

But they kept on going, each realizing that they now had a few precious seconds before the tubs reached them; each wanting to gain a few more yards to the surface. Perhaps Bill Jarvis, the winding engineman was also keen to be finished and away to the match. Perhaps in his excitement he didn't realize just how fast he allowed the great steam-driven engine to accelerate the full set of tubs up the shaft. Perhaps it was the weakened, uninspected wire rope that was to blame – or just fate. The set was still two hundred feet behind them when the first tub jumped the rails. In a split second the seven following spread themselves in the tunnel, tearing at the supports and jamming themselves tighter and tighter. The four men heard the thunderous roar and stopped. But a split second was too quick for them. It was too quick for Bill Jarvis at the controls of the winding engine. Before the thought of yanking the lever that would shut off the steam could activate his muscles, the wire rope snapped a hundred feet behind the men in the tunnel. There was a weird staccato of sound, harsh, hard and metallic as the strands of the rope parted in a fury of relief and flew like a frenzied snake toward the source of their agony. There was no time for the men to reach a manhole. In the instant it took to stop and look back it was all over. The wire strands moving at vicious speed scythed through them as though they were made of paper.

At the surface, the crowd around the football field had grown quickly from a handful to three hundred or more as kick-off time approached. It was a good turnout with almost a hundred of the supporters yelling for Northbank Rangers, a pit team from near the Tyne, seven miles away. They had arrived by charabanc, on bicycle, by cart or had just walked and when the teams finally appeared from the yard at the back of the Fat Ox, the exuberance of their respective supporters lifted to a crescendo.

Tommy Nesbitt felt grand as he danced about, jumping stiff-legged and nodding his head at imaginary balls as he loosened up. There was a bunch of giggling female admirers near the newly whitewashed goalposts who were waving to him and he gave them a wink and a demonstration of his shooting power. He felt the importance of the occasion when he saw Tomlinson standing with Dr Jenkins and the owner of Northbank pit. Then Dr Kinghorn appeared. He was pleased. They were all there and all their eyes would be on him when he scored. He would show them how to play football, how to win – without Norman or the frantic support of his father.

The referee fortified with a small rum from the pub blew his whistle and waved them to the centre but the shrill note was overpowered by a long, low ominous blast from the colliery hooter. For a second the whole world seemed to freeze as the note went on and on, moaning its message that there was a fatal accident at the pit. Dr Jenkins gripped John's arm. It was a vice-like frightened grip. "Come on," he whispered urgently.

They snatched their bags from the car and ran toward the pit yard. John did not ask questions. The silent, sober mass that ran with them told him everything. Mallory was waiting at the mouth of the drift. He was a tiny man with a puggish, stiff face and he fidgeted anxiously as they approached. There was a hollow, ashen look to him and his lips were twisted downward as though he was on the brink of vomiting.

"It's terrible – terrible," he whined. "It's like a butcher's shop down there. Four of them, chopped to bits."

"Where are they?" Jenkins roared.

"In the drift," Mallory bleated.

Jenkins spun him round and gave him a push. "Come on, man," he growled, "get us to them."

John followed into the black, gaping hole, his legs like rubber, his heart pounding from Mallory's concise description and the fearful awesome surroundings that enveloped him. He felt as though they had descended to the centre of the earth by the time they reached the first body. It was covered with a brown blanket from the ambulance room.

"Dead?" Jenkins asked Mallory.

Mallory nodded.

"Are you sure?" he said as he began to lift the blanket.

Mallory swallowed hard and turned away. "It's Ralph Nesbitt ... we found his head further down."

Jenkins let the blanket drop and moved quickly on.

John stared at the mound, unable to believe what he heard. He stood rooted to the spot as a sudden bewildering uselessness came over him.

"John!"

Dr Jenkins barked the word at him, commanding him to move and triggering him out of his stupor. He stumbled down the few steps to the crumpled figures lying across the track and the two doctors began work with an urgent professional silence. John lifted the blanket from a man he didn't recognise and winced at the sight of his injuries. The wire had sliced off his right leg and all his genitals. There was nothing he could do. He was dead. There was a moan from someone as his colleague injected him with morphine and John heard him gently soothe the injured man. He moved up beside him and recognised Robert Fulthorpe, his arms and legs carved open. His eyes had the glassy look of shock and he shivered uncontrollably but he was alive and the bleeding had been stopped with tourniquets. John turned quickly to the remaining man.

"It's no good," Jenkins whispered, without looking up.

"Who is it?"

"Norman."

"Not Norman Nesbitt!" John gasped.

Dr Jenkins nodded as he worked.

John closed his eyes trying to blot out the reality of it, his mind a turmoil of horror and disbelief. He lifted the blanket. Norman lay with a look of surprise on his face. He seemed untouched until he noticed the legs that had done so much for Bolam Blue Star were no longer attached to his body. A wave of nausea swirled around in his stomach. It couldn't happen! It wasn't possible for such an accident!

"Who's the other one?" Dr Jenkins snapped.

John shook his head slowly.

"Is he alive, man?"

"No . . . no, he's dead."

Dr Jenkins moved down and lifted the blanket. He was silent for a moment. He turned his head and looked toward his companion. "Oh Jesus," he whispered.

"Who is it?" John asked blankly.

"It's Sam Usher. He was marrying Miriam Scott next week. Twenty years they've been walking out together . . ." His voice broke off with a long vehement sigh.

They lifted Fulthorpe onto a stretcher and two men carried him away.

Dr Jenkins wiped his blood-stained hands with a piece of lint and stared at John. His face was set hard, drained of colour in the watery lamp light. There was a grim seriousness to him. "Well," he breathed, "you've seen the lot now, son. You know pit life as well as anybody. You've seen them born and how they live and now you've seen how they die. Wish you'd joined the army?"

John didn't answer. He didn't know how to answer. A wild anger pounded in his head at the way these people were treated by fate and by their complacent employers. He stood at the mouth of the drift and looked at the silent agonized crowd. Ruth was there, so were the two football teams, waiting in huddled pathetic bunches. He knew that there would be no cup final that day. The purpose of it had suddenly been extinguished, the conflict now overwhelmed by an army of men, women and children, whose souls cried out for news of their loved ones. John could now answer Dr Jenkins' question. He had already joined an army. Theirs.

8

John focused his tired eyes on the morning's *Journal & North Star* and made a cursory inspection of the news, hunting instinctively for items about London. There was little to interest him. A small paragraph caught his eye about an outbreak of smallpox in Gateshead and Durham and there was a photograph of spring crocuses in Jesmond Dene near Newcastle. He turned the page. There was another photo' there; a wide-eyed grinning collection of art students in fancy dress, artificially posed during their annual ball at Kings Hall. He gazed for a moment, trying to penetrate the happy innocence of their faces and remembering with a sardonic smile his own unblemished student days when ideals were simple and life was an uncomplicated ritual of work and play. He had seen the dark side of life; the ill and diseased and the dregs of humanity who had abused their bodies until they were obscene hulks of living flesh, but it was not the same. He had been detached from them. They appeared, then were gone. They were unfortunate objects that were treated with impartiality and skill and in return poured out their trust and gratitude, overawed by the machines and the white coats and the learned, reassuring advice. Now it was different. In a few short months he had learned the true meaning of life and death and the value of both had been thrust upon him as he had never thought possible.

It was barely a week since the accident at Bolam. The experience had caused him to sleep badly, his rest ripped apart by weird, vivid dreams of the macabre that finally woke him panting and sweating with the bedclothes on the floor or in a tangled bundle around his body. Faces; faces he saw, accelerating toward him; growing from a pin-head until in a flash their open, screaming mouths enveloped him and he was in the tunnel – that black orifice of hell, gaping wide, sucking him down into an unknown bottomless void. His father, Smythe, Jenkins, Tomlinson – they all appeared, devouring him into the drift. Then he saw Ralph and Norman, their dismembered bodies swirling past in a whirlpool of red. Entrails; smiling dead faces; wailing, mourning ragged women. Then he was lost in a vast plain of flowers, bunched and domed with glass; the silent, chilling remembrances of a graveyard. Dead themselves, inanimate, impervious to wind and rain in their transparent coffins.

He turned to another page, forcing the images from his mind. He noted the wireless programmes and gave a grunt of pleasure: 4.15 p.m. Music from Tilley's Tea Rooms, Newcastle; 10.30 p.m. Jack Paynes Hotel Cecil Dance Band. He felt a sudden urge to get away for a while, to clear his head of sombre thoughts, to get some gaiety back into his life. He could almost smell the resined dance floor and hear the scrape of leather on it as some band played and a slick, blazered singer crooned into a megaphone, his tinny voice meandering through painted, frivolous arches and around intimate red-clothed tables. But the idea was instantly lost as he noticed the headlines, modestly sized on page four.

COAL COMMISSION REPORT
FINDINGS OF A FAR REACHING CHARACTER
SUBSIDY CONDEMNED
NATIONALISATION REJECTED

Normally such statements would have brought on a slow blink of disinterest before his eyes passed to something amusing or free from the boring prattle of political and industrial argument. He would have dismissed the item, letting the abrasive world go its own way, pushing its existence out of his memory. But on this occasion he read the report with avid interest. Men he knew were involved; Tomlinson, Edward Sneed, the remaining Nesbitts. The whole village of Bolam and a thousand like it would wilt or thrive on the dictum of Samuel and for the first time in his life he felt as vulnerable as they.

For three weeks the scent of crisis had been gathering momentum. A. J. Cook, Secretary of the Miners' Federation, was reported with growing regularity in the press, his demagogic utterances dissected and analysed. Herbert Smith, president of the same organisation, gave forth with blunt, aggressive warnings. Baldwin struggled to appear neutral while the organisation for the Maintenance of Supplies built itself up alongside the official government effort. Communists had been jailed and demonstrators screamed for their release. Rallies at the Albert Hall called on the armed forces and police to ignore the acts of the British striker. The thunderclouds were gathering.

John finished the article and digested its contents slowly, trying to equate the salient points first with Tomlinson and then with the miners. The Commission critized the industry in general saying that it had ceased to be remunerative. It criticized the owners for their old and badly maintained collieries and stated that an amalgamation of smaller mines was essential. The list of ills was long and complex but the remedy was not to be nationalisation. The remedy was placed firmly on the miners' overburdened shoulders. The continuance of the subsidy was rejected. A reduction in pay as a temporary sacrifice was, to Samuel, the only solution to the malaise. In contrast he advocated that when prosperity returned there should be annual holidays with pay, family allowances, more pit-head baths, profit sharing. A promise of sugar after the nasty medicine.

John exhaled noisily as he folded the newspaper and slapped it down on the breakfast table. Dr Jenkins continued with his kipper oblivious to everything except the plate in front of him and the occasional view of Ethel. Only then did he stop eating, watching her like a doleful hound would watch its master.

"Have you seen the morning paper?" John asked.

Jenkins nodded as he chewed.

"What do you think?"

His companion looked up and observed him with a loose-jawed nonchalance. "About the smallpox?"

"No," John replied irritably, "about the Samuel Commission, The findings are reported in here."

A look of disappointment crossed Jenkins' face and he put down his knife and fork, placing them with slow deliberation while his tongue hunted among his teeth.

"John," he said finally, the word short, almost a command, "would it surprise you to know that I have not read it, that I will not read it and what's more I couldn't care less what it says."

There was silence for a moment as the two men gazed at each other, Jenkins faintly amused by the puzzled expression of his assistant. "I am much more interested in the outbreak of smallpox," he continued. He gave a knowing nod across the table. "You should be too."

John's brow tightened. It would be different when Tomlinson came to cry on his shoulder. He would be interested then. "Will you say that to your friend?" he asked.

"No, no I will not," Dr Jenkins answered softly. "Nor will I say it to anyone else." He laid his hands flat on the table and leaned forward. "John, listen to me. Listen to a man who has, if nothing else, the experience of living and existing in this area for a lifetime. I accepted you into this practice for a number of reasons, most of them – in fact all of them – selfish ones." He sighed and his red face sagged into a sad smile. "I have personal problems, John, you must have realised that. I drink too much. I do that because when I am sober I have no confidence in myself – as a man I mean. There's something that's been driven out of me over the years. How? You may ask, or by whom?" He nodded. "By Ethel, she's done it. She's taken my mind and manipulates it to suit herself. Or she did. It was a last gasp effort, John. You came here and I was almost frantic with worry that you would not like it. You're a good doctor, John. The area needs someone like you. I need someone like you. Just having you here is a tonic. You've put some authority back into the place and you've given me back some of my self respect."

"Why don't you sack her?" John said persuasively.

Dr Jenkins' face stretched into a hopeless grin and he shook his head slowly. "I can't John. I risked her leaving when you came. I can't give her up. She's making my life a hell, but I'll not let her go. She'll come around sooner or later. She's been a wife to me as well. You understand?"

John nodded.

The old doctor smiled. "But enough of that. As I said, when you arrived and I knew your backround, I worried about you. I had visions of you leaving after a week. I wanted you to like the place and the people and fit into the community, for what it is. But take care, John, I can see the signs. Don't take sides. We as doctors are neutral. We deal with humans whatever their position. It's easy for anyone with a conscience to be on the side of the underdog, but in our profession it's dangerous. Take Tomlinson's advice, John, and stick to what you know about, it's so easy to become involved and then find you can't extricate yourself. Let them all get on with what they've got to do and you watch from the touch-line. You were like that when you first arrived."

John's mind flooded with memories of Bolam, of the people, of the accident. He remembered the rough, squeaking handcarts carrying the three dead men up the lane. The women at their doors clinging to their wide-eyed children and turning away in tears of relief when the carts passed them. He remembered the haunted bravery of Ruth and the wild, screaming emotion of Miriam Scott. Then there was the funeral; the silent procession, proud in their sorrow, in rented black; the Union banner held high, faces scrubbed, shoes borrowed and polished. There was an overwhelming dignity to their act and the dignity was magnified by their aura of common suffering. John looked hard at his companion. "I'm afraid I'll have to disappoint you, sir," he said in a whisper. "To hell with the smallpox!"

There was a monastic silence in the Nesbitt's house that had continued almost a week. The three of them ate their meal of dumplings and stew. Even the activity of their cutlery was genteel and quiet as though to generate the usual noise would be indecent. They ate automatically, the intensity of their private thoughts obliterating the view from their eyes like some overpowering daydream. The shock of losing her father and brother had wrung Ruth dry of outward emotion. She sat stiff and white faced, her clouded eyes heavy and red. In a way she knew they would die in the pit. For years the premonition had been with her but she had always dismissed it as a foolishness brought on by the memory of her grandfather, two uncles and a cousin who had perished in the winning of coal. All at different times; each bringing its own engulfing unhappiness. She looked to her two remaining brothers and thanked God that they had been spared. But for how long? How long? Alan sat pale and hunched, picking at his food, a pained uncertainty on his face. Tommy had a grim anger locked into his features and she knew that inside him he seethed with hatred for the pit, for Tomlinson and everything connected with him.

Mallory had called on the previous Sunday morning, the day after the accident. He was proper and correctly sympathetic. He was offered a cup of tea and took it, seating himself at the foot of the two coffins.

"Well, y've nowt to worry about," he said with a forced sigh. "W'll be payin' fifteen pound for each burial. They'll be seen off properly." He looked to each of them in turn, an innocent expectancy on his face as he waited for the grateful nods of relief.

Tommy raised himself from a stool in front of the fire. "Y'll be payin' more than that," he barked, "there's compensation as well."

Mallory shuffled uncomfortably in his chair. "I'm afraid not," he mumbled, "it was an unfortunate accident but . . . but there can be no question of full compensation. Of course there would have been," he added hastily, "if they had been where they should have been. They were not at the face and they had no business in the drift at that time of day." He shrugged. "If they had been at the face they would be alive now and not . . ." He nodded toward the coffins.

Tommy took a step toward him, his eyes wild with anger. "The Union'll say different," he snarled, "they'll fight you like they've done before."

Mallory gave a reluctant smile and his voice hardened. "I'm sorry, but they cannot win." He took a breath through his nose. "Your father and brother were not at their jobs. It appears as though they were sneaking off early – probably to see the football match."

Tommy's face twisted into a savage snarl. "You're a pig, Mallory," he yelled, "you're a swine. Get out! Get t'hell out of here!"

Mallory's eyes rounded and he blinked furiously. He moved quickly around the coffins toward the door. Alan ran upstairs while Ruth watched, numbed and impassive.

"I shall take these insults, Tommy Nesbitt, and put them down to the fact that you are not in full command of your senses . . ."

Tommy cut him short as he closed the gap between them. "Pig! Pig!" he screamed.

Mallory accelerated toward the door ". . .because of your bereavement," he gabbled, as he stumbled into the lane.

There was a rattle on the sneck and the back door opened, bringing Ruth back from her remembering. She heard the deep gentle voice of Edward Sneed and saw his rough, craggy face break into a soft smile.

"Aye Ted," she whispered.

"I've brought a few things," he said, laying a packet of biscuits, a half pound of lard and a small tin of condensed milk on the table. "It's not much . . ." His voice trailed away as he hunted for words.

Ruth stood up and hugged him. She buried her face into his thick rough neck and sobbed.

"Howay now, lass," he said, patting her back, "if we can't help each other who's to help us." He turned to Tommy as Ruth broke away. "It's you I've come to see as well, lad."

"Aye Ted, what's up?" Tommy said solemnly.

"Seen the paper the day?"

Tommy shook his head.

Edward pulled a folded, grimy *Journal* from his jacket pocket. "Read what Mr Samuel and his cronies have to say."

Tommy took the paper and sat on the stool by the fire. After a while he looked up. There was a glint in his eye, a wry, sarcastic smile on his face. "So it's to be less wages after all."

Edward nodded, "But not without a battle royal. You an' the Union lads'll see to that a'll bet."

Tommy's voice trembled with conviction. "You're so right, Ted. We'll drop with hunger before we'll give in this time." He glanced at the paper again as a sudden surge of excitement gripped him, then he looked up at his neighbour. "We'll get a meetin' organised at the pub . . . Y'll help us, Ted? We need every man jack there is. W've got to organise ourselves now, so we're ready . . . for hell t'break loose."

"Easy lad," Edward said with a gentle persuasiveness. "I'm with you all the way but don't fly at it. Wait, wait for Cooky and the big noises in London, they'll call the tune."

Tommy stood up and thumped a fist against the iron surround of the fire. He stared unblinking into the flames. "I'm sick of waiting," he said through clenched teeth. "They want a fight. They've given themselves months to get ready for a fight. Now they think they're strong enough to do battle. Well let's get on with it!"

Edward smiled as a tenuous flurry of envy came over him. He was a quiet man with none of the billowing spirit that exuded from most of them. He lived his life as best he could. He shared it with Nellie and tried to keep her existence as free from hurt as possible. She had had her share in the past. He thought about his two sons and how they would have made up for his lack of fire. They would have been like Tommy. They would have been crusaders, of that he was sure.

"Take your time, bonny lad," he said, "there's nowt we can do just now. Bide your time. And if you hear from the big fella, take no notice."

"The big fella?" Tommy queried. "Who?"

"Y'know, him that shakes hands as though he's sleepin' with yer."

"Tilmouth?"

"Aye. I've told you before lad, watch him. He's up t'no good. He's a trouble maker if ever there was one."

Tommy's lips thinned. He sighed and rubbed his eyes wearily. "I know, I know. He's a damn' communist; he said so himself. It's a massacre that crowd want, not a strike. Don't worry, Ted, if he comes back he'll not be lodgin' here."

"Is it to be a strike then?" The words were quietly spoken and came from Alan.

The two men looked at him.

"Seems like it, son," Edward said, "they want us t'work for next to nowt."

"Canna help?" Alan asked eagerly. "I want to help."

Tommy gave out a dry, mocking laugh. "It's man's work, Alan. There's nowt y'can do but stay away from the pit. When the strike's called y'll be out like the rest on us." He looked to Edward. "Mebbe w'll not get the chance to strike. Tomlinson might have a lock-out like he threatened last year."

Alan stood up and moved towards them. There was an agitated frown on his face. He had been tortured for weeks by the memory of Tilmouth and the secrets he knew the man carried with him. It was imperative that he pleased him – just in case he returned, just in case he decided to tell them. "Please," he begged, "I'm strong now. I'll do anything to help – anything."

His brother gazed at him for a moment. For the first time the combination of his voice and the mincing sway of his movements formed a hint of suspicion in his mind, a flicker of dread then an instant rejection. But he remembered his wide staring eyes as he mopped around the baths watching the crowds of soap-covered naked miners, laughing and singing and oblivious to his attentions. Again he dismissed the shocking thought as quickly as it had germinated but it left a shadow on his mind that was more permanent.

"D'you really want to help, Alan?"

Alan smiled and nodded.

"Even if it means losin' your job at the baths?"

"I don't care."

"Why – don't you like it there?"

Alan hesitated for a second as the memories surged back of the bewildering, uncontrollable feelings; excitement, pleasure juxtaposed with fear, shame and confusion. "I hate it," he said firmly.

Tommy's face broke into a slow smile of relief, he pulled his brother to him. "Good lad," he said with a joy that he had not felt since before the accident. "Why, aye y'can help – can't he Ted? He can help all he wants."

Alan turned his head to see Ruth, expecting a warm look of approval, but she was not even with them. She stood forlornly by the table, her shoulders drooped, wrapped in her own world of misery and despair.

The village of Bolam lay like some mysterious unexplored shadow as the faint, pink smudge of late sunset was smothered by the nocturnal clouds that gathered on the horizon. Only the configuration of the pit and its ancillary buildings were visible; black, hideous shapes that seemed to thrive with the night; the boilerhouse chimney dominating the scene, silently gushing forth smoke into the still air and reminding all and sundry that beneath its awful rigid form, it lived and was king.

John swung the Sunbeam off the road and set himself for the bumpy ride toward the cottages. There was nothing that showed the trauma of the week before. It was as it had always been except the population was a little less. The pit, the people, the atmosphere had returned to normal. Most of them had come to terms with sudden, violent death. It was part of their lives, a version of Russian roulette that was played each day. When from time to time there were losers, the mourning was intense but brief. It was not so for one person, however, and John Kinghorn knew it. The thick layer of shock and grief that had been spread upon Ruth's already weakened spirit had bitten deep into her soul and John realised the growing symptoms that could undermine her health completely. He had hunted his mind for an excuse to help her out of the rut in which she was gradually becoming immersed but nothing came that was not blatantly obvious and could perhaps be misconstrued. Yet on that particular night he couldn't care less. He had the car and the distance between him and Plessey House was increasing by the second. He was intent on an evening where he could forget about pits and doctoring and the troubles of life. He wanted to find music and laughter and hear the chink of fine glass. There were jokes to be heard and songs to be sung and wine to savour. He had a sudden pang of conscience when he stopped the car at the bottom of the quiet smoky row. It would have been grand if he could have invited them all to join him. He was in that sort of mood. But he couldn't, it was just a fanciful thought. It would have to be Ruth or nobody.

It had been just as John had predicted. Evening surgery was over quickly but even so Charles Tomlinson arrived just as he finished and gave him and Dr Jenkins a full appraisal of the Commission's report. His feelings were mixed. He moaned at their criticism of the condition of collieries in general, praised their wisdom in recommending a cut in wages and scoffed at the future benefits which were advocated.

"Hah! I'm one step ahead of them," he barked at a subdued Dr Jenkins. "They say 'pit-head baths', I say we've already got them. But will that stop the Bolam crowd from yelling for more?" He sneered at the two doctors, "Not on your bloody life. They'll listen to Cook. They'll believe anything he tells them." He ground his teeth in anger. "Mindless idiots – the lot of them!"

Dr Jenkins glanced at John, giving him a sheepish, watery look that was a premature apology. "Easy, Charles," he said. "Baldwin hasn't had his say yet. Samuel's report is only a guideline for the Government."

"Guideline!" Tomlinson snapped. "Christ Almighty, if it's taken verbatim I could wind up sucked into Daleman's North Tyne complex and be lost without trace." He sat down and held his head between his hands. "There's going to be trouble. I told you months ago. We've got to stand firm though, see it through. It's got to be less money and longer hours at least – or we'll all go under."

John turned away in disgust, but the words burned to get out. He spun on Tomlinson. "So you're going to cut their wages," his voice was low and thick with contempt. "Well done. They're living just above starvation level and that's too good for them. You're going to knock them back to pre-war standards. God! You'd have made a successful slave trader . . ." He breathed in noisily, wanting to say more, abuse crowding his tongue for utterance but he resisted in deference to Dr Jenkins whose silent plea for civility got through to him.

"How do you know about wage levels and what not?" Tomlinson asked with surprise, ignoring the insult.

"I listen, I enquire, I find out things that interest me," John answered curtly. He didn't wait for a reaction. He turned to Dr Jenkins. "May I take the car?"

Jenkins shrugged. "Yes, I suppose so. Why?"

"I want to see Fulthorpe at the Infirmary."

"Tonight?"

"Why not," he said with a trace of hopelessness as he turned toward the door. "I might go to the pictures or something afterwards. Goodnight, gentlemen."

There was silence for a moment after he closed the door on them. Tomlinson sighed and viewed his friend warily. "You don't agree with him, Bob, do you?"

Dr Jenkins didn't give him a direct answer. He reached for the whisky bottle. "Ah, he's young," he said as though the question was preposterous. "He's learning how to come to terms with life as it really is."

"And how is it really?"

Jenkins swallowed his drink. "Bloody awful I suppose," he whispered.

Ruth answered John's knock but there was nothing from her, not even a flicker of surprise. She stood, her face blank and tired waiting for some explanation of his presence.

He smiled at her. He was pleased he had called no matter what. The idea had occurred to him as he backed the car out of the garage that he should have some company. At first he thought of Tomlinson's daughters, but their giggling, flirtatious manner scared him. They were desperate for a husband, a lover, a male to quench their untapped desires. And then he thought of Ruth. She above all needed some of life's pleasures. She seemed to carry the stigma of everything that was wrong and unjust in the village. To give her some inkling of the luxuries of the world would be a blessed act, spiritually gratifying, morally satisfying. He didn't question his conscience further.

"May I come in?" he asked.

"Of course," she whispered, her voice flat and uninterested.

He tried to appear casual, light-hearted, but the act clashed with his natural feeling of regret at her bereavement. He felt suddenly awkward and embarrassed in the tiny room, dimly lit and crowded with the basics of frugal living.

"Well?" he said, flapping his arms down by his sides. "How are you, Ruth?"

She dropped her gaze to the floor. "All right I suppose."

He tried to be diplomatic. He wanted to chat to her, to ease the question into his conversation as though it was a foregone conclusion but he knew it was hopeless. His every action seemed so obvious, so fabricated, so rehearsed and blatantly patronising.

He looked into her green, wondering eyes that observed him with a patient calmness. "Ruth, I am going into Newcastle. I have the car. I have to see Robert Fulthorpe at the Infirmary. Will you come with me? We can have a bite to eat and see a show or something . . ." He stopped and waited for a reaction.

Ruth sat herself on the stool in front of the fire. Her face broke into a sad, weary smile. "You want me . . . to come with you, Dr Kinghorn?" she said, her voice questioning what her ears had heard.

"Yes Ruth," he said, finding renewed confidence. "I want you to come out with me. I want you – us to enjoy ourselves. Will you?"

She ran a hand through her hair and down to the nape of her neck. "Me? Eatin' out in Newcastle? Going in a car?"

"Yes, yes," he answered eagerly. "We need to get out of this place, Ruth. We need to remember what it's like to laugh. I've forgotten and so have you. You'll come, won't you?"

She stood up, her head a whirl of excitement. "But the lads – they've gone to a meeting they won't know . . ."

"Leave a note. We'll not be late."

The positiveness in his voice swayed her, and the surge of pleasure at his asking. Yet she still wanted to say no as her mind crowded with doubts. Clothes, manners, all the frightening proper ways of the city filled her with dread.

He saw the sudden hesitation in her face and tried to quell it quickly. "Please say yes, Ruth. I'm not going without you."

She wrung her hands in an agony of indecision, her self-conscious imperfections battling against the overpowering urge to accept. Her eyes, brimful of tears, stared at him as though he was an hallucination, a dream that would vanish in a flash and send her wild, miraculous imaginings crashing into abject disappointment. But he was real; he was standing there and she could not allow herself to refuse. "But what will I wear?" she asked of him, her voice weak and childlike.

He sat himself in the rocking chair and loosened his coat. "What about that pretty dress you wore at the surgery?"

Her face brightened. "Do you really like it?"

He gave her a broad reassuring smile and winked. "It's tip-top."

She blushed as the wisp of intimacy between them suddenly came to her. She walked to the foot of the stairs. She was positive now, her mind was made up, her doubts without meaning. "I'll be as quick as I can," she whispered.

John rocked gently, his feet splayed out and his arms nestling comfortably across his chest. There was a warm glow of pleasure in him as he waited. He couldn't care less that her dress was of little better quality than his London clique would wear for mucking out the stables. The woman in it, with her simple unsophistication, had a strange chemistry to her, a quality of truth that he had never seen in his past friends. For once he didn't bother to analyse his feelings. For once they were clear and made sense.

It was a week later when Robert Fulthorpe was discharged from hospital. His injuries, compared to the others, were amazingly slight. The fickle ways of chance had left him with lacerations of the limbs and he had lost the knee-cap from his right leg. He had been lucky; other than stitching scars and a stiff leg he would be normal. When John called on him that day he was laid out on an ancient protesting brass bed, yelling oaths at his wife and children and lamenting his fate. He praised the Lord for his deliverance and in the same breath cursed the pit that had almost snatched his life. When John entered the bedroom his family departed but the verbal barrage continued.

"Oh, Dr Kinghorn," he wailed. "Yea, though I walk through the valley of bloody death . . ." He wiped at his brow with his podgy hand, gasping as though he was breathing his last. "By Christ," he croaked, "if it wasn't for the faith in me I'd be a gonner, doctor. Jesus saves! Jesus saves! Tomlinson and that rat-trap of a pit – I hope he gets a boil on his arse the size of a turnip."

John ignored his rantings. He examined the dressings regretting that the hospital could not have kept him longer but considering that he had been continually spouting doggerel since he regained consciousness he could understand their keeness to be rid of him. He was a man John could not take to. His hypocrisy was greater than even Tomlinson's.

"I have been spared for better things, doctor," he continued. His voice was a hoarse whisper of emotion. "The Lord in his wisdom has chosen that I should see that sod Tomlinson get his just reward."

"You'll get your just reward if you don't rest those legs – and that tongue," John said sharply. "You want to walk again, don't you? Or do you want to be like Nellie Sneed?"

Fulthorpe's face grew suddenly angry. "Now here, you young pup, don't take that tone with me. I know my rights. I'm not a County Councillor for nowt, you know. You're paid to look after us, keep us healthy, not tommin' around with the village girls and bossin' us about. You're as bad as that shit Mallory. There's a whole nest of you's up there at Allington. You're all too big for your boots."

John itched to hit him, to sink his fist into the flabby redness of his face, for the insults and the insinuation about his relationship with

Ruth. He stood dumb with rage, biting his teeth, fighting to keep control. He turned and grabbed his bag. "Good-day," he growled.

He stamped down the bare stairs, the withering rage in him making his head pound. How did he know about Ruth? In the two hours or so he had been home it could only have been his wife. He had given him no hint on the night he went to the hospital and left Ruth waiting in the car. Did all the village know? Did they all have the same opinion? He hadn't bargained for the eagle eyes of Maudy Fenwick. She had seen him the week before; she had heard the car and stood with her little nose pressed against the glass of her window. Then she saw him return, not alone but with Ruth Nesbitt! Her head withdrew into her shoulders as her beady eyes filled her mind with all the sexual delights that scared her yet tortured her with the want of them. She bit her lip as desire warmed her loins. Men! Men! – The cause of all her torment. She had to tell someone of the sins of the flesh.

John looked around the room. Fulthorpe's wife sat rocking and sewing, any flicker of vitality long since washed out of her by her overpowering spouse. Their children rolled around the floor, barefoot and grubby. Wilbur, the eldest, observed him with a wariness borne from the pain of their last encounter.

"Try to keep him still or he'll open those wounds," he said as he walked to the door.

Mrs Fulthorpe nodded, her tiny face still peering at the action of her needle. "Will he get back to work?" she asked.

John stopped. "It'll be a while yet."

She nodded again, satisfied; well versed in hunger and hardship.

John walked along the Row intent on visiting Nellie Sneed, anger still simmering inside him. His mood had gone sour after the elation that had lasted a week. The reserved shyness and fine, quiet charm of Ruth had sent a tingle of fascination through him during their evening out. She had radiated some strange purity as though even to touch her would be a violation of some inviolable law. Yet she relaxed on the way home, her pleasant ordeal over. She seemed at ease and happier than he had ever seen her, but still a long way from the vibrance that her years commanded. There was nothing more to it than that. Her shyness returned as he said goodnight, the significance of such a moment bringing to her mind perhaps something more than polite words. It had been a good evening, enjoyable and proper, and he knew he would ask her again but as he lifted the sneck on the battered, brown door of the Sneed's house he wondered if it would be wise.

Nellie greeted him with her usual smile and Edward, home from the pit and working at the hessian, welcomed him with a wave. There was no need to make the tea that day. It was brewed and ready. John poured himself a cup and walked around to Edward. The mat was almost completed. "God, that's a fine bit of work," he breathed.

Edward smiled. "It's taken some doin' doctor. I'll be glad t'see the end of it."

"You're a craftsman Ted. You'd make a fortune selling those."

Edward chuckled. "Who'd have them? There's only us folk who can afford nowt better. It's only rags."

"Rags or not, it's a beauty."

"For the lads' room," Nellie croaked.

John turned to her. "Yes Nellie, for the lads' room. They'll like that in their room. Your Ted's a very clever man."

"Aye," she answered in her flat, singing manner.

Edward continued working and John moved back to his wife. "Come on then, milady. Today you're going to stand up. Right?"

She looked up at him, belief in his words unquestionably showing on her face. She took hold of his arms and her frail, wasted legs twitched ready for her effort. Her toothless mouth was sunken and tight and her eyes were small, round beads of concentration.

"Up Nellie!" he commanded. "Come on – up! Up!

It took her almost five minutes to raise her bottom off the chair. John gripped at her bony elbows, taking some of her scant weight.

"Look!" he yelled to Edward. "Look at her!"

Edward left the table and stood blinking with disbelief. "Eeh Nellie," he whispered, "you've done it."

She flopped with exertion and John let her sink back into the chair. "Good girl, Nellie," he said, patting her shoulder. "You're doing just fine."

"Aye," she said with a hint of pride.

There was a sad smile on Edward's face. "Will she walk again doctor?"

John gripped his enormous arm. "I think so. She must keep trying. You'll have to try her every day."

Edward shook his head. "It's no good, doctor. She'll not try with me. There's only you who can do anything with her."

John patted her hand. "Is that right? Won't you try with Ted?"

She hung her head and shook it.

"Ok. Nellie. We'll do it then. Just me and you. All right?"

"Thank you, Doctor Kinghorn," Edward said humbly. "We've no right to such help."

"I would say that you miners have more right than most."

"I wish there were others with that opinion."

"You mean Tomlinson?"

Edward lumbered slowly back to the table. "Aye," he said warily.

"Him and his kind."

"Is there going to be trouble?"

Edward fished among his pile of rags. He sighed, a deep regretful sigh. "I don't know, doctor. Depends on a lot of things – talks in London and whatnot."

John nodded. "How will you manage if there's a strike?"

Edward shrugged. "Won't be much different to how it is now."

The doctor tutted and made for the door. He turned and looked hard at the gentle man. "I'm on your side, you know that don't you?"

Edward's eyes were dull yet they had a deep understanding in them. "I think I know that, doctor. I've told others as much."

"Who?"

"Tommy Nesbitt."

John frowned. "Why Tommy?"

"He didn't like the idea of Ruth being out with you. Said you were not our sort. Said you were of Tomlinson's class."

John's eyes narrowed. "You tell him different," he hissed, anger boiling up again. "Ted, you damn well tell him different."

Edward's eyes began to sparkle. "Because of us or because of Ruth?"

"Because of all of you!" he yelled.

Edward smiled.

"Aye," Nellie sang.

It had been a long day. Evening surgery dragged on until after seven, aggravating John's despondency. He was still smarting from the comments of Fulthorpe and Tommy Nesbitt. He had thought he was close to them; he had imagined their acceptance of him as a formality as and when he chose. But it was not to be like that. He realised he was nothing more than their equal, perhaps not even that. Their history of exploitation had welded them into a select, interwoven community, naturally cautious and proud of their heritage of defiance. He was only a man among men and an unproven outsider separated from them by a class distinction which in John's mind was rapidly being refined to a false, valueless level of "the haves" and "the have nots". He rang the little bell and relaxed when there was no response, sitting back letting his thoughts chase themselves around his mind. Then, with a sigh he sauntered into the hall. He examined some obscure plant in the glass outhouse that was sprouting with the warming spring, then turned to lock the door. The figure at the other side of the glass startled him for a second. It was Alan Nesbitt, pale and dishevelled, his eyes heavy and red and a profound unhappiness on his face. He stood in a tattered work jacket, still and trancelike as John opened the door.

"Alan. What's wrong?"

He made to speak, his lips moving but there was no sound.

"Come on into the surgery. Tell me there."

He shuffled forward and John finally sat him on the chair in front of his desk.

"Now Alan, tell me what's wrong. It's not Ruth is it, or Tommy?"

Alan slowly lifted his head. There was an agony of inner conflict on his face. "No," he said, his voice barely audible, "it's me."

John leant forward. "Are you ill?"

His head went back and his mouth opened as though he was giving out a silent scream. "Yes – no. I don't know," he gasped.

There was something about him; some intangible signal that told John his trouble was not physical, that he was wracked by some torment of the mind.

"What is it, Alan? You've come to me for help. If I can, I will."

His head wavered as though he was forcing the words to be spoken. There were tears in his eyes and his clenched fists showed the white of his knuckles. He thumped his chest with them. "Give me something, Doctor Kinghorn. Give me some medicine to take away the hate that's in me."

"The hate? For whom?"

"For myself – for the things I do and the things I want to do."

"What have you been doing, Alan?"

He buried his head in his hands and the answer came in a halting, muffled voice. "The baths – all those men – naked. It's wrong, I know it's wrong but . . . but I can't help myself. I watch them – I want to touch them. Do you see doctor? Do you see now!"

John sat back, stunned, his mind racing. He blew a long, low whistle from his lips. He had read about such things; he had had one brief lecture that touched upon the psychology of it; he had seen what were purported to be men – women swaggering around the West End. "Queens", "nancy boys"; they were objects of ridicule among his crowd. Surely Alan Nesbitt could not be like that. He was young, an adolescent, his maturing instincts still jumbled and searching for their correct roles.

He spread his hands on the desk as he hunted for words. "Yes, I see, Alan," he said. "How long . . . how long have you felt this way?"

There was no answer.

"Since you started at the baths?"

He nodded and let his hands slide away from his face. "But before as well," he whispered, "before . . . always . . . but worse now. Today was worse."

John's brow tightened. "Does Ruth know or Tommy?"

He swallowed hard. "They know nothing. How could I tell them? How could I tell anyone?" His face twisted in desperation. "Have you some medicine, doctor? You're the only one who can help me."

"I can give you nothing, Alan. There's no medicine except what is within you. You must fight it. Force it out of your mind."

He sobbed again. "I can't. I've tried for so long. Oh, doctor, you've got to help me. I just want to be normal."

John stood up. Again he felt a frightening uselessness. "There is nothing I can do. I wish there were. Fight it, Alan. Get yourself a girl. Take plenty of exercise and fresh air. That way you'll drive it out of your system."

Alan's jaw dropped and he blinked. "You won't help me?" The blank neutral stare spoke volumes. He leapt out of the chair and ran to the door.

"Alan! Come back!" John yelled.

But it was no good. By the time he got to the outhouse, he had gone, running wildly out of the village and away.

John rubbed a hand over his tired face. He could go chasing after him, but to what good? His tangled emotions would have to right themselves. Yet a feeling of frustration came over him at his inability to help. He realised the searing torture within him that had forced such an admission and he thought of Ruth and how she would cope with the shame of it all should he be found out. He wanted so much to break through their closed ranks and be identified as a champion of their cause. He could treat their boils and coughs and calloused backs but now that was somehow not enough.

He locked the door and turned wearily back into the hall, his mind a whirlpool of uncertainty. He noticed the rolled object propped in the corner but he passed it without a second glance. He stopped short at the grandfather clock and turned again, a puzzled frown on his face. He recognised its form and colour. It was a large mat woven out of rags and tied with a piece of brown twine. He pulled at the knot and it unrolled. Quickly he laid it out on the hall floor. There could be no mistake. There was no other like it. It was Edward Sneed's magnificent six month effort.

There was a little scrawled note tied to the string. It said: For Dr John Kinghorn from Nellie and the lads.

He cried like a baby.

9

It had been a useless meeting. The crowd of miners at the Fat Ox had allowed it to slump into a harangue of heated, aggressive argument, uncontrolled and roudy. Rumours were rife and exaggerated; ideas ridiculous, the product of wondering, desperate men. Tommy strained his lungs to surmount the rising cacophony but it was no good. Even the four-fingered whistle of the irate barman was lost among the solid roar of angry voices. Finally Tommy gave up. He looked around him at the shoal of open mouths and shook his head. It was hopeless. Only Alan and Edward Sneed were in control of themselves; Alan cowering by his side and Edward as placid as ever, strong, silent and understanding. Suddenly Tommy leapt up and pushed his way to the door. He thrust his hand into the pockets of his trousers and kicked fiercely at a stone as the muted melee continued inside. Alan and Edward appeared but they did not speak. Their silence was for Tommy and his ever-thwarted efforts to marshal them all into some form of coherent unit, should the strike become a reality. But they were getting nowhere.

As the lengthening days of March wavered before letting April smother the remnants of winter it seemed inevitable that the summer sun would shine on a troubled country. The strength of passion of Cook's speeches accelerated into a frenzy after the Samuel report was rejected by the Miners Federation. The coal owners bluntly refused to discuss reorganization. Longer hours and a reduction in wages was their immovable decision. The haggling continued however, and Baldwin sat back waiting for the two factions to agree among themselves, issuing an ultimatum that, no matter what, the subsidy would end on April 30th.

They set off over the field toward home, leaving the hoarse voices to tire themselves out and soon the noise was lost behind a strong westerly that caused low, stretched clouds to chase across a waning moon. It was Edward who spoke first. He placed a hand on Tommy's shoulder.

"Don't fret, son," he said "They're good lads really. They're just het up. They'll see sense by an' by."

Tommy gave out a bark of derision. "What good will they be

fightin' among themselves? Christ man Ted, if it's to be a strike, we've got t'be ready – not like before – not like 21 an' . . . an' all the rest." He waved his hands wildly in the air. "We've got a soddin' month to build up something. To let the country see that we're solid to a man. Cook's sayin' it but nobody's doin' it. Not an effin' word from the Federation or the T.U.C."

Edward patted his shoulder. There was a chuckle in his voice. "Eeh, Tommy y've got it weighed up, lad. There's not much slips by you. If only the lads . . ."

He stopped as a lull in the wind brought the noise of a car engine to their ears. They looked to the Rows and saw the yellow beams searching the contours of the road and low walls of Maudy Fenwick's shop.

"It'll be the doctor," Edward whispered. "Somebody's bad."

Tommy stopped. "Aye, which bliddy doctor though?"

"What difference," Edward said, more as a statement.

" 'Cos it might be Kinghorn and he might be out t'see Ruth."

Edward tutted. "So what?" he said gently. "He's all right, is that lad. He's for us. I've told you before."

Tommy grunted. "Mebbe so, but he's not our kind. He's got those high flyin' London ways. He should stick to his own. Let him poke those two turkeys of Tomlinson's and leave us to ourselves."

Edward's voice was firm. "He's a gentleman, Tommy. Y've no cause t'say things like that."

Tommy waved away the statement with a growl. He turned to where Alan trailed along behind them.

"Alan," he commanded. "Run on ahead and see who's at the house."

"Right Tommy," came the eager reply and was off and ahead of them, holding onto his cap against the wind.

It was another five minutes before they reached the house. The back door was open and the murmur of voices came from within.

"The bastard," Tommy whispered. "I was right."

"Easy Tommy," Edward chided. "They're young. Let them be."

He ignored him and stamped inside.

With a sigh Edward lifted the latch on No. 8, wondering all of a sudden if Nellie was all right.

It was not as Tommy expected. As he burst into the room he could not believe his eyes. Ruth stood by the fireplace, a sour smile stretching her lips. There was a stranger sitting at the table, a sharp featured young man, thin, with flesh of putty and a dark shadow of stubble. His hair was black and limp and his eyes narrow and arrogant. He stared up at Tommy and smiled crookedly, vapidly.

Alan was at the far side of the room, his face white and his eyes big and round as he stared down at another figure in the rocking chair. The face turned slowly to observe him. There was no mistaking the gaunt features and eyes of polished ebony.

"Hello there, Tommy. We meet again," said Kenneth Frederick Tilmouth.

Tommy stood for a second, breathing noisily as icy fingers clutched at his heart. "Oh it's you," he muttered. "You're back."

Tilmouth stood up. "Yes, I'm back," he said in his sugary voice. "And I've brought a friend. I've told him all about you, Tommy, and what a good lad you are. Meet Ron Brooke."

Brooke rose from his chair, the twisted smile still locked on his face. He held out a hand and Tommy reluctantly took it. It was a cold hand, clammy and insipid and the rubbery nod of his head made Tommy's flesh creep.

"There now," Tilmouth said, sitting himself down again. "We couldn't come North without coming to see you. In fact Ron's been quite looking forward to it. Haven't you, Ron?"

Brooke gazed ponderously around the room and nodded quickly.

"I'm afraid we can't put you up this time," Tommy said urgently. "You know about . . .?"

"About Ralph and Norman? Yes, I read about it. I'm terribly sorry. They were great men. But don't worry about us," he gave a nod in Brooke's direction. "We're staying in Newcastle. We've taken some rooms there. And we've driven up, you know. We need the car – we've got to be mobile."

Tommy hardly dared to ask the question. "Will you be in these parts long?"

Tilmouth shrugged. He seemed jovial, flamboyant even. "Oh, a while I think. There's work to do, Tommy. There's a revolution on the way."

"There's a strike on the way – that's all I know."

Tilmouth gave forth with confident enthusiasm. "That's true – that's true, Tommy, but it'll be more than that. The workers of this country are going to rise up like never before. They're going to devour the bourgeoisie. They're going to eliminate the parasites." He gave a cute, knowing grin. "It's in the wind . . ."

"You're wrong," Tommy countered. "The workers of this country want nothing more than a livin' wage. They're prepared to suffer to get it. They'll use the only weapon they've got that's right t'use. They'll strike. If it comes to bloodshed it'll be others that have caused it."

Tilmouth held up his hands in mock surrender. "All right, all right, I take your point. Nevertheless, there is work to do. If nothing else, the strike must succeed. The coal owners must be defeated once and for all."

Tommy sighed. "We agree on that point anyway."

Tilmouth sat back, pleased with himself. "We agreed on a lot of things last time, did we not? It was only when the ideals were condensed into a collective term that you lost your faith. You chose to call it by another name – any name would do."

Tommy ran a hand through his hair as right and wrong suddenly merged in his mind, then split into a thousand ill-defined facets. "I follow Cook," he said at last, "Cook is our man."

"And Cook follows Lenin. He's said so himself," Tilmouth said with a dramatic softness.

It was pointless arguing further. The man was too quick, too experienced. Tommy looked at the two of them in turn, angry with himself that he had no plausible answer. "At least he's only interested in gettin' a fair deal for the miners," he growled.

Tilmouth's face lit up. "And so are we – aren't we, Ron? In fact that's why we're here. We want to tour the area – all the pits in Northumberland and Durham. We want to drum up the noise of protest so that it'll rattle the doors of Parliament. That's all Tommy. But it's a big job, that's why I've brought Ron. We'll split up where necessary and cover the whole of the two counties." His brow furrowed and he flicked at his nose with a forefinger. "But I'll need more help, Tommy. Ron's a stranger to these parts. He needs a guide. Know anyone who might like to show him around?"

Tommy shook his head. "No – there's nobody," he said positively.

Tilmouth stared at him, his deep, dark eyes unblinking. Then his lips parted and stretched, creasing his face into a contortion of joy. "What about Alan?"

"Alan can't," Tommy snapped, "he's workin' at the pit now."

"Oh, that's all right; just a few hours at night perhaps, and a weekend or two."

"No!" Tommy yelled.

Tilmouth spun around. "What does Alan say about it?"

Alan bit on his bottom lip. His eyes flicked from Tommy to Tilmouth to Brooke. His knees trembled with fear and yet he couldn't say no. Tilmouth had him, his devilish smile and the knowledge behind it controlled him.

"Oh yes, please Tommy. I want to help Mr Tilmouth and Mr Brooke. It'll be grand. Please let me go, Tommy. It'll be helpin' us as well."

Tilmouth's eyebrows lifted as he turned back to his brother. "Well there you are now. There's a real keen lad. He's not a kid now, you know. Let him give us a hand."

Tommy glanced at his sister but she was lost among her own thoughts. He slapped hopelessly at his thigh and shrugged. "Oh, please your bloody selves," he whispered vehemently.

It took only a split second for Tilmouth to gauge Brooke's expression. It was one of triumph.

John knew he shouldn't have accepted the invitation. In fact if it hadn't been for Dr Jenkins' persuasion he would have been on his way to Bolam even sooner. As it was, he had reluctantly given in and subjected himself to an evening of tongue-biting at Tomlinson's house. It was as though their every word was somehow a subtle ridiculing of his allegiance. Tomlinson himself muttered on about the high probability of a strike and that it might not, after all, be a bad thing.

"Cut losses while the slump continues, y'see Bob," he said with a sniff and a forced laugh.

Clarrie, his wife, made trite remarks, fingering her beads and bowing her head toward John, straining an effervescence into her voice. "Then we can all go to Antibes for the summer."

Their daughters were no better. The fact that the dispute would almost certainly degenerate into a general strike seemed to thrill them. They saw adventure and novelty in it. A class war tempered down to a safe, exciting conflict of wits and determination. Thoroughbred against mongrel. Righteous David against the uncouth Goliath. They gabbled with schoolgirl vigour about having joined the O.M.S. and being trained to drive lorries at Newcastle.

"We'll keep the old country's heart ticking," Grace gushed.

Clarrie clapped. "Bravo," she bleated with pride.

John made his excuses as soon after dinner as manners would permit. There was little resistance. Dr Jenkins was past caring, lost in a plush armchair with a brandy glass in his hand.

Tomlinson saw him to the door and there was a hint of pity in his voice as he bade him goodnight, but John ignored it. He walked quickly to the village letting the wind purge his mind of their complacency. He thought of Ruth, as he had done for most of the evening and compared her company with that of his recent hosts. He knew then that was where he should be. Her quiet, reserved character, free from the artificial trappings of affluence put her high above his kind. Her quality of truth humbled him. He passed Plessey House and turned at the corner toward Bolam feeling an exhilaration in him as he looked towards its cowering drabness. He had seen her in the last month, spoken to her lightly and casually, but he was determined now to ask her out again; to draw from her some of her inner excellence that made his heart sing and his mind swirl into new depths of happiness. It had to be – no matter what her brother or the villagers had to say.

The car parked at the bottom of the row puzzled him for a moment. It was a Morris saloon, mud spattered and travel-weary, but its presence was forgotten by the time he approached No. 10. It was Tommy who answered his knock and in the instant of recognition it was as though he submitted to John's determined stare.

"I've come to see Ruth, Tommy," he said without hesitation. "Is she in?"

Tommy seemed to hold his breath, on the verge of some pre-rehearsed comment, then he sagged, his iron features melting into condescension. "Come in, doctor. Why not? Come in and join the bliddy rest. It's half-way house the night."

He was into the room before Tommy's comment made sense. It took only an instant for him to observe Ruth's sad smile and Alan's wince of alarm before he turned away. The two strangers gazed at him, Tilmouth with raised eyebrows as though on the verge of a pleasant surprise, Brooke smiling and biting at his bottom lip. John felt suddenly foolish. It seemed as if they all knew the reason for his visit.

He turned back to the door. "I'm sorry," he whispered. "I didn't realize you had visitors."

"No! don't go!" Tilmouth stood up and took the harshness out of his order with a hungry smile and a whining qualification. "Don't leave because of us. You're more than welcome. Isn't that so, Tommy?"

He didn't wait for an answer. He held out his hand. "I'm Kenneth Tilmouth. This is Ronald Brooke."

"John Kinghorn," John muttered.

Tilmouth nodded. "Didn't I hear the word, 'doctor'?"

"That's right."

"Ah! A man of letters." He turned his delight around the room. "A doctor – of philosophy, of law, of medicine?"

"Of medicine," John growled, perturbed by the silent awe of the Nesbitts. Yet it was not hard to see why. The man had some nerve-tingling mysticism to him, a heavy shadow of shrewdness behind his smooth, dominant bonhomie.

Tilmouth's face changed to mock concern. "There's no-one ill, I hope." Then he smiled again. "Or is it a social visit?"

John glanced at Ruth. She was looking away, arms folded in front of her, her face neutral. "No – no, there's no-one ill," he said vacantly.

"Splendid!" Tilmouth said with joyful sarcasm. "Then sit down, Doctor Kinghorn, we're all friends together."

"No – it's late," John countered, "I'll come back another day."

Tilmouth tutted as he opened the door into the scullery. "Perhaps we'll meet again, doctor."

John turned. He gazed into Tilmouth's black eyes then took one last glance at Ruth. There was still no response. "Perhaps," he snapped, then closed the door on them.

There was silence for a moment, then Tilmouth spoke again. "You surprise me, Tommy," he whispered. "I had no idea you had intellectual friends."

Tommy snorted. "He's not my friend. He fancies Ruthy here."

Tilmouth hummed a note of understanding. His mind galloped. Affairs of the heart were almost as useful as flaws of character. His eyes narrowed. "Interesting – very interesting," he breathed.

John strode quickly down the row, disappointment, anger and bewilderment all struggling for gratification. There was something familiar about the stranger. He had seen him before, heard his voice. But where? And why was he visiting the Nesbitts? What business had he there which allowed him and his silent colleague such smarmy jurisdiction over them? He tried to dismiss the problem from his mind. He sighed and shrank into his overcoat as the wind howled along the lane, banging doors and sending obscure litter soaring through the night like weird, misshapen bats. He passed Fulthorpe's house. Fulthorpe's voice was raised and irate and the obscenities came with rapid regularity. There was the sound of children crying and his wife sobbing. He shook his head forlornly remembering again Fulthorpe's comments. By the time he reached the parked Morris he was flooded with doubts. Perhaps his notions were misguided, his feelings misplaced. Perhaps he had no right to involve himself with anything but their diverse medical problems. But his misgivings were shortlived. The wind brought the sound of hurrying footsteps on its lamenting voice; sharp, urgent, female footsteps. He stopped and peered back through the gloom of the lane and then his heart lifted. The dull, brief illumination of the cottage windows picked out her fleeting form. It may have been his imagination that showed the need of him on her face from such a distance but it didn't matter. In a few short seconds there was nothing in the world but Ruth and a blustering wind that tried in vain to part them.

It was a loud, cheery voice that woke Robert Fulthorpe from his slumber. He surfaced into consciousness with the voice jarring his drowsy mind and he blinked as the daylight stung his eyes. With a guttural yawn and a grunt of annoyance he manoeuvred his fat body to a sitting position and swung his legs over the edge of the bed. He looked down at his right leg that stuck out stiff and straight from beneath the mound of his belly and grimaced at its flabby varicosed form as he rubbed at the scar-ridden knee joint in an effort to ease the ache that constantly nagged at it. The incessant noise from below told him immediately that it was Saturday. The high-pitched, excited exuberance could only be that of Raymond Bennett, the collector from Goldsteins. He yawned again and scratched at his hairy shoulders, listening to Bennett's muted wisecracks that made his children laugh and charmed his gullible wife. He sneered at the floorboards before silently mimicking the smile and the jocular patter that he knew was Bennett's calling card. The collector would be expecting his weekly payment to come oiled on his polished words – but not that day. It was weeks since Fulthorpe had earned a penny. The six pounds three shillings collection that had been presented to his wife shortly after the accident had dwindled to five or six shillings. He hadn't had a drink or a smoke since his return from hospital. The County Council had managed without him. No, the clagger man could wait. He wasn't taking their last.

Eagerly Fulthorpe grabbed at his pants and pulled them on as a tardy cockroach wandered out from under the bed. Viciously he stamped on it with the heel of his left foot. There was a crackle as it burst open and the mess of it clung to him. "Ye little bastard," he hissed, his mood getting worse. His lips thinned as he scraped his foot along the floor, leaving a smear and the crumpled remains for his wife to clean up. He reached for his walking stick and pulled himself onto his feet. He limped to the door. "So endeth all bastards," he muttered, then with afterthought and bitter amusement, "The Book of Fulthorpe. Chapter one, verse one!"

The thump from upstairs stopped Raymond Bennett in mid sentence. He glanced to the ceiling then grinned. "Aye, aye, here comes Long John Silver."

Fulthorpe's children had to busy their mouths among their forearms to smother the laughter but when they heard the ponderous clump as he descended the stairs a frightened solemnity came over them.

"What cheer, Bob?" Raymond yelled before he was at ground level.

"Canny – until you woke me up," Fulthorpe growled.

Raymond ignored his mood. He had had years to get used to it.

"How's the leg?"

Fulthorpe grunted as he lowered himself onto a stool. "It gives me what you give me."

"What's that?"

"A pain in the arse – that's what."

Raymond laughed.

"Aye y'can laugh," Fulthorpe interjected, "but y'll not be laughin' when you leave. There's nowt for you today. We've got bugger all, so y'can take that fancy suit of yours and that fancy lip and get on your fancy bike and piss off."

There was nothing but amusement from Raymond. He took all their jibes in good heart. There was no point in getting angry. That would be bad for business and he knew after all the years that the insults were as good as "God bless you".

"What a pity, Bob," he said keenly, reaching for the catalogue, "and I've got just the suit for you that would have them gasping at the Council meetings. Straight from London – a Savile Row special at a special price. Two guineas or two bob a week."

Fulthorpe's eyes narrowed and for the first time Raymond sensed that he was causing him hurt.

"I've told you, Ramey, we're skint." His brow tightened. "Christ man, I've never worked for weeks – you know that. Four bob Guardian Relief won't feed a spuggy."

Raymond nodded, serious now. "Yes, I know. Forget the suit – and the payments. I'll cook the books so's old Goldstein won't have a fit." He sighed. "I'm an expert at doing it for you lot at Bolam. Pay it off when you get started. O.K.?"

Fulthorpe gave a curt nod.

Raymond rose to go. "I hope it's soon Bob. Why don't you see Mallory about some light work?"

Fulthorpe snorted. "He dishes out work like a man with no arms."

Raymond smiled again, "Cheer up you old bugger. Try him, man. y've nothing to lose." He threw a boiled sweet to each of the children and winked at Fulthorpe's wife. "Ta-ta for now. See you next week."

"Get in as much as you can 'cos y'll get nowt when the strike comes," Fulthorpe yelled after him.

His grinning face reappeared around the door. "What a change that'll be!"

Fulthorpe coughed and hawked and spat a great gob of phlegm into the fire as Bennett's cheery whistle faded down the lane. He sat for a minute gazing at the sizzling mass, his bottom lip loose and wet. Slowly he turned to his wife who was at the far end of the room with her eternal needle. He eased his aching leg to a straighter position.

"What you doin'?" he barked.

She raised her tiny, timid face. "Just sewin'."

"Well pack up an' press them scabby blue pants of mine."

"Where're you goin'?"

He scowled. "T'see if I can get set on – that's where."

"I didn't know Mallory was that fussy."

He drew himself up to his pompous best. "T'hell with Mallory. I'm going to the top. I'm going to see Tomlinson."

It took him almost an hour to hobble up the rough, uneven road and into Allington. The pain in his leg seemed to sear his whole body, annoying every nerve that was in him but he kept going. It would be worth it, he was sure. A desolate, hollow feeling had settled on him after Bennett's departure. He felt suddenly unclean, tainted with the misery of it all, his image in the community tarnished and decrepit. Soon there would be no money for food and the impending strike meant weeks, perhaps months with a few shillings Guardian Relief. He had to get a job. He had to have a few pays, however small, so that when the strike came he could to some extent keep the respect he thought he had. And surely Tomlinson would help him. After all he thought, hadn't he handed him his hymn book every Sunday for years? Hadn't they exchanged smiles as he passed the collection plate to him, and there was always a gracious nod from his wife on their way out. Surely that counted for something.

He stopped on the red gravelled drive and gazed reverently at the imposing house. He wiped the sweat of exertion from his face with the sleeve of his coat then limped forward, mentally setting himself for some pleasantries and a man-to-man discussion about his capabilities. His knock seemed to echo through the house and he heard the faint barking of a dog from deep within. It seemed an age before the door opened and he forced his nicest smile when he saw the curious face of Clarrie Tomlinson peering out at him.

He moved his walking stick nervously as he shuffled his feet. "Good morning, Mrs Tomlinson. I wonder if you remember me. I'm Robert Fulthorpe."

Clarrie stiffened and fingered her beads, a look of distaste on her face. "No, I don't think so. Can I help you?" she asked haughtily.

"The church," Fulthorpe said eagerly. "We've met at the church. I'm from Bolam, but I'm a sidesman at the church."

Clarrie drew back. "Oh yes, I remember. From Bolam, you said. Yes, yes," she added dreamily.

"It's Mr Tomlinson I'm wanting to see. Could he spare me a minute?"

She frowned. "I don't know Mr er . . . He's rather busy."

"It's important."

"Oh is it? Well I'll see. Would you wait there please."

Fulthorpe beamed. "Of course. Bless you."

She gave him a look of disdain and closed the door. It was almost five minutes before it opened again.

Tomlinson knotted his brow. "Yes, what is it?" he snapped.

"Ah Mr Tomlinson, it's me, sir, Robert Fulthorpe from . . ."

Tomlinson cut him short. "I know who you are and where you're from. What do you want?"

"I was wondering if you might be able to get me set on again at the pit. I was a rolleywayman until the accident but the leg's a bit stiff just now. I was wondering if you might have something light for me. I'm pretty fit except for the leg."

Tomlinson held a hand over his eyes as though he were shielding them from the sun. There was a look of boredom on his face. "My dear sir, are you not aware that Mr Mallory is the man to see."

Fulthorpe nodded petulantly. "But . . ."

"But nothing," Tomlinson barked. "See him – and do not bother this household again."

The door slammed shut and the words on Fulthorpe's tongue that started as persuasive niceties turned instantly to abuse. He shook with rage. "Effin' bastard," he hissed at the door. "Rotten sod!" He turned and limped quickly away, the pain in his leg deadened by the anger that consumed him.

There was no mistaking his mood when he got home. He threw open the door and instantly bellowed at his scattering children. His wife did no more than look up. She knew the reason for his ire. She could have told him the outcome before he even went. He stumbled over to the mantelpiece and grabbed at the scratched tin tea-caddy that bore the face of George V. He pulled off the lid and snatched the few coins that were inside. He threw the tea-caddy onto the table and made for the door again.

"Don't take the money, Bob," his wife yelled frantically.

"I'm takin' the money," he snarled. "Bugger you. Bugger everything. It's a drink I need." Then he stopped. His eyes twitched once as he noticed the small square of paper on the bottom of the tea-caddy. He picked it up, examined it and glanced menancingly at his wife. It was a pound note, folded carefully and stuck down with glue.

"So!" He breathed, "holdin' back, eh? And me without a drink for weeks."

"No! Don't take that," she wailed. "It's for food for the bairns."

"It's for me!" he yelled. "I'm drinkin' the soddin' lot!"

He felt better after his fourth pint. The first three had gone down in fifteen minutes but he took his time with the fourth, enjoying its taste and the mellowed sensation it brought. He sat back and relaxed, comforted by the feel of the pound note as he fingered it in his pants pocket. The bar seemed quiet. A few of the local miners stood in groups discussing or opinionating on the latest news from London but he did not get involved. He was not in the mood. His encounter with Tomlinson had left him cold and uninterested in everything but the fleeting immediate enjoyments that a few shillings could bring.

"Where's everybody th'day?"

The barman jerked his head toward the wall. "Out the back. There's a school going."

Fulthorpe swallowed and fingered the pound note again. They were throwing pennies; perhaps with a little luck he could win a week's wages. He hurried outside to a patch behind the back yard of the Fat Ox. There was a crowd of about fifteen there and two young lookouts. Willie Cox was in the act of throwing when he joined them. Two pennies, polished bright from constant rubbing spun high into the air and wondering faces elevated upward following their flight, then moved downward to examine the outcome. It was two heads. There was a whoop of delight from Willie and a groan from the others. Willie's "bebber", a friend who organised the bets, stuffed a handful of coins into an already bulging pocket.

"Right," Willie cried. "I'll cover a pound."

The bebber collected eight half-crowns and there was a sudden silence as Willie rubbed the pennies against his lapel. "Come on now, come heads for your da'," he whispered. The coins flew skyward from his index finger and sparkled in the sunlight. The faces swivelled up and then down.

"Onesers," somebody yelled as they landed a head and a tail.

Willie threw again. It was two tails. There was a yell from the crowd and the eight winners crushed forward to receive their even money winnings from the bebber. It was almost an hour later before Fulthorpe got a chance to throw and he had been dying for the opportunity. Betting against the "hoyer" he had won another pound. His luck was in, he was sure. But he was still cautious. "I'll cover a pound," he said.

"Who's bebbin?" somebody yelled.

"Me!" Fulthorpe snapped. "I'll do me own."

He took eight half-crown bets and offered up a silent prayer as the crowd gave him room to throw the pennies not upward but almost horizontally, a method known as the "coal-house hoy". He flicked the coins forward and they landed head up. With a sigh of relief he pocketed the money.

"A pound again," he yelled. Again he won. He was sweating now, excited by the weight of assorted change that tugged at his jacket. His leg began to ache but he ignored it. He hopped around with his stick looking into the dismal faces of the men who had lost the best part of their hard earned wages, revelling in their misfortune and his own good luck. The crowd had grown, attracted by the yells and groans and there was thirty or more by the time he took his next throw.

"Come on y'sinners," he squawked. "I'll cover two pounds this time."

The bets were laid and there was a pause as Fulthorpe gurgled with anticipation. Then he became serious. "Oh Lord, look down on this thy servant," he whispered as he rested his stick against his leg and placed the pennies on his finger.

"Come on!" someone yelled angrily, "hoy the bastards."

He threw them, carefully, and they spun almost in slow-motion. The crowd descended on them like a pack of devouring wolves.

"Two effin' heads," Willie Cox snarled, his winnings dwindling away.

Fulthorpe blinked, unable to believe it. He clawed at his collar. His mind swirled with visions of the new suit Bennett had offered and the drinks he could buy his colleagues at the Council.

"Any bugger got money left?" he yelled, flooded with confidence.

A few turned and wandered off but most stayed, determined to chance their last silver and recoup some of their loss.

"It's three this time," Fulthorpe taunted. "Any daft takers?"

Willie rummaged in his pocket. "I'll take a quid of that."

Fulthorpe chortled. "Any more?"

Reluctantly they placed their small bets and he threw the coins. There was a tremendous cheer.

"It's tails! It's bliddy tails!"

Fulthorpe swam into the crowd. His heart dropped to his boots. It was tails and he had lost the throw.

He paid out three pounds, his face long and sour, then waited till the crowd had spun for the next thrower. He had to bet the rest. He couldn't let a fortune of six pounds slip away like that. It was more money than he had ever had. But he was too keen. He bet a pound and lost it. Then ten shillings and another ten. It wasn't long until his prayers were billowing skyward and his pocket contained one hot, moist half-crown. Frantically, he placed his bet and watched the two pennies sail into the air. He almost sat on them in his eagerness to propel his stiff leg out of the way. He looked down and his fat face seemed to shrivel up. There were two heads. The hollow, sickening feeling of despair was with him again. Slowly he pulled himself up and limped through the swarming crowd, a withering rage bringing tears to his eyes. He had nothing left. He had used every scrap of money they had. There was nothing for food; there was nothing for anything. With a drooping hopelessness he made his way slowly back toward the Rows. It took a few minutes for the uncomfortable feeling inside his trousers to make its presence felt. He stopped and rubbed at his thighs, then unbuttoned the front of his trousers. "Oh no!" he whispered. His last pair of underpants, patched and sewn until there was little of the original, had finally disintegrated. He staggered home holding his stick in one hand and clutching at his pants with the other. The ultimate degradation. It had been a bad day.

It was a worse day for Tommy Nesbitt a fortnight later. He sat at the table brooding over the whereabouts of Ruth whom he hadn't seen since his return from the pit, wondering, still with a trace of discontent, about the increasing number of times she was flitting off with her doctor friend. Yet, even he could see the benevolent change in her. She looked better – healthier, happier. But there was still the nagging doubt about that relationship. Was it right? The gulf of status could not be breached by fancy words. The mixing of the two breeds could cause only further unhappiness. He worried about Alan as well. He had been almost too keen to join Tilmouth and Brooke and the latter had spirited him away too often for Tommy's liking. As for Brooke himself, his insipid but smooth mannerisms smacked of some cheap corner-end trickster and filled him with an indefinable, puzzling apprehension. Then there was the industrial trouble. The T.U.C. and the Miners Federation had tried in vain to persuade the coal owners to consider reorganising the industry. But it was not to be. The Government remained publicly neutral and on April 13th the Owners posted notices at pitheads terminating existing contracts at the end of the month. There was a fever of wondering throughout the country and an ominous taking of sides. The sabre rattling was all but over and there seemed little else but conflict and misery for a long time to come.

Tommy threw down the newspaper after reading a report of Cook's latest fist-clenched oratory, frustrated and angry by the lack of coherent organisation among the miners. It was as though the Federation was convinced of some eleventh hour settlement that would eliminate the need for any arrangements to strengthen their cause. But he was sure they were wrong. He was as certain as Cook and Tilmouth of the need to stand firm against the coal owners. The opportunity had presented itself; fortuitously or otherwise and there should be no question of compromise.

He sat forward on the stool, his hands clasped in front of him and his head bowed as ponderous thoughts weighed down his mood. There was activity outside, the sound of conversation and the noise of footsteps but he took no notice until the door opened and the murmuring voice of Kenneth Tilmouth caused him to sit up.

Tilmouth came first, his comments stopping abruptly. Brooke followed, some wild delight giving his face the look of a madman. Alan was last. He appeared between them, his arms hanging loose, his face ashen and the sinews of his neck tight. His eyes were large and round, shimmering on the brink of tears, holding an excruciating horror in them.

Tommy jumped up. "What in hell . . . ?" he gasped, but he was stopped in mid sentence as Alan surged forward. Tilmouth made a wild grab to stop him but he wasn't quick enough. In a flash he was past his brother and leaping up the stairs, an agonising wail issuing from between his clenched teeth. Tommy gazed stupidly from Tilmouth to Brooke, his reasoning numbed and a prickle of fear bathing his skin.

"What's happened? What's wrong?" he pleaded, as the knot loosened in his throat.

Tilmouth stood for a moment, his face rigid and his breath coming noisily from his nose. He flicked his eyes at Brooke who was for once impassive then turned to Tommy. "Sit down," he said with a gentle menace. "I have something to tell you."

Tommy sat, wanting answers without the rigmarole of argument. Brooke took a seat at the table, his head resting on an upturned palm, observing him intently.

"We have a problem," Tilmouth snapped, "A serious problem, Tommy. It concerns Alan and Ron. But like most problems, it has a solution if one applies reasoning and a measure of logic."

"Don't give me any bliddy cack!" Tommy yelled. "What's got Alan like that?"

Tilmouth sighed. His face became hard and ruthless. "Your brother has some strange ways, Tommy. He has not, it seems the natural instincts of a man. He took certain . . . certain liberties with Ron here."

Tommy's blood turned to ice. His eyes closed on the scene before Tilmouth had finished. He somehow knew the statement was coming. He remembered the suspicions that had only nibbled at him weeks before but he could still not bring himself to believe. These men were evil – devils vomiting filth and corruption.

"You lie!" he roared.

Tilmouth nodded, unperturbed. "Oh, but Tommy," he continued with smarmy confidence. "The blame does not only lie with Alan. Ron sort of encouraged him, if you know what I mean." He patted his companion's shoulder. "You see Ron's like that. He has traits which are not altogether acceptable in this society of ours. He's even been to jail for it. But you didn't like it there, did you, Ron?"

Brooke gave him a rapturous look and shook his head.

"You wouldn't like it if you and Alan had to be locked up would you?"

He shook his head again, an imbecilic grin on his face.

"But you wouldn't mind if it was to help the cause. You'd gladly go to jail for the cause – wouldn't you?"

This time he nodded.

Tommy leapt at him but Tilmouth shouldered him away as his hands reached Brooke's throat. He landed face down on the floor and in the instant it took to pick himself up he knew his actions were useless. He knew exactly what Tilmouth had in mind and the way he had engineered it.

"Don't be a fool," Tilmouth snarled as he stood between them. "As I said before, the problem can be solved. We want something from you, Tommy. In return, we will keep silent and keep your brother free from scandal and jail. What do you say?"

"Alan!" Tommy bellowed.

There was no answer.

"Leave him be," Tilmouth said. "He's up upset but he'll get over it."

Tommy ran up the stairs. He threw open the bedroom door. The room was empty.

"Alan!" he shouted again. He noticed the open window and the easy climb down onto the scullery roof. He had done it himself many times as a boy. He walked slowly back downstairs. "He's gone," he whispered.

"Not gone," Tilmouth sang. "He'll be back shortly. He's just upset."

Tommy slumped down on the stool, his mind a shattered, numbed vacuum of emotion.

"The cause needs you, Tommy. It needs you badly," Tilmouth whispered with a tremble of excitement. "The lock-out notices have gone up. The revolution is about to begin."

"What do you want me to do?" Tommy breathed.

Tilmouth shot a wide, excited look at his companion. "Well now, that's better. Let me see," he said, slowly stroking his chin with a forefinger. "We need recruits, Tommy. People who need to be convinced that their salvation lies only with Communism. Not only workers but intellectuals. What about that young doctor who's keen on Ruth?"

10

It was warm for April. A day when winter is a faded memory and the pleasant sun looks brand new and shines down on a hushed, grateful Earth. John Kinghorn lay on his back, his drowsy mind mesmerised by the smell of fresh, sprouting meadow grass and the distant softened chatter of larks. The air was heavy with peace and nature and it lulled him into the sensation that he was as one with the sky and all creation. He reached out and found Ruth's hand, holding it gently, rubbing her slender fingers with his thumb as contentment soothed away the tensions of Bolam. He opened his eyes when a whisper of mechanical sound came to him but he lay still, searching only the area of blue above. Finally it came into view, a minute, silver aeroplane almost motionless, buzzing determinedly across the vastness; lonely, like a waif searching for a home. He watched it until it merged with the haze and its sound blended with the peace, feeling that the pilot, perhaps alone, could have no greater isolation than he and Ruth had at that moment. He sat up and drank in the scene that had earlier taken his breath with the sheer, raw beauty that was Northumberland.

They had driven less than forty miles westward out of Newcastle and it was a different world. A straight tree-lined road that followed the route of Hadrian's Wall, the remains of which stood strategically on the green, undulating hills as it had almost since the time of Christ. This was England at its natural best. Unsullied by time or progress, oblivious to everything except the seasons and the daily whims of weather. The road climbed gently upward, stretching the view until the multitude of yellows and greens swam into a delicate milky purple far away on the brink of eternity. It was by chance they found the lough. They parked by the roadside and carried their picnic past outraged sheep protesting their presence with deep bleating. There were startled rabbits who sat up, then, fled, and larks who rose from the ground with a twitter of alarm. They climbed a sloping hill towards the remains of the Wall which snaked and dipped unbroken along its highest contours. At last they reached the top and stood for a moment in silent admiration. Their eyes followed the Wall on its meandering course to the East, and saw for the first time Crag Lough, a random mirror of blue, snug from the world, fresh from the womb of creation.

The hill, which was steeper to the East, ended abruptly with the Wall and then there was a sheer drop of one hundred and fifty feet of jagged, scree-littered rock to the Lough at its base. It was as though they had invaded some secret holy place, known only to God and the Romans. The stillness was like a heady wine, the vista divinely architectured.

"Who could have thought," he murmured.

"Thought what?" Ruth asked.

"That such beauty could be so close to the ugliness of industry."

"You're surprised that it can be like this?"

"Amazed!"

Ruth shook her head as she gazed into the distance. "I'm not. I knew it would be like this. When I was young I watched the sun sink into the hills and wondered what it was like away from the coal and dust. I knew it would be like this."

He looked up at her, to where the sun shone through her hair and warmed her gentle face. There was sadness there again. It could not be disguised. "Let's leave Bolam, Ruth," he said suddenly. "Let's go somewhere else. Let me show you what the world's really like."

"Is it better than this?"

He looked around again. "No, not better."

"Then I'll stay," she said with a soft smile. "Alan might come home . . ." She sighed. "He's out there somewhere."

John lay down again and stared into the sky, wondering about Alan, afraid to tell Ruth of the torment that had dragged him to the surgery that day. He couldn't bring himself to load her fragile spirit with more shock. She had lost her father and brother in the accident. Then her favourite had left home. The tattered shreds of her work-worn mind that he had fought to keep healthy were fraying again. He knew that. She ate little, slept badly. She was in danger of rejecting the world, withdrawing mentally from the life that caused her so much anguish. Then he thought about Tommy and the visit he made with Tilmouth the week before.

Dr Jenkins was taking the evening surgery when Ethel burst into the study, her face white with controlled anger. "There are two men to see you," she snapped, her nose wrinkled with disapproval. "They're from Bolam. One of them is . . . a Nesbitt," she added vehemently.

Her anger pleased him. It was obvious that the front door approach of anyone from the pit village was a gross breach of her personal rules and he played on her annoyance: "Well, well," he said with a grin, "show them in, would you please."

Her face darkened. "They're waiting at the door," she whispered with an arrogant lifting of her nose.

John ignored her. He stood up and walked to the door ready to shout a hearty invitation, his mind preoccupied with supremacy over Ethel rather than who of the Nesbitts was calling and the reason for the visit. His brow furrowed when he saw Tommy's hang-dog expression and Tilmouth's gaunt face and excited eyes.

"Yes?" he said cautiously. "You want me?"

"We would like a little talk, doctor," Tilmouth said with spreading pleasure. "That is . . . if you can spare us some of your time."

"You'd better come in," John murmured, mystified by Tommy's guilty silence. He led the way, blankly following Ethel's mute, hurried exit. "Well now," he said as he closed the door, "what do you want to say?"

Tommy thrust his hands into his pockets and looked at the floor. "Where's our Ruth, doctor?" he asked bluntly.

John frowned. "Ruth? She's with Mrs Jarvis. I asked her if she would watch her for a while. The woman had a bad delivery this . . ."

Tilmouth interrupted him, spinning around from where he closely examined the shelves of books, "Oh, come now, Tommy," he chided "we've more important things than that to tell Dr Kinghorn." He gave an ingratiating smile. "We have here a busy man. Let us get straight to the point."

"That would be an excellent idea," John retorted, angry at Tilmouth's flowery sarcasm.

"It is said that you have a certain affinity for the miners of Bolam," Tilmouth said with a sharp positiveness. "That their problems are your concern. That you have aligned yourself with them in their struggle for justice and that your interest in Ruth is more than a medical one. Do I speak the truth?"

John was taken aback by the hard, snapping statements. His mind raced, then his anger flooded back. "Damn you, Mr Tilmouth," he growled. "What in hell has it to do with you?"

Tilmouth clasped his hands behind his back, "It intrigues me, Dr Kinghorn," he looked around the room. "You live here with all the trappings of luxury, yet you let it be known that you support a class struggle far removed from your breeding. There are troubled times ahead, doctor. I am here to help the workers of this community. I do not just talk about it. I intend to be instrumental in their victory, to carry their colours unashamedly. Would you do that?"

John shrugged. "I don't know what you mean."

"I mean that words alone are useless. Vague allegiances are worthless. If you believe, you must be prepared to broadcast that belief, to act on it, to live by it."

"And who are you to be telling me this?"

Tilmouth smiled. "I am a man who believes in certain ideals; that the working class should be the masters of their own destiny, that men of vision and conscience will eliminate suffering in much the same way that you can with your medicines."

At last John saw him clearly. In a flash of understanding he recognised the man for what he was. He turned to where Tommy stood still and apprehensive. "So you've joined the fanatics. I credited you with more sense."

"Hah!" Tilmouth shouted in triumph. "You see, Tommy, the man is a shallow advocate. There are many of them. They are afraid to stand and be counted. Tell him Tommy – tell him to prove himself to you and Ruth and the people of Bolam."

"I need to prove myself to no-one," John interjected before Tommy could speak. "I know nothing of your kind except that they thrive on trouble. I want nothing to do with you or your misguided plotting."

Tilmouth nodded. "So be it, Doctor Kinghorn." He turned at the door. "Perhaps it would be better if you stopped deluding these people and yourself. They need friends who will back them up to the hilt, people they can rely on for support – isn't that so, Tommy?"

Tommy followed him out. He gave John a reluctant, unhappy nod, which could have been somewhat explained if he had heard the short conversation between the two men after their departure.

They were well down the road before Tommy spoke. Tilmouth seemed far away, lost in some inner amusement. "Is that the way you hope to win friends?" he said with a sneer. "You're a bloody amateur."

"You think so, Tommy?" Tilmouth answered lightly. "We shall see. Let him think on it. If we succeed, all well and good." He shrugged. "If not, we have lost nothing. We have done nothing but plant a seed. You, Tommy may have to do a little watering."

John gripped Ruth's hand harder, interlacing his fingers among hers as he wrestled with the memories of that evening. There was something rotten about Tilmouth and Brooke and their interest in the Nesbitts. They had something to do with Alan's departure, of that he was sure. Yet he had quizzed Tommy that same night after they had left and he had returned with a heartbroken Ruth from a fruitless search of the area.

Tommy had been edgy and aggressive. He would hear nothing against Tilmouth. He became furious at the idea of informing the police. "He said he was leaving," he shouted. "He's sick of pit life. He's old enough to know his own mind. Let him go. Christ almighty he might be back in a day."

"But why? Why?" Ruth sobbed.

Tommy sighed, his face twisted in anger. "I don't know," he whispered hopelessly. "I just don't know."

John blew out a long, wondering breath that seemed to help Ruth conclude her mental search of the distant hills. She lay beside him and the warmth of the sun and her nearness faded the conundrum from his mind. He turned his head and opened his eyes. She was looking at him, their noses almost touching.

"Why are you staring?" he whispered.

"To make sure you're real."

He put his hand to her cheek. "I'm real."

She held his hand on her face. "Sometimes I feel that one day I'll wake up and you'll be gone . . . like the others."

He shook his head gently. "I'll be here."

She gave a wistful little smile as she convinced herself of the truth of it.

"Won't you ever go back to London?"

"Not without you. Not in a thousand years."

There was contentment on her face as he kissed her. He could feel the tremble of emotion that came from her, a refined, beautiful sensation. Then she clung to him, holding his head, his neck, his body; clawing him closer, finding unknown strength in her passion.

It could have been the last day of the millennium.

Ethel Friar sat in her room and smiled when she heard the revving engine of the car as it was manoeuvred out of the garage. She smiled because she knew who was behind the wheel and who was left in the house. At first, when she had managed to piece together the snippets of chit-chat that came from the waiting room about her young adversary and Ruth Nesbitt, her loathing of him increased. Her imaginings of the intimacies between them made her want to claw his eyes out; not from any atom of jealousy but from the fact that anyone in such close proximity to her who could desire a girl from such a place as Bolam must be depraved, debased, capable of unimaginable atrocities. But now she saw some merit in it. She was glad to know that he was out of the house, away with his tart. It meant that she could be alone with her doctor and the growing enjoyment she was beginning to feel at his hungry desire of her could be prolonged and frequent. It would take only a little more time, she was sure, and his quelled instincts would burst in a deluge of anticipated ecstasy, swamping everything, his sense, his reasoning and his will to renege. Then she would be free of the intruder and the influence he had on her domain. She would be rid of his alien presence and his growing familiarity with the Bolam rabble that was causing them even to call socially at Plessey House. Yes, she knew she would win in the end. She knew his need of her. It was in the air as she passed him, on his face, recorded with his every movement. But she had been surprised by his fortitude. After all the long weeks of his bleating, persuasive cant, he had still held out against her. Not much longer, she thought, it can't be much longer and then there would be victory and peace of mind and a delicious satisfaction. The noise of the car faded into the distance and there was silence. She knew her doctor was downstairs and where he would be sitting and what was on his mind. Soon Tomlinson would call and then he would leave and there would be just the two of them alone and apart in different rooms. But not for long. She would answer his mental plea – in part anyway. Just enough to allow the delirium of temptation to excite his body. That would be all for that night. She turned to the mirror and began preening herself.

Dr Jenkins twitched nervously, toying with a piece from the chess board, waiting for the interim visit from Charles Tomlinson and trying to forget the fact that Ethel Friar was somewhere within the walls of the house and waiting her turn. Tomlinson's visits had increased during the last days of April and for all his chummy, casual openings it was never long before his voice became low and dark as he recounted tales of outrageous happenings and his bravado cracked. Each time he mumbled news from London and seemed to gasp for reassurance and moral support. It was as though he was in a quandary that was not of his own making. The events, while specific in their meaning, were somehow opaque in their significance to him. As for Dr Jenkins, he was becoming heartily sick of the whole affair. He was caught in the middle of two factions and did not want to be drawn into either. He had Tomlinson on one hand and his assistant on the other, diametrically opposed. He had to pay lip-service to both, for nothing else than to keep his relationship with each alive and fruitful.

The latter half of April brought little but depressing news that rumbled of anarchy and revolution. Headlines about the Duchess of York giving birth to a daughter called Elizabeth Mary were soon ousted by foreboding articles concerning the industrial front. The deliberations of the Mining Federation and the coal owners had continued negatively as the month drew to an end. Baldwin at last stirred himself and called a meeting between the two parties but each refused to give an inch. Just the day before, however, the T.U.C. met the Government to consider a compromise by the owners. They had decided to accept a national minimum wage set at the 1921 level provided the miners worked an extra hour per day. Inevitably it was rejected. It meant a reduction in pay of 13 per cent. The activity in

London had been frantic as the last hours of the month ticked away. The King presided over a meeting of the Privy Council and declared a State of Emergency. The Government ordered regional authorities to be ready. The O.M.S. handed over membership records to the Government. There was to be a confrontation the like of which had never been seen in Britain. There would be no more "Red Fridays". There would be no calm before the storm.

Dr Jenkins could wait no longer. He let the chess piece drop onto the table then poured himself a large whisky. Tomlinson was late. He was sure he'd have arrived sooner, bursting to tell him about the latest developments and the first day of the miners' lock-out. He'd half expected him to arrive at the surgery begging for the reactions of his patients to the fact that they were now without work and without wages. He gulped down the liquid, letting its smooth warmth sooth his frayed nerves and asking himself why he should be on edge. It had nothing to do with him, yet he couldn't help himself. Like it or not he was caught up in the same atmosphere of tension that quietly nibbled at every man in the country. It was the frustrating uncertainty of it all, the lethal excitement of a time-bomb.

He heard the clock in the hall strike ten but by that time he was past caring about Tomlinson. The alcohol in him had reduced the world to a cosy sanctuary full of soft colours and uncomplicated thought. The study door opened and it took a minute or two for it to register in him that it was Ethel. He waved his arm loosely at her. "Ethel, so you've come at last," he murmured.

She gave a thin contemptuous smile when she saw his stare. "So your visitor hasn't come tonight," she said with a gloat of ridicule.

He hung his head and shook it.

"I wonder why?" she mused as she moved toward him.

He looked up and observed her from eyes that were puffed and bloodshot. He gave a little juggle to his shoulders. "He's busy. He's got other things on his plate just now."

She knelt beside him. "Do you really think that, Bob? Do you?"

He nodded.

Her eyes narrowed as she moved her face closer to him. "I don't," she whispered. "It's him – it's Kinghorn. Tomlinson doesn't like him. He's sick of the drivel he spouts about that lot at Bolam. He thinks you agree with him, Bob. He thinks you're for that lot with Kinghorn. That's why he hasn't come. He won't come back. You've lost a good friend."

Dr Jenkins became agitated. He shook his head wildly. "No – no, it's not that."

"It is, Bob. Think of what you're losing. Think of us and what it was a few months ago."

He breathed noisily through his nose. He turned his head and tried to kiss her, his fumbling hands grasping at her breasts but she pulled away.

"No, Bob," she breathed. "Not until you see sense. Kinghorn will ruin everything. Why, he's even had miners at the door – in this very room. He's out now with that Nesbitt girl. He'll be fornicating with her at this very moment. In your car, Bob. Do you realise that?"

Again he protested. "You're wrong Ethel, you're wrong. He's young, a good doctor. Why? Why?"

He was more drunk than she thought. He slumped forward mumbling some weak, unintelligible words and she came nearer, putting her lips to his ear. "Get rid of him, Bob," she whispered. "Get rid of him . . ."

It was raining. A steady downpour that hissed into the ground and made music among the pipes and gutters of the crowded, ancient buildings lining the banks of the Tyne at Newcastle. It was night and Alan Nesbitt stumbled aimlessly over piles of rubbish and rubble that littered the narrow lanes. He was soaked to the skin, his sodden clothes clinging to his body in an embrace that had long since ceased to be uncomfortable. He moved slowly through the darkness, letting his feet pick their way among the junk, disturbing rats that squealed and ran, not knowing where he was or where he was going. He knew the river was near. He could hear the gush of a sewer amplified by a falling tide as it spewed its contents into the murky depths. The fetid stench that accompanied it was thick and reached down to his stomach but he carried on, passing dark, warped sheds and warehouses that loomed and leered at him. He came to the river's edge and stood for a moment watching the dim lights on the far bank snaking across the black, racing water. There was a ship further up, lying low and ghostly at the staithes. There was activity there; the sound of voices and the grating rumble of coal sliding down a spout and into its belly. He turned away, not wanting to be seen, not wanting to see. The night was his friend, its darkness his disguise. Soon he was back among the labyrinth of claustrophobic lanes that rose with the banks of the river. His feet clattered over the wet cobblestones that rang in their nightly loneliness and his tired eyes began their search for some hole or doorway where he could rest. The path narrowed, the buckling brick walls closing in on him. Ahead there was a lamp fixed to a corner. Its glass was broken, the mantle gone, leaving the flame yellow and licking idly at the wet air. Cautiously he approached it, using its feeble glow to pick out some possible refuge. He could see a gap in the wall, the division of two buildings. There were steps leading upward, dozens of them but he had only climbed a few when he noticed the crumbling brickwork on his left revealed some sort of open area behind it; a yard perhaps or the foundations of some house that had given in to the appetite of time. He climbed over the wall and nervously lowered himself down until his feet felt the ground. He turned and squinted through the night, vainly trying to see. Instinctively he knew he was not alone, but in the flash of realisation it was already too late. There was a hand over his mouth and an arm across his neck. His head went back and a pain seared his throat. He gasped for breath, sucking in the rancid smell of sweat and filth.

"One sound and I'll effin' break your neck – d'you hear!" The voice was hoarse and panicky.

Alan nodded quickly and the hand over his mouth relaxed and slid away.

"Who are yer? What yer doin' here?"

"Lookin' for somewhere to sleep, that's all," Alan whined.

The arm tightened around his neck. "You sure?"

He nodded again, unable to get words from his mouth.

"Who told yer about this place?" the voice barked.

"Nobody," he croaked. "Honest. I just saw the gap in the wall."

The arm was slowly released and he was gripped now by the scruff of the neck and dragged across rough stone-littered ground. "Come on, y'sod, let's have a look at yer."

He could make out a low jagged hump ahead. There were baulks of timber sticking up, canvas draped among them, an old bedstead lying at an angle, the wreck of a drayman's cart beside it. Soon he knew the reason for it. An old carpet that reeked of cat's urine was pulled to one side and he was thrust into some black enclosed space that drummed with the rain and the terrifying shuffle of unknown human bodies. The smell made him retch. It was the smell of death on the living, a putrefying cocktail of filth of every description.

"Now," the voice growled. "Let's see what we've got."

A match rasped across a box and burst into life, then the stump of a candle was lit. Alan cowered where he fell, afraid to look. There was silence and then a deep, liquid chuckle.

"Well now, it's a lad; in a sorry state too. And here was me thinkin' it was the law."

Alan could bear it no longer. He had to look, to see what evil place surrounded him. There were seven of them including his captor. The other six lay huddled around the ashes of a fire. He couldn't believe the state of them; no more than bundles of rags with matted, long hair and skin that was covered in layered, hardened dirt. One seemed to be asleep yet his eyes were wide open, staring sightlessly upward. Another scratched at his woolly beard and among his ragged clothes, as though there were demons eating him. The rest lay prone, silent and disinterested, one holding an empty bottle to his chest as though it was his first love.

"Y'like our little hotel?"

Alan turned his head toward the voice that came to him with amused interest. He seemed a younger man, younger than the rest, perhaps twenty-five or thirty. He was a pathetic sight. His hair was wet from the rain and hung in cloying brown strands down to his shoulders. His eyes were sunk deep into the dark sockets of his emaciated face that was white and lifeless except for his chin which spouted a short, shaggy beard in clumps as though he were some mangey animal. Yet his smile which showed brown stumps of teeth stretched his face into a wiry pleasantness, a humble understanding softness.

It did not allay Alan's fear. He looked quickly around him again. "Let me go, please," he begged, on the verge of tears. "I didn't mean any harm."

The man crouched down at the entrance to the shelter. He chuckled again, "Don't be scared, young'un. Y're one of us it seems. Kip here the night."

Alan closed his eyes. "No, I want to go. I want to be by myself."

The man nodded knowingly. "What ya done son? Pinched the collection box? Put your hand up the teacher's skirt? Ran away in disgrace – eh?"

"No – no," Alan yelled. "I'm just . . . I just want to be left alone." He began to sob.

The man opened an old haversack and rummaged inside it. He held out a piece of cracked dry cheese and a chunk of bread. "Here eat this, then get them wet clothes off."

"I'm not wet," Alan said quickly. "I'm all right."

There was a profound understanding in the man's voice. "So you're a shy one, eh? You don't fool me, bonny lad. How long have you been wandering? One night – two?" He offered the food again. "Here take it."

Reluctantly Alan began to eat. There was the taste of fust but he didn't care. It was the first solid food for three days. The man sat down and relaxed stretching his cloth-wrapped feet towards the ashes. "Want some advice, son? Go home, take the medicine, face up to life or you'll wind up like this lot. Thieves, meths drinkers." He kicked at one of them opposite him. "See him there – sleeps twenty hours a day, the other four he's drinkin' and spewin' all over the place. Well to do at one time, they reckon. Had a shop somewhere that went bust. Then his missis pissed off wi' the kids. Couldn't face it, you see."

"I'll never go back," Alan whispered vehemently.

"Me neither, but I would if I were your age."

"What did you do?" Alan asked, afraid really to know.

The man laughed out loud. "Me?" He looked upward. "Not much – not enough to hide away like this. But you see it's catching, the more you hide, the worse you're afraid to come out in the open."

"I'll never go back," Alan repeated.

"Want to talk about it?"

He shook his head.

"Ok son, sleep on it. Me – I'm out lookin' for work the morn. Nothing strenuous, mind, just a few bob before the bliddy country falls to bits. I don't drink their rubbish but a pint goes down a treat if they'll let me in the pub."

"I've got money," Alan blurted. "I'll give you some if you'll let me go."

The man sighed. "You are a green one. Lucky for you I'm no thief either. If one of these buggers was interested enough to listen they'd have the lot by now." He thought for a moment. "I'll tell you what. Here's a good deed for you. A couple of bob would come in handy. That's a good night's kip at the Sally Army hostel. A wash and brush up to make myself a bit presentable for a job and crack bang, y'll get the money back. That is if you're still around."

"I need a job as well," Alan said, feeling a strange affinity for the ragged character.

"Couldn't be better," he said. "We'll both go to the Sally Army and we'll both look for a day's work. How's that?"

Alan gave a hesitant nod.

"Good!" he said. Then he paused. "How much money have you got?" he asked quietly.

"About a pound."

The man laughed, his face creased with merriment. "I've just had a brainwave, son. For that pound I can get us togged out at Piercey's secondhand shop, smartened up at the Sally Army and with a bit of luck a job that'll pay money y've never dreamed of. We'll make their strike put us on easy street. Haven't you seen the posters all over town?"

Alan frowned. "No. What's the job?"

He laughed again. "Y'll see, bonny lad. Y'll see the morn. What's your name, by the way?"

"Alan Nesbitt."

He held out his grimy, blunt fingered hand. "Jim Dyke. Now sleep well, son, tomorrow is our lucky day."

Alan stretched out. His new acquaintance blew out the candle and they returned to darkness. He lay listening to the wheezing, shuffling bodies near him, trying to ignore the smell that exuded from them. There was a rasp of expelled wind from one of them, then another gave a bleating cry as though he was looking death in the face. The rain stopped and it turned suddenly silent. He was where he should be, he thought. He wasn't fit for anything better.

"Not a penny off the pay! Not a minute on the day!"

The chant grew louder and stronger, falling into poetic metre, rolling through the village houses causing children to stop their play and wives to stand and ruminate as though the sound was some foreboding death-knell. It carried up the road and into Allington, halting conversation, striking fear into some and wondering into others. It was like the noise of an approaching army, the measured crunch of advancing feet, bringing apprehension and awe.

Edward Sneed stood silently among the fevered miners watching the glazed, somehow bitter triumph on Tommy Nesbitt's face as the sound of defiance reverberated around him. He had heard Tommy speak; spout foolishness to them; whip them up into a frantic mob and it saddened his heart. It was obvious that Tommy had been coached by Tilmouth; that he believed in his extremes and had been converted to a cause that could only breed on violence and suffering. Edward was disappointed. Tommy was a champion among them. For years his ideas for justice had been simple and sane. The exuberance of his youth had stirred the complacent, his keenness and interest in their welfare was a cause for pride. But no longer. He had gone too far; his enthusiasm was being fed now by dangerous men and his gullible years snatched at their feasts of glory and success. Edward was in no doubt about the battle ahead. He knew the attitude of the miners had to be strong and hard. There would be weeks of hunger and want. There would be argument and demonstration and finally someone would win. That was how it should happen. Perhaps they would receive their just reward, perhaps not; but whatever, it was a dispute that should be fought within the law. History dripped with the blood of men who had been caught in the absolute of conflict, he knew that all too well. With a doleful shake of his head, he turned and plodded back toward home.

He was almost to the Rows when the chant stopped and gave way to a tremendous cheer, but he ignored it. It would only be Tommy, he thought, giving forth with some other grand notion that had set their pulses racing. He reached the back lane of First Row and squelched through the mud and pools left from the downpour of the previous night, his mind mulling over the immediate problems of food and coal to keep Nellie comfortable. There would be no more Smart's pies for a while, he resolved, they were a luxury that could be done without. He hoped his wife would understand. The sight of Doctor Kinghorn coming from the Jackson house stopped his train of thought and he called out a subdued greeting.

John beamed. "Ted. How are you?"

He shrugged. There was a wistful amusement on his face. "Canny doctor, I suppose. How's the new babby?"

John glanced at Jackson's door. "Oh he's fine. Ruth's there; giving Mrs Jackson some help. She's had a rough time."

"Aye." Edward said softly; "She's a good lass is Ruth, doctor." A glint came to his eyes; "She could be a lady, that lass. She could mix with the best on them."

"I know it, Edward. I know it well," John replied.

Edward nodded, understanding that he had caught the meaning of his statement.

"Have you been to the meeting?" John enquired, looking up the lane for signs of the others.

"Left it in the middle. Couldn't bear to hear anymore."

"I heard them yelling. They're working themselves up, aren't they Ted?"

"Tommy's workin' them up. Tilmouth's been fillin' him full of rubbish."

John rubbed pensively at his chin. He gave an exasperated sigh. "Why, Ted? Why has Tilmouth such a hold on him?"

Edward's rough, craggy face seemed tired. He shrugged. "I don't know," he whispered on his exhaled breath. "Perhaps it's the times we live in, doctor. Perhaps he has visions that only young eyes can see. When you're young you think you'll live forever. To change the world seems an easy task."

John's lips tightened. "Ted, I feel so damned useless. I want to help, but I don't know what I can do. I've said my piece to Tomlinson and Dr Jenkins, but short of joining Tilmouth's henchmen . . . what is there?"

Edward smiled. There was a quiet admiration in his eyes. "You can do what you have been doin'. Just look after us, doctor. Care about Nellie, Mrs Jackson here, Ruth and all the rest."

"But it's not enough."

"There's nothing any of us can do except be convinced that we are in the right. There are men in London at this minute who have the real power, the power of millions of trade unionists behind them. They've tried to sway the Government and the coal owners. They feel like you."

The conversation stopped as a crowd of whooping miners surged into the lane. They ran, yelling and cheering, to their houses, jumping and waving, overjoyed by some event or news. Ted caught hold of Will Forrest as he galloped by them. He was a young man, twenty or so. His scrubbed face glowed with excitement and his blue eyes shone with some inward delight.

"What is it, Will?" Edward asked urgently. "What's happened? Is the strike off?"

"The strike?" Will shouted eagerly, "No, man, the strike's not off. The T.U.C.'s just had a ballot. They're supportin' us up to the hilt. The whole country's out at midnight, Monday."

Edward let him go. He turned back to John. His face was grim yet his eyes now had a sudden, staring blaze to them. It was as though he had been fired with some brilliant, frightening thought. "Well now doctor," he breathed, "looks like we're a force to be reckoned with after all."

11

The atmosphere in the Palace Theatre, Newcastle, on Saturday May 8th seemed far removed from a country deep in the turmoil of a General Strike. The place was packed with people enjoying the show "Still Going Some," with Eddie Emerson, the Kentucky Singers, the Melody Mixers and Ten Georgian Peaches. They laughed and clapped and when the fire-curtain dropped at the interval, the buzz of conversation was relaxed and light-hearted. There was nothing amiss. It was like any other Saturday night, even busier than some, with the air a blue haze of tobacco smoke and the faded, painted advertisements on the fire-curtain silently extolling the virtues of Ovaltine and Sloane's Linament to the contented crowd.

In the true tradition of Theatre, the bright lights and swirling multi-coloured costumes offered some refuge from the troubled world outside. The Tuesday before, the country had woken to an eerie silence. Railwaymen, transport workers, iron and steel workers, printers and building workers remained at home. Two and a half million men were idle. Trains and buses were still; factories empty. For a while it was as though the world had died in its sleep. The early morning crush and push of men to their place of work never happened. The clank of trams and the host of factory whistles were loud with their absence. But only for a while. The Government's nine month preparations were at last put into practice. Warships steamed into position off the Tyne, Humber and Clyde. The Army moved into the cities and took over the distribution of food. Armoured cars trundled noisily among the masses of private vehicles. O.M.S. volunteers, guarded by armed soldiers, unloaded cargoes from docked ships and drove lorries, buses and trains. But life went on amid the swarms of pickets and angry crowds incensed by the demarcation of class that struggled against them to keep the nation on its feet. There were minor incidents of violence; bricks hurled through the windows of the few trains and buses that managed to run; the odd tussle with police and their recruited "specials" who were paid over a pound a week more than the wage of the locked out miners. A fuse had been lit on Tuesday May 4th. Its length was unknown.

The orchestra struck up in the Palace Theatre and the curtain rose to enthusiastic applause. John Kinghorn glanced at Ruth. She was enjoying every minute. Her face was bright and riveted on the stage, agog at the spectacle before her. He felt a smug satisfaction inside him. He couldn't help it. He was happy in her company, at ease when she was near him; filled with an indefinable pleasure at her warm loving ways. Yet to take her out of Bolam, to the city, where he could impress her with its life and gaiety was done for more than just therapeutic benefit and the ritual of courtship. The novelty of it all to her was an amazing experience. It was as though she had been blind and could now see, entranced by the wonders around her, absorbing in her quiet way the quintessence of everything that before had been a girlish dream. And yet it was nothing. A meal in a restaurant; an hour in a picture house or a theatre. To her it was the life of a princess – and it was his doing. Despite the frustrations of Bolam, he had achieved something and it was precious to him in all respects.

Eventually it was the finale and even he had managed to forget the dejected populace of Bolam who now wondered about the Rows, kicking their heels, bored and depressed by their plight. The show had been good, a mixture of songs and jazz, jokes and dancing and the crowd had loved it. As the clapping stopped and the audience began to stir themselves, a man appeared on the stage and held up his hands for attention. He was a small, round man, dressed in an evening suit and bow tie. His hair was flat and shiny, his face red and harassed. A sudden silence descended on the shuffling crowd and he dropped his hands, holding them across his chest as though he was about to break into song.

"Ladies and Gentlemen," he shouted in a tinny voice that belied his stature. "Would you please keep your seats."

There was a wondering drone from the audience.

"There is some trouble outside. A riot of some sort. The police are in attendance but I advise you to stay within the theatre until the street is cleared."

Some made light of it as they returned to their seats, others grumbled. Ruth gripped John's arm as they sat down. She was afraid. "What can it be at this time of night?" she asked.

John shrugged, then smiled reassuringly. "It won't be much. Some demonstration or other must have got out of hand."

She put her arm through his and held him closer. He sat for a moment staring forward, then pulled his arm free. "I'd better go out, Ruth. I may be needed. You stay here and wait for me."

She tried to protest. She didn't want to be left alone but he was out of the row and up the aisle before she could stop him.

A uniformed attendant was at the doors. "I wouldn't go out there, sir. There's war on."

"I'm a doctor," John snapped. "Let me out."

The man pulled a face and opened the door just sufficient for him to squeeze into the street. He hadn't been exaggerating. He stood for a second unable to believe the scene a hundred yards to his left. The street seethed with people, the night rent with screaming agony and hoarse yells of fury. It was a pitched battle. Hundreds of cloth-capped civilians reeled among what seemed as many policemen: a vast, boiling cauldron of fighting, kicking and punching as the truncheons flew up and down and fists found mouths and boots a soft vulnerable groin. It was a scene from hell and a shiver of disgust ran through John that became a tremble he could not control. He moved forward in a daze of disbelief at the carnage in front of him. A man staggered past him, blood spurting from his left ear. John made a half-hearted attempt to stop him but he was pushed away.

"Eff off," the man growled in his angry remorse.

He came to the edge of the fighting, blinded to the danger by a withering rage at the degradation around him.

"Stop it!" he bawled. "For Christ sake stop it!"

No-one heard him. He ploughed into the thick of them, gazing like some mindless idiot at the flaying hands and feet and the action of the truncheons as they cracked down on dodging heads. He stumbled over a prone body but he didn't bother to look. His mind was knotted with the horror of humanity and its animal actions. He stood circling on himself, his eyes filled with the scene of blood and twisted frenzied faces as his fellow countrymen tore at each other in a battle spawned on poverty. Then he came to his senses. In front of him there was a man on his knees shielding his head from the battering that came from a "special". The striped arm band denoting his rank moved quickly as his truncheon lashed again and again at the man who crouched helplessly with his face on the road. John gave a great shuddering sigh and grabbed at the "special" from behind. He yanked at his shoulders with all his strength, pulling him away from the fallen man. Without looking behind him the "special" resumed his battering. Again John went for him. He grasped a handful of his fine hair and there was a squeal of pain. This time he turned, his baton raised, ready to lash out at another agitator. There was just an instant before it flew down and connected with John's head near his right eye. His mind seemed to burst open in a million vivid threads of light as he lost consciousness. But in that instant he recognised his attacker. With a strange sensation when time becomes valueless, a second or a hundred years, he drank in the crazed, wild face, warped with its flood of bestiality. The thin, delicate features suddenly returned with a look of fear. Then the world was gone for John Kinghorn and Alan Nesbitt turned away to pastures new where he could eke out more revenge on the people that had given him life and the torture of living it.

It seemed a long time before he became fully conscious. Deep in the chasms of his mind, John knew he should wake up but it was like surfacing from the bottom of some dark ocean bed. He strove to reach the surface, away from the darkness to a shimmering pool of yellow and finally he made it. He was in hospital, he knew that instinctively. He was sitting in a chair with Ruth beside him and a policeman on his other side. Why he was there did not register for a moment, then with a rush it all came back to him. He opened his mouth, ready to gabble out the news that he had seen Alan, but stopped himself. The circumstances of their meeting would do Ruth no good and it would rekindle all the worry that was gradually being lifted from her. He felt at his head. It was sore and swollen above his eye and covered with an adhesive plaster.

Ruth got hold of his hand. She had been crying, but her green, luminous eyes shone behind the well of tears. "You're all right, John," she said gently. "You're in hospital but the wound is only slight."

"I know," he mumbled. He looked around him and down at his blood spattered coat. "God, it was awful, Ruth. I've never seen such carnage. How long have I been here?"

The policeman cleared his throat and looked at him sternly. "Half an hour, sir," he said dramatically. He seemed a dowdy sort, in need of a wash. Crumbs clung to his moustache and there was a brown sliver of nicotined saliva at the corners of his mouth. "Yes sir – half an hour or thereabouts," he added. He thumbed open a note book. "Now, if you feel up to it, I'd like to ask you some questions about this evening. Would you tell me in your own words what happened?"

A hospital trolley came through the casualty ward pushed by two nurses. The unconscious patient's head was swathed in bloodied bandage. Another followed; then a man staggered in, helped by a friend. His left arm dangled loosely in the ragged confines of his coat.

Visions of the riot came back to John in vivid detail and anger surged through him with such ferocity that pain seared at his already aching head.

"Damn you," he snarled. "You tell me what happened. Why this?" he asked pointing around the ward. "What happened to cause this. A disaster? An explosion? A pack of wolves?"

The policeman sat back and looked down his thin nose at him. "There was a riot. Surely you remember that. A mob tried to stop a food convoy. The police acting in the course of their duty stopped them from breaking the law." His lips twitched into a fractional smile.

"You were found among that mob. Now would you kindly explain your presence there."

"I've told them, John. I told them when I found you," Ruth whispered.

The policeman drew in his chin. "Yes, but I want it from him now."

John sighed with exasperation and hung his head. "I am a doctor," he said savagely. "I was in the Palace Theatre when we were told of the trouble outside. I went out to tend to any casualties. I was hit myself – by one of your mob. An official thug!"

The policeman wrote, breathing slowly and noisily through his nose. Finally he said "Name and address?" John told him and he scribbled it down. Then he looked at him with cold heavy-lidded eyes. "Go on, get goin'," he snapped, "and think yourself lucky that it'll be taken no further."

Ruth helped him to his feet.

"Where's the car?" he asked.

"Where we left it."

He nodded. "Come on, let's get out of here."

"And take some advice," the constable shouted after them, "keep away from things that don't concern you, young man. These are bad times."

John turned, snorting sarcastically, thinking of some apt remark that would adequately portray his contempt but the tightened grip of Ruth's hand stopped him. The policeman stood watching them for a moment, waiting with stiff-necked authority for some abusive remark and when it didn't come he sneered and moved officiously to another of the hapless injured.

Outside, the night air was cold and the city subdued. John's mind streamed with thoughts of Alan and wrestled with unanswerable questions about him. It seemed preposterous to think that he could have taken such a job and he began to wonder if he had in fact been mistaken. The whole episode began to take on strange nightmare qualities, yet he knew it had been disgustingly real. The words of the policeman rang through his head and the similar comments of Tomlinson and Dr Jenkins. By the time they reached the car a wild, angry stubbornness ate at him. He drove home at speed incensed by the sickening society that looked down on men struggling to live by their labour; the bigotry that branded them as evil and himself as a meddlesome, misguided samaritan. He felt deeply ashamed of his kind and their ignorance of the facts. He glanced at Ruth. She was sitting quietly by his side. She sensed his look and turned her face toward him. In that momentary glance he saw everything that was rare and good in the world. Serenity, kindness and understanding. If only they knew, he thought. If only they damn well knew . . .

It was nearing lunchtime on the following Monday. It was a fine day, warm, with the sky blemished only by wisps of remote cirro-stratus. John Kinghorn left the village of Bolam and walked slowly toward Allington. For all the summery weather his mood was sombre. He tried to convince himself that Nellie Sneed was progressing, that her efforts after all the weeks would be successful. Yet he was worried. The gradual improvement that he expected had not come to pass. After her initial strained movement there had been no advance. He tried to reassure her, to make light of the disappointment he knew she had. He attempted to keep her will strong and confident but the doubt and sad understanding on Edward's face made him wonder for the first time whether it was all in vain. Perhaps the events of Saturday night added to his frame of mind. The memory of it all seemed to dull his wits and fill him with an irascible feeling of anguish that could only be sated by some involvement in the miners' struggle. Yet what could he do? There was nothing to relieve his torment. Dr Jenkins had lectured him when he saw his wound and his discoloured eye and Ethel Friar had mocked him with her silent expertise. He was in a limbo that tore at the roots of his soul.

Bolam had been quiet during his visit. Most of the men had gone across the field to yet another of their meetings to yell and fume and fortify their ardour. Even Edward Sneed had gone, excited in his gentle way. John felt for them. The strike was not an all-powerful weapon. The Government's well-laid plans were running as smoothly as could be expected. The O.M.S. did their job with frantic enthusiasm. Many titled people clamoured to join in the wizard game of doing menial work. To them it was one enormous jolly prank to be able to clip a train ticket or don a boiler suit and oil railway engines. He thought of his family back home and how remote they were in every sense of the word. He imagined their joy at getting their hands dirty, their smug patriotism fed by a history of arrogant domination. He shook his head. He had doubts about the outcome of the strike. As much as he tried not to, his reasoning said the Establishment would win.

The noise of cheering carried through the warm air and he stopped to look back at the dark patch gathered near the Fat Ox. There was something pathetic in the sound. Its source seemed diminutive now, lost, striving for willing ears. He began walking again, wishing that the day had never dawned. It would have been better if Sunday could have lasted forever. That was his first thought when he woke that morning. He had wanted to perpetuate the day before when Dr Jenkins had somewhat reluctantly lent him the car yet again and he drove north with Ruth. They were soon clear of pit heaps and silent industry and out into the vast canvas of countryside, leaving the bitterness and trauma of the riot behind. They followed the coast for a while before turning inland to Alnwick, then on eastward again to the sea and Bamburgh. He had seen ancient castles and the splendour of untamed coastline. Great scimitars of yellow beach bordered by rolling dunes whipped by the wind into harmonic curves and long, arced breakers that unfolded onto the sand with a slap and a sizzle of expended energy. There were fishing villages and fields of sprouting crops, reeling blackbirds and hovering gulls. And finally Bamburgh Castle itself. An enormous fortress built on a great mound of basalt that seemed to have lurched out of the beach during some primeval cataclysm. The castle stood proud and dignified and could have been Camelot itself. They seemed to be a million miles from the unrest. They walked and talked and lay among the long marram grass, listening to the sea and the cry of the gulls. He had loved her there among the loneliness of the dunes and she gave herself with unashamed pleasure, true to her character, allowing her natural feelings to dominate her without fuss or false attitude. He relived it all as he continued toward Allington. The supple willingness of her limbs, the beauty of her freckled breasts, the warmth of her young body. Yes, he thought. Monday should have never dawned.

He saw a man standing near the gate of Plessey House and recognised immediately the tall, gaunt figure of Kenneth Tilmouth. He clenched his teeth as he approached. He was in no mood to waste time arguing against his smooth fanaticism.

"Good-day, Dr Kinghorn," Tilmouth said with icy friendliness, his smile a parody of sincerity. He waved toward the house. "I called to see you." His face changed to mock unhappiness. "But that . . . that woman wasn't very obliging."

"Are you ill?" John fired the question at him with bored disinterest.

The smile returned. "Ill? Me? No, Doctor." He cocked his head slightly. "But I see you've had an altercation with something – or someone."

John felt at the plaster near his eye. He stared hard at Tilmouth trying with all his mental power somehow to probe beyond the outward assurance. "If you're not ill, what do you want?" he said curtly, unable to make sense of him.

Tilmouth shrugged slightly and shook his head. "Nothing much, Doctor," he said with amusement. "I heard about your misfortune in

Newcastle. I came to see how you were." His face changed suddenly to a narrow-eyed seriousness. "And whether the sting of the enemy had left its mark. I see it has, Dr Kinghorn. Look at yourself in the mirror and magnify your wound a thousand times, a million times. That is the treatment of a master to his slave. That is the contempt which we bear. That is the reason for our struggle!"

John left him standing. He swung open the gate and stalked down the path. He could take no more. What Tilmouth said was right, yet his absolute beliefs twisted everything into a hotch-potch bordering on religious mania. His own allegiance had limits. Its parameters were newly formed; based on humanity by an outsider looking in. He could not even begin to digest Tilmouth's intimate, all-consuming doctrine. He followed a creed founded on usurpation and a promise of Utopia and John knew deep down inside him that the whole concept was irrational; an unachievable dream.

John stopped for a second and watched him as he walked away. Tilmouth was casual, at ease, as though enjoying the air of the day. John let out a long shuddering breath of exasperation and forced his mind to other things feeling, yet not wanting to feel, that the advice that streamed from his elders had some merit.

Upstairs Ethel Friar let the curtain drop back into position. She heard the door slam below and her mind raced. Yet she could make nothing of it. For a second time the stranger had called and asked for John Kinghorn. But why, why? she asked herself. What mischief did they plot? Angry at her inability to know or to come to some conclusion she wafted down the stairs and set herself for another lunchtime of aloof, forced tolerance.

The crowd gathered on the football field near the Fat Ox were in full voice as Tilmouth slowly approached them. They were compacted now into a tight knot around Tommy Nesbitt, their faces drained of colour as they roared their defiance. Tilmouth was pleased. When he had left them to visit John Kinghorn they had been loosely-bunched, hesitant, worried. But not now. There was an aura of power in the air. He could sense the magnetism of their want drawing them closer, torturing their minds for satisfaction. And it made his nerves tingle. This was the force of revolution. This was the sound of freedom.

He squeezed himself among them, drawing contentment from their hoarse cries, seeing their clenched, raised fists as his own creation. He soon forgot about the young doctor. There would be more occasions to speak to him, to coax his persuasion out into the open for all to see. It would come, his intuition told him so.

Tommy Nesbitt waited until the yelling died away. He had spoken for almost an hour and his throat was dry and sore yet he did not want to stop. The response from the crowd carried him on, pumping adrenalin into his blood, filling him with an intoxicating energy that had no motivation from Tilmouth's blackmail. The words that came from him were his own; inspired by their need for justice and fortified by his ire at the treatment meted out to the striking masses. Even Edward Sneed responded to the electric atmosphere. His eyes were wide and glazed; he was hypnotized by the frenzied determination of his colleagues and his calm, thoughtful manner had long since been overpowered.

"This time we will never give in!" Tommy screamed at them. "Let them use their weapons. Let them cudgel us into the ground, but while one man stands, the strike will go on!"

"Aye!" the crowd roared as one.

"The time has passed when we grovel at their feet. We will suffer and they will suffer until this dispute is resolved. But our suffering can only lead to victory!"

The crowd roared again.

"But take heed, lads," Tommy yelled. "We must not weaken. We must not let them see a crack in our solid wall. For if they do, they will exploit it. They will prise it wide open and we will crumble into a pile of dust."

"What about the bloody blacklegs," someone shouted. "Them bastards are workin' against us!"

"Aye!" the crowd bawled angrily.

Tommy waved them silent. "How many? A handful among the millions. They cannot help to break us."

"There's some on the railway," a man yelled. "The trains are still runnin'."

"The trains must be stopped then," Tommy screamed at them. "Stop the trains at the stations."

"The stations are guarded," the man shouted back. "We can't stop them there."

Tommy felt a surge of fury rise inside him. There was an instant of silence as he hunted frantically for an answer. He stared at Tilmouth as he came forward. His eyes were wild with passion. He stood beside Tommy and gazed quickly around at the hushed, breathless faces. "Then stop them in between!" he shrieked.

It was as though they had been forged into a unit of common action. Almost to a man they roared their approval and stumbled forward in a blind surge of eagerness toward the railway lines. Tommy led them on and they followed. Abe Johnson, Robert Fulthorpe, even

Edward Sneed were among the crazed, desperate crowd, their reasoning suffocated by the overwhelming desire for victory.

There were just three men left at the spot. And soon there were only two. Willie Cox stood blinking stupidly at the receding mass. He had suddenly realized what they had in mind and the consequences of their action. He turned and scuttled quickly up the path toward Allington. Tilmouth watched him go. He seemed deep in thought and rubbed the tip of his nose with a forefinger. Then he looked at the stupid, wan smile that spread across the face of Ronald Brooke.

"Where's the car?" Tilmouth whispered.

Brooke nodded toward the Fat Ox.

Tilmouth breathed out. It was a long breath, his mouth open, his eyes full of euphoric imaginings. He put an arm around Brooke's shoulders. "Come on my friend," he said with a satisfied grin. "I think we have just about overstayed our welcome."

Willie ran as fast as his little legs would carry him. His body ached and the air burned its way into his scarred lungs long before he reached the village but he kept going. He had to find someone, anyone who could halt the crowd's wild rampage. They were intent on stopping a train – by force if necessary – and Willie, after all his years on the railway, knew all too well the dangerous consequences of their mood. The police came straight to mind but he did not relish their reaction. He thought of Tomlinson but knew that the miners would sweep his protests contemptuously to one side. He came to Plessey House and clung to the gate for a second before he stumbled to the door.

John sat ruminating in the study. He felt listless after a lunch that he had not tasted and had been eaten in silence. Dr Jenkins was out, along the road at Tomlinson's house. He had dashed eagerly away after a telephone call that Clarrie's malaria had returned. Suddenly the urgent banging at the outhouse door snapped him out of his daydream and had him leaping to his feet. The sweating, gasping face of Willie Cox told him there was trouble before he had swung open the door. He heard an incoherent croak and almost carried Willie into the surgery. "What is it?" he demanded.

Willie wallowed in a chair, flinging his arms around as he struggled to speak." The lads," he panted "all het up . . . gone to stop train."

A prickle of fear played across John's skin. "How? Where?" he whispered urgently.

Willie shook his head. "Dunno – down the line – they're crazed – they'll do anything."

"What can they do? Can they block the line and cause a crash?" John shouted at him.

“Aye, aye, anything. There’s loose sleepers and all sorts,” Willie gasped.

“Christ,” John breathed, looking helplessly around as his mind galloped to find a course of action. It did not take him long. In a moment he was out of the house and running toward the railway lines at the other side of Bolam colliery.

The crowd of inflamed miners surged along the polished tracks that shone in the afternoon sun. Their fury had been fed by the sight of a gang of platelayers who they stoned and chased from the scene. Tommy Nesbitt strode along at the head of them, his fists clenched and white, turning now and then to face the excited cries of his mates, drawing them on, screaming for revenge against all and sundry who defied them. There was a hut near the edge of the track and they swarmed around like angry bees. It took only a few blows from hefty boots and the door splintered. The hut was full of tools; hammers, spanners, picks. With a roar of triumph they armed themselves.

“Come on, lads,” Tommy yelled. “We’ll stop the wheels turnin’ We’ll pinch the soddin’ track!”

A great cheer rippled among them and they began to work on the line. Soon a forty-five-foot length of rail had been removed. Edward Sneed and Robert Fulthorpe levered at it and it slid sluggishly down the embankment.

“Here’s a train!” someone cried. “There’s a train comin’. But it’ll not go much further.”

They stood silently now, heaving air into their demanding lungs, then moved backwards down the track. Their frenzied eyes watched; their ringing ears listened to the slow chuff of a moving train. The noise grew louder. Its size grew bigger, blasting black smoke and white steam into the blue sky. On and on it came and the miners stood mesmerized by its inexorable course.

“That’s not a goods train,” Edward Sneed whispered to himself. “That’s not a goods train!” he bawled down the line. “It’s the Flying Scotsman!”

The green, clanking dragon journeyed on, pulling coaches with over two hundred people on board. Suddenly it lurched then rose upward, trembling with its power. There was a screech of noise and a spray of sparks. It lurched again, then toppled on its side, sliding still forward with a deep growl that drummed against the ears and shook the earth. Three coaches behind it bucked and yawed, then crashed sideways. There was a cacophony of noise; glass, wood, metal all in an anguish of torsion. The rails ahead of it reared and buckled, twisting themselves like some unearthly limbless reptile. The engine finally came to a halt, embedding itself into the side of a brick building. The deafening crescendo fell away. The three coaches lay still, ruptured and tangled. There was only the sound of vented steam and spinning wheels and the hesitant cries of the injured.

John Kinghorn stopped his running and stood in frozen horror unable to believe the vision or the noise that came to him. The miners of Bolam were stiff, rooted to the spot, paralyzed by the enormity of their deed. Then again, as one, they turned and ran; past him, away from the scene, their faces white with shock. John saw them all as he sprinted toward the wreck. He felt like screaming abuse at them; at Tommy, at Fulthorpe who moved his stiff leg with surprising speed, at Edward Sneed of all people. They all fled, a hundred or more haunted faces, back to Bolam to pretend and convince themselves that what had happened was not real.

The noise was heard for miles. All of Allington and all the innocent of Bolam ran toward the steaming destruction. Even Ethel Friar ventured out. Not far, but far enough. In fact she was out soon after John Kinghorn and the stumbling, tired figure of Willie Cox. She saw it all. She stood stiffly, looking toward the village of her birth. She saw the fleeing miners and she recognised them. Then she turned and walked sedately back to her sanctuary.

It was almost seven o'clock before John finished. It was a miracle that no-one had been killed. It was a greater miracle that injuries were relatively slight. There were cuts and bruises and people with shock. John worked blindly on throughout the afternoon, oblivious to the swarms of angry passengers that had descended from the remaining coaches and reviled the village women who attempted to help them. Ruth was soon by his side and Dr Jenkins arrived, puffing and panting and with a grim realization on his face. Finally there was silence. The crowds dispersed, the travellers left in batches by car, bound for Newcastle to continue their journey. John looked around him at the railway officials and the policemen who had gathered there. They were stern, quietly examining the wreckage, muttering ominously among themselves. He turned and took Ruth's hand, leading her slowly back along the lines. They passed Dr Jenkins but there was nothing said. There was no call for words. They were like strangers.

It was Ruth who spoke first as they were nearing Bolam. Her voice was faint and he gripped her hand harder to stop the tremble that coursed through her body.

"It was Tommy, wasn't it, John?"

This time he could not keep it from her. He looked into her green luminous eyes that were wide with foreboding. "It was Tommy," he whispered, "and all the others."

"How did they do it?"

He shrugged. "I don't know, Ruth."

"Will they be caught?"

"I don't know that either."

Her fist flew to her mouth and she bit at her finger as the significance of it gelled in her mind. A lump grew in John's throat. There was a sudden fear in him. For her, for her brother and all the men of the village. Indeed, it was a Monday that should never have dawned.

Edward Sneed sat by his fireside, gazing at the cold ash-filled hearth, his heart heavy with worry and regret. It was two days and two sleepless nights since the incident on the railway line and the noise and the sight of it were still burned into his brain. He still couldn't accept that it had happened and that he had lent himself to the cause of it, yet he knew with a sickening certainty that somehow he had been there and had torn at the rail with all the savagery of a mad dog. He looked to his wife who sat opposite him. She had no idea of what had happened. She could not notice or comprehend the torment that nagged at him. Her face was blank and still, her unadventurous thoughts, simple and satisfying to her. In a way he was pleased. He took the load entirely, leaving her undisturbed, keeping her free from hurt; yet his agony was not only from what had been done, it was the consequences that were to come. The future was a terrifying prospect that he could not bear to explore mentally. Perhaps it was not as black as it could be, he thought. On the Monday night under the cover of darkness a whispered message brought them together again. Soberly they discussed their plight and Tommy, a subdued hunched figure in the night, rehearsed with them an excuse for the authorities that they were nowhere in the vicinity at the time of the crash. Some were doubtful, others concocted their own stories and slunk back to their homes with the wild hope that no-one would be implicated and the wrecked train classed as an unfortunate accident.

There was a harsh banging at the door and Nellie jumped. Slowly Edward walked to answer it. He was not surprised at the sight of a uniformed policeman. The village had seen many of them during the last two days. They were calling on everyone; questioning them, taking statements, generally probing.

"Edward Sneed?" the constable asked.

Edward hesitated, then nodded, his face solemn, his eyes bright with emotion.

"May I come in?"

He stood to one side and allowed the man to enter, forcing the guilt from his mind.

Nellie became agitated. Her knees jumped under her skirt and her head wobbled on her frail shoulders. Edward had forgotten about her. He scooped her up. "I'm sorry," he said. "My wife – she's not well. She does not take to strangers. I'm sorry." He carried her upstairs and laid her on the bed. He stroked her rough grey hair. "Easy, bonny lass," he whispered, smiling gently. "Don't fret. I'll be back directly."

"Now, Mr Sneed," the policeman said with due seriousness when he returned to the kitchen. "We are making enquiries about the train that came to grief near the village. Can you tell me anything about it?"

Edward sat on a stool and looked at the floor. "It's a terrible business," he whispered.

"It is that, Mr Sneed. A foul business. Do you know what or who could have caused it?"

Edward shook his head slowly.

"Are you sure?"

Edward looked up into the stiff, grave face. "I know nothing."

The policeman sniffed. "Where were you at three o'clock or thereabouts on Monday, May 10th?"

Edward felt a hot flush rise to his cheeks. He leant forward and rested his thick arms on his knees. "I was behind the Fat Ox . . ."

The policeman cut him short. ". . . and you were watching the whippet racing."

"Aye."

"And your witnesses will be Abe Jackson, Robert Fulthorpe and the rest of them, eh?"

"Aye," Edward said weakly.

"Did you see the derailment?"

"No, no but we heard it."

"Did you then go to the scene of the derailment?"

"No."

"Why not?"

Edward shrugged, "It was just a noise. We thought it was something shuntin'."

The policeman's lips thinned. "I should remind you, Mr Sneed, that it will be better for you if you tell the truth. If the inquiry tomorrow shows that the train was deliberately caused to crash, the guilty parties will be most severely dealt with."

Edward closed his eyes. "I know nothing," he said again.

The policeman left. Edward shut the door and rested his back against it. He felt sick and his head swam with the abject dread that flooded him. He turned his eyes to the ceiling. "Oh Nellie," he whispered. "What have I done to you."

Next door Tommy Nesbitt took refuge in his bedroom. He had had the same visit and told the same story but on top of that he had endured repeated questioning from Ruth and John Kinghorn until he could take no more of their "whys" and "hows". He felt bad enough without the constant tears and censure that poured from his sister, but there was more to it than that. John Kinghorn knew they were there on the line, He had seen them all. He had the power in him to thrust them all into jail. But would he do it? Was he the shallow advocate that Tilmouth had called him? True, he had said not. He had reassured him during the last two days that he would say nothing of what he had seen. With a bitter smile Tommy realized that his test of allegiance had taken on a terrible importance.

He lay on his bed for an hour or more, a thousand and one things running through his mind. Tilmouth, Alan his brother, the strike and their struggle for justice which seemed at that moment dwarfed by the magnitude of the immediate problem. The voices that came from the lane did not register with him for a moment. They were noises that blended with his heavy thoughts and were not deciphered in his mind. But suddenly the word "strike," was heard and understood. He began to take notice. The voices were hard and angry. He sat up and heard the words: "The strike's off. It's been called off." He dashed downstairs and into the lane. Edward Sneed was crouched down near his door, quietly watching the growing activity of his workmates.

"Is that right, Ted?" he asked, feeling a rare burst of elation. "Is the strike off?"

"Aye," Edward growled.

"The Government's given in?"

Edward shook his head. "The T.U.C.'s given in. The General Strike's over. We're on our own now."

Tommy gritted his teeth and slammed his fist against the stonework of the house. It was impossible. He couldn't believe it. Yet it was true. During the previous week the T.U.C. negotiating committee had, unknown to the Miners' Federation, been in deep consultation with Samuel and others to produce a settlement. The terms, offering little new, were rejected by the miners when they learned of them. The T.U.C. somewhat overawed by their newly discovered power were anxious to end the chaos they had caused. On May 12th the strike was called off and the miners left to fight their own battles.

And for the village of Bolam more harrowing news came the following day. At a Ministry of Transport inquiry held at Newcastle, it was proved beyond a doubt that a length of railway line had been deliberately removed by persons unknown causing the Flying Scotsman to crash.

12

It was three weeks later when Ruth started coughing, yet she thought nothing of it. Her tiredness had returned but she was sure that was because of the worry that had kept her awake for more nights than she could remember. The severe sweating that she endured seemed to be only when her spirits were at their lowest. But when the pain came to her chest and a gentle irritation caused her to cough, it was a summer cold not worthy of mention to John. The weeks had been long and fraught with hunger and a never-ending fear that a knock on the door would take her remaining brother.

Yet Tommy had returned to his old self. As each day passed his confidence grew. The investigations by the authorities had petered out and the men of Bolam began to forget it had ever happened. Their minds were filled again with defiance and their hours were spent rummaging on the pit heaps for bits of coal for the fires and around the countryside catching rabbits and pigeons and anything else that was edible.

Ruth was luckier than the rest and she knew it. John brought her groceries more than weekly but she refused most of them. Some bread she took and an occasional tin of condensed milk but little else that would put her above her neighbours. He made sure Nellie did not starve. Whatever Ruth did not want he took next door and to other houses where there was special hardship. And she loved him for it. For his kindness, for his concern and his never-ending attempts to cheer her up. He took her out of the village as often as possible, away into the hills and countryside of a Northumberland he had grown to think of as his own. But for some reason it was becoming increasingly difficult for her to pretend. Her smiles and gay attitude that she forced upon herself to match his own happiness were false. She could not rid herself of the dread that was forever inside her or the wondering anguish that smouldered when she thought of Alan.

They were sitting that night with their backs against the car and their feet almost touching a stream of clear water that ran fast and bell-like over smooth stones and away past drooping ferns to join the River Blyth farther south. It was a warm night. A smell of wild garlic came from the glade on the opposite bank and buttercups bent and bobbed with heavy-laden bees. John was at ease, He felt happier than he had done since his arrival. For all the suffering of the village, the secret he had kept to himself had given him a new affinity with them. He felt closer than ever before and his feelings for Ruth were fixed and unalterable. Even the hostility at Plessey House had ceased to bother him. In fact since the incident of the train, Ethel Friar's outward distaste for him had increased and even Dr Jenkins became cool and seemed only grudgingly to tolerate him. He knew he was now classed as of the same ilk as the villagers but he didn't care. He was amused by the fact that he irritated them, that he was a cause of embarrassment to his employer and his friends. He did his job thoroughly and to the best of his ability. It would be hard for Jenkins to sack him without an extremely awkward admission.

Ruth rolled her head lazily around and looked hard at him. "When will it end, John?" she said, her voice flat and despondent.

"What – the strike?"

She nodded.

John found for his pipe and examined the bowl. "Soon I think. When the power stations and the gasworks use up their reserves they'll be ready to talk shop." He smiled at her. She seemed lethargic all of a sudden. Her face was pale, her shoulders round as though without the support of the car she would fall over. He nipped the end of her nose. "Stop worrying," he said with mock sternness. "Doctor's orders. Come on now."

She cleared her throat. "I'm not worrying – just wondering."

"Then don't wonder. It's not good for you." He put his arm around her but she was limp and did not respond. "D'you know what I've got planned for after the strike?" he said lightly, trying to oust her melancholy.

She turned her face up to him. "What?"

"A holiday – that's what. You and I are going off to London. I'm going to show you around and show you off." His voice dropped to a low, ominous exaggeration. "We'll even darken the door of that notorious household known to be inhabited by the Kinghorn family, where Mrs Kinghorn has been seen on a broomstick and her husband keeps catching his tail in the doors of the underground."

Ruth laughed. Her head went back and she laughed and he laughed with her. But then her laugh changed to a cough, a quick uncontrollable cough. She brought her hand up to her mouth and bent forward. It lasted no more than five seconds.

"Ruth, are you all right?" John said urgently.

She nodded and took her hand from her mouth. There was silence for a moment as they both stared at the streaks of blood among the phlegm. John went cold. He wiped it away quickly with his handkerchief.

"Ruth," he breathed, "how long have you had this cough?" He stood up and she followed. He opened the handkerchief again. There was no mistake. Silently he cursed himself. He saw her now in a completely different light. "How long?" he demanded.

"A day or two, that's all," she said casually. "Is it bad?" She coughed again, trying to hold it back.

He looked at her then held her to him. It became bluntly clear to him now. The pale, tired face that was thinner; the droop of her body. All the symptoms that he had put down to her mental state had matured into a physical one. And now a cough. How could he have been so stupid? Yet he had to make sure.

"Ruthy," he whispered. "Let's get back to the surgery. I want Dr Jenkins to see you."

"What is it, John?" she queried.

He said nothing. He led her to her seat. She asked again but this time her voice was shallow and spiritless. He drove away. "I'm not sure, Ruthy. But something like that needs investigating."

They spoke little on the way home. Ruth coughed intermittently with her mouth shut, trying with all her might to suppress and disguise her condition. But it didn't matter. John, with a chill of dread inside him, fought against the images of a life without her near him.

Plessey House was quiet as John opened the door. It seemed to have an unusual stillness to it, an eerie feeling of finality. Yet he had noticed the light at the study windows as they drove up and prayed that Jenkins was there and still sober. Quickly he ushered Ruth into the surgery and lit the lamp, and she stood like a bewildered child in the middle of the floor as he hunted the desk drawer for a stethoscope.

"Take off your coat, Ruth, and step on the scales," he said with soft authority.

She obeyed and he slid the weights carefully along until the arm was still and level. It took him a few minutes to find her record card. She had lost ten pounds since her first visit to him. He examined her thoroughly, questioning her, searching his mind for the slightest clue that could aid his diagnosis. Finally he sat on the edge of the desk and ran a hand wearily through his hair while she dressed.

"It's consumption, isn't it, John?" There was a brave acceptance in her voice.

He looked at her then hung his head. "I don't know for sure. It could be. It may not be," he said with weak hopelessness. "There are tests . . . we'll do tests, Ruth, to find out, but I want Jenkins to give his opinion. He's got a lifetime of cases to draw on."

He held out his hand and she came to him, clasping it in her own. They stared at each other for a moment then she clung to him, her face buried in his shoulder. He shuddered with anger, silently cursing the unfairness of it all, enraged that one life could hold so many miseries.

"Give me hope, John," she whispered. "Give me some hope. I need hope."

He eased her away from him, holding her shoulders at arms length. His brow tightened.

"There's hope, Ruth. There are drugs, sanatoria, rest and good food. Whatever happens I'll see you through this, Ruth. You've got to believe me."

She fought back the tears that threatened and composed herself somewhat.

"Come on," he said. "Let's see Jenkins."

He led her through to the study but it was empty. There was still a trace of tobacco smoke in the air and an empty glass near the chess board.

"Wait here a minute," John murmured, moving the newspaper from the settee.

She sat herself down on the edge of it, holding her hands nicely on her lap and looking around with the awe of an intruder. "Is it all right for me to be here?" she said with a humble uncertainty.

John, was already striding toward the door. "Of course it is. If Jenkins is in bed I'll get him up."

The door opened before he got to it. Ethel Friar stood looking into the room. She seemed to take a long, slow breath and hold it as her narrowed eyes flashed from one to the other. Her face drained of colour and her mouth turned downward.

"Where's Dr Jenkins?" John asked in cold monotone.

Her eyes riveted themselves onto him, then she blinked and sagged as though she had awoken from a dream. "Dr Jenkins is out," she whispered.

"Where?"

"At Mr Tomlinsons," she breathed, her eyes widening.

"For dinner?"

She shook her head, and turned her gaze back to Ruth.

John knew exactly how she felt. He could almost see the abhorrence oozing from her skin. But he was in no mood for her petty domineering ways that night. "Come in, Mrs Friar. I want to introduce you to someone," he said with gentle menace.

She swallowed and drew back a step, revulsion written all over her.

"I said come in, Mrs Friar!" John barked at her.

She moved slowly into the room, her head cocked slightly to one side, her hands gripped tightly in front of her.

John smiled at her back. "This is a friend of mine, Mrs Friar. This is Ruth Nesbitt from Bolam. She is my guest, Mrs Friar. She would like some tea."

Ruth began to shake her head but John overrode it. "Would you be kind enough to make some tea, Mrs Friar, for Miss Nesbitt. She is waiting to see Dr Jenkins."

Ethel opened her mouth to speak but her jaw trembled and she said nothing. She was white as she turned. There was fury in her face as she passed him. "Yes, Dr Kinghorn," she hissed.

"Thank you," John snapped as he closed the door on her.

Ethel filled the kettle and sat watching it as it began to sing and steam on the hob. She stared at its brown form, trancelike and placid. She knew what she had to do. After weeks of mental battle her mind had been made up for her. She had no qualms now. It had been the last straw. He had brought his village woman to the house: she had been sitting there in the study as though it was her natural habitat. The greatest insult of all was that she, Ethel Friar, was waiting on her – her, an animal from Bolam! John Kinghorn had pushed her to the brink. She could abide no more of it. In a last desperate effort to conserve thirty years of subtle gain she had only one course of action open to her.

She was calm as she served the tea, almost nice, with the inner satisfaction of a mind made up. She left them to it and ventured outside the confines of Plessey House yet again. But this time she had good reason. She threw a shawl across her shoulders and walked slowly down the road toward the house of Police Sergeant Connelly.

John paced up and down in the study. He had tried to relax, to be patient but it was useless. All during the long day his mind raced and his body was tensed as he waited for news. He looked at his watch. It was ten minutes to midnight and he tried to face the fact that he would not hear the result that day. Really he had known that for four or five hours but as the time passed the fact became more and more definite. Yet Dr Wear at the pathology laboratory had promised him the result that day and he clung to the hope that he had been busy and might still ring him.

They had not waited long the night before. Dr Jenkins arrived home smelling of whisky but still sober enough to show cautious surprise at the sight of Ruth sitting in his study. He seemed nervous and worried as John explained the situation. He fidgeted constantly as he listened, glancing toward the door as though any second Ethel would appear and destroy them all with her stare. He nodded quickly, confirming that he understood each item of John's observations, plainly broadcasting his anxiety at Ruth's presence.

"Will you examine her?" John asked as he finished giving details.

The old doctor sniffed and rubbed a finger under his nose. He lifted his red, tired face and turned his dull, watery eyes to Ruth. "I don't need to, John," he said as though giving a gruff apology. "I can tell b'looking at her."

Ruth hung her head. "Thank you, Dr Jenkins," she whispered.

Jenkins sat down beside her. His lips were bunched and his chin wrinkled as he silently reproached himself. He took her hand and patted it. "I'm sorry, lass," he said. "You've had some knocks these last months. Y'll need rest, you know. Good food and fresh air and rest." He gave a sad smile. "But then I might be wrong. It's been known before."

Ruth shook her head. "I don't think so, doctor."

Jenkins sighed. He looked around, still patting her hand. "It's a funny life, Ruth. Sometimes the price for living it is too high . . . too high."

John took a sputum sample in the morning and drove to Newcastle with it. He harboured the weak hope that it would be negative but even then it would be by no means conclusive that she was free from tuberculosis. If it was negative there would be more tests and more anxious hours of waiting. That day had been an ordeal for him and even then he was none the wiser.

Dr Jenkins watched him as he paced back and forth. The clock in the hall struck midnight and he lifted himself from the chair with noisy effort. He walked stiffly to the decanter on top of the piano and began to pour.

"One for bed?" he asked John.

"No thanks," John said vaguely.

"Y'll have one for bed," his companion replied. "And so will I. We both need it."

They stood facing each other as they raised their glasses and when they were empty Dr Jenkins spoke. "It's late. Y'll hear nothing tonight."

John nodded. "I know."

"What'll become of her, John?"

"How do you mean?"

"She'll not improve living in Bolam. You know that."

"She'll have the best there is," John snapped. "I'll get her into the best private sanatorium in the country."

"It costs money. A great deal of money."

John shrugged. "I'll get the money. I'll borrow it from my parents."

Jenkins took his glass. "Would you do that for Robert Fulthorpe or Miriam Scott and the like?"

John turned away. "How could I, for God's sake. Ruth's different. She's something special to me."

Jenkins nodded. "Privilege is sometimes a matter of luck, isn't it, John?"

John didn't react. He looked at his watch. "I can't wait," he snapped. "I'll never sleep. I'll ring Reggie Wear at home. Have we his number?"

"It's in the book, but he'll not thank you for a call at this time of night."

"He can please himself. I've got to know."

Jenkins yawned. "Hurry up then and we can all get to bed."

The phone rang for a full minute before it was answered. There was a bored sleepy voice at the other end. "Yes, what is it?"

"Doctor Wear?"

"Yes."

John began to tremble. "Look, I'm sorry to disturb you but I've been waiting for the result of the sputum test."

The voice became angry. "Who the hell's that?"

"John Kinghorn from Allington. You promised the result today."

"Christ! Can't you wait till morning. It's not your own, is it?"

"Have you got a result," John demanded.

"It's a beauty. Pulmonary tuberculosis. Now can I please get some rest."

The strength ebbed away from John's feet. Meekly he hung up the ear-piece and turned silently away.

"Positive?" Jenkins whispered.

John nodded.

"I thought so. I'm sorry, son."

Suddenly a harsh banging at the front door dispelled any further thought of Ruth. Jenkins growled to himself as he hurried down the passage. "Who is it?" he yelled as he pulled out the bolts.

"Open up, it's the police," came a voice from behind the wood.

There were three of them standing there, strangers, burly straight-backed men.

"Dr Kinghorn?" the leading constable enquired bluntly.

John walked to the door, his brow furrowed with puzzlement. "Yes, what do you want?" he asked vaguely, in no mood for pleasantries.

"I'd like you to accompany us to the police station, sir. I have here a warrant for your arrest."

"Arrest?" John yelled incredulously.

"On what charge?" Dr Jenkins sang with all the ridicule he could muster.

"Displacing a railway line and endangering the lives of passengers!"

Ethel Friar heard it all. The charge, the raised heated voices, the scuffle and the slamming of van doors. She sat up in bed with her hands tucked gleefully between her raised knees. For the first time in many months she felt a warm glow of security.

Robert Fulthorpe sat alone in the kitchen of his house watching the settling embers of a fire that had been kindled with twigs and wood and bits of stony coal picked from the heap. It had burned reluctantly, giving off a scant, smoky heat that was hardly sufficient to boil a kettle. It had warmed some water though. It had given the neutral liquid some bite and his wife and children drank a cup before bed to smother the hunger pangs until sleep dulled their craving. His own stomach rumbled incessantly and it seemed even louder in the quiet of the night. Without thinking he rubbed at it in a vain attempt to ease the noise of its displeasure. He looked down at his stiff leg that was stuck out, poker-like away from his body, and cursed its uselessness as he inspected his ragged trousers and limp, sweat stained shirt for signs of further degeneration. He felt the way they looked; worn out, tattered, a tired excuse for the real thing. He was thankful his fellow councillors could not see him. He dreaded the thought of them being able to view the reality of his means. It was unthinkable that their subtle derision of him could be confirmed. Yet at one time it had not mattered. He could stand among them in his precious, shiny blue suit and speak his mind. He had confidence; his voice carried authority and they listened in dutiful silence. But not now; something had gone from him, left him a wondering introvert, doubting his own thoughts and words and deeds. Since the derailment he had been a frightened man, scared of his own shadow, full of debilitating torment.

The rumpus started down the lane almost at the same time as the banging on his door and he went cold as the realization came to him. The night was suddenly laced with crying, swearing and hard, barked orders. He knew the cause of it immediately. His sleep had often been split asunder with dreams of it. The moment he had been expecting for weeks had arrived. Yet he was not afraid now. From somehow deep inside him, there issued a calm acceptance of his fate. He opened the door and limped back into the room without so much as a glance. His wife and children crept wide-eyed from their beds and stood crouching on the stairs at the sight of the policeman.

"Robert Frazer Fulthorpe?"

Fulthorpe nodded.

"Get dressed," he ordered. "You're under arrest."

Fulthorpe's wife let out a weird shriek of distress and the children sobbed and clung to her.

Fulthorpe stood straight and erect. His red, flabby face was proud and pompous. He turned to his wife. "Cissie, get me blue suit," he whispered.

He dressed carefully, changing into a clean shirt that was fractionally more sound that his old one and putting on a tie.

"Come on, come on. Hurry up," the policeman droned.

Fulthorpe buttoned his jacket. "I'm a councillor, you know," he said haughtily. "And a sidesman at the church."

The policeman was not impressed. His big hand gripped Fulthorpe's podgy arm. He gestured with his head. "Come on. Let's get goin'."

And, led by the policeman, Fulthorpe limped dejectedly away.

Farther up the Row Edward Sneed woke suddenly from his sleep and at first he couldn't tell what noise had disturbed him. It was quiet except for the nasal snore that came from Nellie but that was something he normally didn't hear. He lay in the darkness, staring sightlessly upward, listening intently. There was nothing; just a slow grunting from his wife and the warmth of her frail body beside him. Then he heard it again; a cry of anguish, a chilling voice cutting its way through the night. The sound of banging doors came to him and running feet and strange guttural orders. He sat up, blinking toward the window, his imagination swirling wildly. And then he knew. He was sure he knew the reason for it all. The shock of it stunned him for a moment then he silently leapt from the bed and stood at the window, screwing his eyes to the left to see down the lane. A lump came to his throat and his limbs trembled. It was as he thought. He could see them – uniforms, strangers and the milling, protesting villagers. They were working their way up the lane. He knew what they were about and with an overwhelming surge of regret he knew they would come for him. He turned away and lit a stump of candle that stood on a cracked saucer. He watched the dancing light swell and fill the tiny room with its feeble glow. Nellie slept on, her wrinkled face just visible among the bedclothes.

"They're comin', Nellie," he breathed. "They'll be comin' for me." His eyes filled with tears and he clasped his hands to his chest. "They'll take me away and lock me up and I won't see you. Not for a long time. I won't be here to see to you, hinny." He knelt beside her and shook his head. "What'll become of you, Nellie? How will you manage? If the lads were here you'd be all right. I'm sorry, bonny lass."

He put his head beside her for a moment and felt the tears chase themselves across his face. The thoughts of her left to random help were unbearable. She would waste away in an agony of unhappiness and, no matter what, it was a prospect he could not allow. He knew what he must do. There was no other choice. He returned to the window. They were getting closer and the noise of them getting louder. He picked up his pillow then gently stroked her rough hair. "Sleep well, Nellie," he whispered. "The lads will look after you."

He lowered the pillow slowly down but his arms locked with it an inch from her face. He was frozen, his mind a turmoil of indecision. It was a minute or more before he threw it savagely away. "I can't, Nellie," he sobbed. "I can't do it."

Downstairs a clenched fist thumped again and again at the door. Edward raised himself. He pulled on a pair of pants and a shirt. "They're here," he said softly. "Be good, Nellie."

He bent over and kissed her. She did not wake. He blew out the candle and with a wave in the darkness he wiped his eyes and clumped steadily down the stairs.

The lane was in pandemonium as Edward was led out. Tommy Nesbitt appeared as he passed. His face was white with shock and anger. There was a policeman at his door and another behind him. Ruth stumbled out after them and turned her face to the wall, her body heaving with uncontrollable grief.

"Ruth! Ruth!" Edward yelled as he was bundled past.

For a second she turned to the voice. "See to Nellie, Ruth," he begged. "Please! Please!"

He could not tell if she heard. She became lost among the crowd, wide-eyed from their sleep, screaming and crying in the shocked bewilderment.

They were grouped together at the bottom of the lane. There were seven of them in all lined up against the side of the Black Maria. Edward Sneed, Robert Fulthorpe, Tommy Nesbitt, Abe Jackson, Wilbur Forrest and two other young ones barely out of their teens.

Tommy looked around him. "Is this it?" he bawled. "Where's the rest? There was a hundred to choose from. Why us?"

"Quiet!" a policeman barked.

"It's that sod of a doctor," Jackson shouted. "The bastard shopped us."

"Quiet!" The order came again with savage menace.

The doors of the big Black Maria were opened and the prisoners hustled in. Inside the men could not believe their eyes. John Kinghorn sat forlornly in a corner handcuffed to an impassive constable. His shirt was torn and there was a sickly pallor to his face.

"Jesus – not you!" Tommy said with a high pitch of amazement.

John nodded. Then he gave a snort of mirthless amusement.

Tommy threw his head back and laughed and with the laughter came derision "Oh, Christ, no!" he said. "Is there no end to their stupidity?"

John suddenly imagined that perhaps there wasn't. And it frightened him.

13

The long, straight corridor had its brickwork freshly distempered in apple green. It gave off a pungent smell that was different from the rest of the prison and that fact was the only thing that registered with John Kinghorn; that and the crisp echo of his footsteps on the stone floor. He was used now to the barred windows and heavy studded doors that kept him from the outside world; to the silent warder who trod in his wake whenever he was allowed out of his cell; to the thick mess that passed as food and the vile brown liquid looking like tea but tasting of rancid fat. In two weeks he had become a different man. His anger had dissipated; the ignominity of his status no longer bothered him and the stiff coarse suit that went with it was almost comfortable. But his attitude had not come by chance. His first night in the cells at Gosforth Police Station had produced a fear in him that he had not thought possible. It was a claustrophobic terror, a frenzied panic nurtured on the thoughts of Ruth and the fact that he could not get to her, to help her; to engineer her recovery. The frustration in him sapped his strength and left him numb beneath his seething silence. Then there was the official charge at Newcastle and the imposing ugliness of Durham jail. It was ironic, he thought, how such a beautiful city could surround the awesome building. The sheer lunacy of the charge against him made him look forward to the trial. In his anger he was keen to see the law ridiculed with his innocence. But now he was different. The seven miners were undoubtedly guilty to some extent: he had seen them there among the frightened faces that fled from the terrible scene. Yet during the long hours he had to think and dissect his thoughts he realized he was as guilty as they. Everyone was to blame. All the upper classes who took their fine living as a birthright; all the complacent ostriches who pulled the strings of industry; all those who grew fat and content from the labour of their underlings. They were the guilty ones but their crime was within the law. It was only Ruth who made the thought of acquittal worthwhile. She was ill. She needed him. She was alone now. In one fell swoop she had lost the last of her loves and whatever the outcome of the trial it was unthinkable that he could lose her without a fight. Somehow he would persuade his father to lend him money. Somehow she would have the scant recompense she deserved.

He came to the end of the corridor. The warder behind him barked a quick order, "Left turn!"

He turned left into a corridor equally as long as the last. There were visitors, the warder said, when he came to his cell. "Highly irregular," he added. "Must have friends in high places," he said with cutting sarcasm. For a moment Ruth came to his mind but it was almost impossible to hope, so he walked now with a blank, careless automation.

"Halt!"

He stopped and the warder opened a door on his right. There were two men in the divided room. When John saw them he had to clench his teeth as a surge of emotion came from nowhere. They both stood with the solemnity of mourners. One was a stocky, distinguished, ageing man with bushy eyebrows and steel grey hair. The other was tall with a long neck and gangling limbs that had not been left in youth. It was William Fitzgerald Kinghorn and Roger Smythe.

John stood for a moment, drinking in memories yet somehow seeing them as strangers.

"John," his father whispered. "My God, you're thin."

From somewhere within him John managed to smile. He controlled the urge to turn and run and hide himself away from them. "You look fit, father – and you, Roger, all brown and healthy looking. Too much of that spa water gives you wind, you know."

The pair of them looked sheepishly at each other and forced a nervous laugh. Then his father frowned.

"Christ Almighty, John, this is a fine how-do-you-do," he said in a wavering voice. "Your mother's ill with it, you know. It's been like bedlam. The phone goes every minute. Friends and damn' newspaper men."

"Tell her I'm sorry."

"Sorry!" his father exploded. "For what?" He pushed his head forward. "You're not guilty, are you? I mean you weren't really mixed up with those blasted ignorant miners – those rogues who almost killed a train load of people."

"Yes I am. No I wasn't."

Smythe hung his head. His father blinked stupidly. "What sort of tomfool talk is that. Did you help to crash that damn' train?"

John sighed heavily. "No," he growled.

His father looked relieved. He smiled and crossed his arms in front of him. "That's better. I knew it. You've been a fool, John. You should have never left home. You were made for better things. Now look – I've been in touch with Sir Rupert Charnley, he's agreed to defend you. You'll be free and clear in a fortnight. He's coming up . . ."

"Tell him not to come."

"What!"

"Don't be an idiot, John," Smythe whispered. "He's the best money can buy."

John shook his head. "I don't want him – unless of course you've hired his services for us all."

"All?" his father snapped. "Who's all?"

"The miners who were charged with me."

His father closed his eyes as though he couldn't believe what was happening. "John," he sang, "John, you're my son. It's you I'm interested in. It's you I want to see clear of this awful mess. I'm not paying good money to help ragged, idle criminals."

"Then help me, father. I need some money. There's a girl at Bolam, the pit village near Allington. She means a lot to me, father. She's got tuberculosis. She needs help – treatment at a sanatorium. She's got to live. Save your money – forget Charnley. I'm innocent, I'll get off anyway, but I need you to help her."

His father gazed sullenly at him and then at Smythe as though to ask "Is he mad?" He turned back to his son. His voice was dry and clear. "John, you are talking rubbish. This damn' prison has twisted your senses. Do you really expect me to fork out cash and send a common pit woman to a sanatorium. There would be a queue a mile long at my door if I did that. For Christ's sake pull yourself together, man. I'm not a charitable organization."

John felt his panic returning. "Please father," he begged. "I'll pay you back somehow. She means more to me than anything in the world. You've got to help her. You don't know her, you see – if you did you'd find her something special."

"I'm sorry, John," his father snapped with finality. "This is ridiculous. I don't think we have much more to say to each other. Perhaps after the trial when you can breathe some decent air, you'll come to your senses. I bear no grudge. You're welcome back home at anytime."

John stared at him for a moment and then he turned and ambled toward the door. He knew it was useless to labour the point until he was free.

"Goodbye and good luck, old chap," Smythe said with an insipid smile. "See you in the dock!"

"Enjoy it, won't you," John said with bitter amusement. "And thanks for the letter."

Smythe frowned. "I'm sorry, John. I really am. I've been so busy."

"Haven't we all," John muttered as the warder followed him into the long, green corridor.

It was the last day of June when the trial took place at Newcastle Assizes. The court was packed and the atmosphere almost crackled with expected drama. All eight of them pleaded not guilty and they listened in nervous silence to reports by Railway officials and various policemen. Edward Sneed looked bewildered. Robert Fulthorpe sat stiffly upright, his double chin pulled hard against the collar of his shirt. John listened intently to every word. He was outwardly calm but there was a constant tremble deep inside him that he could not control. The others were scared, their eyes wide and round, their faces ashen with their ordeal.

They had their say. Each one of the miners admitted that they were there but that there were many others who were involved. No-one could recall or chose to name the men who actually loosened the rail and lifted it out. John told his story in exact detail but it was Ethel Friar who rocked the proceedings. Calmly she picked out Kenneth Tilmouth from a selection of photographs and gave evidence of his visits to Plessey House. She identified the seven miners as some of those she had seen immediately after the derailment. The court was in an uproar. John could not believe his own ears. He tried in vain to shrink away from it. He had told the truth but her version sounded better. There was more logic to it. It seemed somehow easier to accept. He fixed his gaze on her. She was smug, at ease, enjoying every minute. And he hated her for it.

That night he came to terms with his fate. In the eyes of the law all eight of them were guilty. He knew it. He had sensed it. He could see it on the faces of the jurors. They had impassive faces, but their eyes were cold and stared disapprovingly at them. It was the same look on his father, on Smythe, Jenkins and Tomlinson. They knew now that he was guilty and during the long sleepless night he accepted the inevitable. At last he was one of them and for all his love of Ruth he drew some pride from the fact that they shared a common destiny.

The next day the judge, a diminutive, spectacled man began his summing up. His voice was shrill yet grave as he began to speak amid a straining silence: "Gentlemen of the jury, you have heard the evidence presented to you appertaining to the most heinous of crimes, that of the deliberate derailment of the express train from Edinburgh to London, known as the Flying Scotsman.

"I do not need to elucidate further on the potential carnage this act could have caused had the train not been travelling uncommonly slowly at the time when it came to grief. The fact that it was travelling cautiously, the driver being forewarned of possible trouble, is the one and only reason for the mercifully minor injury list. Let not this fact deter you from a just decision, for the situation, but for the grace of God, could have been one where literally hundreds of men, women and children perished among the wreckage of the aforementioned train and the proceedings here today could have been of an even more serious nature. It is not a flight of fancy that the incident in question could have resulted in the biggest mass murder in the history of this land.

"There before you are Thomas Nesbitt, Robert Frazer Fulthorpe, Edward Sneed, Wilbur Forrest, Abraham Jackson, Thomas Joseph Wilkinson, Edmund Collington and Dr John Kinghorn. All but the last mentioned are miners residing at Bolam Colliery near Allington. These miners, it has been shown by the Crown, were among others at a meeting prior to the derailment and by their own testimony were at the scene of the derailment. All have stated to varying degrees some involvement and all have stated that the intention was not to derail the express train but an expected goods train. And furthermore that their act was not premeditated or designed to cause actual bodily harm to anyone. This point I fail to comprehend as even the goods train would have been manned by flesh and blood mortals equally as vulnerable and innocent as the passengers and crew aboard the Flying Scotsman.

"Your task is not to judge the merits or otherwise of their intentions. You must judge on the evidence presented to you whether these men derailed the Flying Scotsman on May 10th 1926 by the deliberate act of removing a portion of the track. If you decide that this was so you must find them guilty as charged. You can only find them not guilty if in your deliberations you come to the conclusion that the evidence you have heard is unfounded and completely without substance.

"The last member of the accused, namely Dr John Kinghorn, may by his testimony and by the eminent profession which is attached to his name lead you to think that he cannot be directly involved with such men or so terrible a crime. I would however remind you that the evidence brought against him, which although circumstantial, appears conclusive. He has admitted himself of his involvement in the riot at Newcastle upon Tyne on May 8th 1926, where the severity of the rioters prompted police to baton charge in order to bring order to those present. You must remember the evidence of P.C. Reynolds who interviewed the accused regarding injuries he sustained during the riot. You must decide whether the accused was telling the truth when he stated his innocence of any agitation and merely got 'caught up', as he said, in the riot during an attempt to administer first-aid as his profession dictated. Furthermore it has been stated that Kenneth Frederick Tilmouth, a known communist from London, visited Bolam on several occasions and in fact visited Dr Kinghorn a week before the derailment and also it has been said in evidence that he visited Dr Kinghorn only an hour or so before the actual crime was committed. I cannot bring myself to believe Dr Kinghorn's explanation, I can only believe that their meetings were for much darker purposes. There are two other significant factors you must consider carefully. It has been given in evidence that prior to the derailment Dr Kinghorn was overheard to say 'Can they block the line and cause a crash'. The obvious connotation of this statement has been vehemently denied by the accused but there is no doubt that it was said and you must decide in what context it was uttered. The last and probably the most important evidence regarding this man is his actual presence at the scene of the crime. Again he has denied his direct involvement by stating that he was there in an attempt to halt the removal of the track and not assist in it. The fact that he administered first aid to the injured is irrelevant. You must decide, based on the evidence presented to you, his guilt or otherwise. For even those who you may deem to have acted in a supervisory manner only and not actually laid a hand on the rail or the instruments used in removing it must be as guilty as those who physically administered the removal, thus causing the train to leave the rails and crash sideways to the ground.

"You may now retire and consider your verdict."

The silence that gripped the courtroom continued for a second or two. It was a stunned silence as though everyone knew without a doubt the outcome. John watched the jurors file slowly out. His pulse raced as he turned his head to the heavy buzz of conversation that broke out among the public. His father sat forward with his head in his hands. Smythe had a glassy stare of amazement. The village women wept. His seven colleagues looked as though they were about to vomit.

It took the jury only half an hour to find them all guilty and the judge then pronounced sentence.

"Edmund Collington, Thomas Joseph Wilkinson, Wilbur Forrest, you are sentenced to four years imprisonment. Abraham Jackson, Robert Frazer Fulthorpe, you are sentenced to six years imprisonment. Thomas Nesbitt, Edward Sneed, John Kinghorn, you are sentenced to eight years imprisonment."

The court erupted. Women shrieked and fainted. Others sat in a shocked daze. There were angry cries from the men. It took ten minutes to restore order. Finally the prisoners were led away and John felt tears burning at his eyes: not for himself or his predicament but for the men who were with him. Their pathetic lives had known nothing but want and because of that want they had transgressed to an even lower order of things. He felt honoured that he was with them; they were men of a greater quality than his own friends. Only Ruth caused him to look back. His father was standing watching him. Their eyes met for a second and he silently pleaded for him to understand. Then he was back to bars and brick walls and footsteps on a stone floor.

It was late when Dr Jenkins arrived home with Ethel. The sun was low in the sky and its redness spread a warm peace over the ending day. The air was still and carried the heavy scent of lush greenery. There was a strange calmness to the evening, a hushed splendour as though the blushing, swollen orb was setting for the last time. Dr Jenkins was subdued, his face locked in a frown. Ethel stepped out of the car but said nothing. They had spoken little on the journey home.

She was waiting for him in the study after he returned from the garage. He looked at her, unsure of her broad smile. "Let me take your coat," she said soothingly.

Stiffly he turned and allowed her to pull it from his arms. "There now," she whispered. "I'll get you a little drink."

He nodded dumbly and sat down, his mind far away on other things.

"No, don't sit there Bob," she purred. "Play me something."

He walked slowly to the pianola and fitted the "Träumerei" roll and as the gentle notes issued forth she placed a glass of whisky near him then put her hands lightly on his shoulders. She let them slide smoothly up to his neck and around his chin.

"It's all over, Bob," she whispered. "At last it's all over."

Jenkins nodded. His voice was a hoarse growl of regret. "It's damned quiet without him. Didn't you sense that when you came in?"

Ethel smiled to herself. "I told the truth Bob. I could do no other."

"Aye," he said vaguely. "I suppose you did." He shook his head. "He was a good doctor, Ethel. Keen as mustard. I told him not to get involved. But he wouldn't listen. I could have told him that old Nellie Sneed would never walk you know, but he wouldn't have believed me. He was so damned keen. I just let him go."

"Yes Bob, I know. Keep playing for me. It's so lovely."

She left him at the pianola and went upstairs. Within her was a controlled yet wild elation; a continuum of orgasmic delight that held her trancelike in its embrace. But there was one last thing she had to do. The young doctor was gone and after all the years she had revenged her husband. It was a lot for one day, but there was just one little thing she still had to do and she could relax completely and savour her victory. She bent down and rolled up the multicoloured mat that lay at the foot of John's bed and carried it downstairs. There was a garden fire out at the back. It was a large one that had been smouldering for weeks. She heaved the mat onto it and watched for a moment as its weight disturbed the hot pile and sent sparks dancing upward in the current of heated air. She gave a sigh of satisfaction and returned to the house.

The music on the roll was almost finished and Dr Jenkins turned his dazed face to her when she came back to his side. He had drunk his whisky.

"He was a good doctor," he said solemnly.

Ethel smiled. "Of course he was . . . but just not right for you and your friends."

Jenkins brow tightened. "I need another drink."

Ethel stroked his hair. "No, Bob," she whispered gently. "No more tonight. It's time for bed I think. Are you ready for bed, Bob?"

Dr Jenkins swallowed hard. For a second he stared in disbelief, then took her hand and kissed it.

"Come on then," she breathed. "It's been a long, long day."

Ruth Nesbitt poked at the smoky fire. For all the heat of the summer's day she was cold and needed its warmth. There was little wind to draw it and the clouds of fumes billowed out into the room, aggravating her cough until she was forced to sit down and regain her feeble strength. She was weak from her illness and the news of the outcome of the trial had drained from her the last drop of emotion. She had staggered around in a dream, her weary mind unable to accept or absorb any more. Life was a painful ordeal to her and she became suspicious of every moment that passed that did not bring further suffering. Her whole being was now a blank aching sanctuary for memories that did not even stir a reaction within her. Yet for all her troubles she had dragged herself to the house next door and fought to dress and clean Nellie Sneed and sometimes force some food into her mouth. Nellie, in her bewildered panic, summoned the strength of three and Ruth was left coughing and exhausted while her neighbour constantly wailed in her confusion.

At last her breathing came somewhat near normal and the prickling irritation in her chest subsided. She sank back in the rocking chair and closed her eyes.

Her rest was shortlived. Outside in the lane she heard a cheerful whistling and she knew even before the door latch rattled that it was Raymond Bennett, the collector from Goldsteins. It wasn't long before his cheery, oily face poked around the door. "Aye, aye," he shouted.

"Come in, Ramey," she said.

His flash smile changed immediately to a soft, understanding one. "Hello Ruth. Y've heard the news, then?"

She nodded.

"I'm sorry hinny. It's, it's . . ." He shrugged. "It's rotten awful."

She looked away and coughed again, gently.

"How's Nellie, Ruth?"

Ruth shook her head. "Just the same."

He brightened. "I've come for her, you know. I'm takin' her."

Ruth frowned. "Takin' her where?"

"Home – where else?" he yelled.

"Home?" she said with weak puzzlement.

"Aye. There's only mam and me, you know. It's not much, two rooms and a kitchen, but at least she'll be looked after and it'll save you, hinny." He puffed out his chest and winked. "She knows me, she's canny with me. You know that, Ruth." He was pleased with himself. He had an excitement that parried with his overall regret at their plight. "Mam says she can come . . ." He shrugged. ". . . so I'll take her. I've got old Goldstein's car down the lane. Don't ask me how, but I've got it."

Ruth felt a rare surge of pleasure. "Oh that's grand, Ramey. That's grand of you."

Raymond beamed. "She needs a son," he said. He nodded to the wall. "Give us a hand to pack her things, will you, Ruth. I've brought a case with me."

She eased herself to her feet. "Of course I will."

Within an hour Nellie was gone. Her tiny face glowed with delight and her eyes sparkled as Raymond carried her down the lane. For the first time in a month she was calm and happy. Perhaps somewhere in her befuddled mind she remembered that Raymond always promised to take her away.

Ruth waved at the car until it was out of sight and then as the noise of its engine faded to nothing an overpowering feeling of loneliness took hold of her. She walked unsteadily back to the house and slumped down in the rocking chair. She gazed for a long time at the faded photograph of her mother and she cried, without noise, letting the tears silently flow as she felt the need of her mother's comfort more than ever before.

The knock at the door was light, almost a mouselike tap, and she did not hear it. Then it came again, louder and more urgent.

"Come in," she said in a wavering voice.

They came in, their noses wrinkled from the smell of the ash closets, their eyes wide with gazing as though they had entered Aladdin's cave.

Ruth knew the leading man immediately. She could see John in him. It was his father.

He could not disguise his dislike of the visit but he forced some semblance of pleasantness to his face. "Miss . . . er, Nesbitt?"

She nodded.

"I'm John's . . ."

"You're his father."

His lips thinned. "Yes . . . yes I am and this is Dr Smythe." He sagged and frowned at his companion, trying in that one gesture to sum up both a confirmation of her condition and convince himself of his son's attachment.

"Are you well enough to travel?" Smythe asked.

She was puzzled. "Travel? Travel where?"

Kinghorn slipped his hands into his jacket pockets. He took a deep breath and seemed to tuck his chin inside his shirt collar. "You're ill, Miss Nesbitt, and it appears that my son had certain plans for you. Now of course . . ." His shoulders moved and his voice became strained. "Now he can no longer carry them out." He paused and then the words came positively as though he could not wait to be free of them. "John's friend, Dr Smythe here, is accompanying a patient to a sanatorium the day after tomorrow. If you are willing you can join them and stay at the sanatorium until . . . well, let us look on the bright side . . . until you are cured." He gave a pained smile. "Well – what do you say?"

Ruth said nothing. She closed her eyes as a sweet joy flooded her mind. She could find no words, only more tears.

Kinghorn nodded. "You will have nothing to pay and the journey to Switzerland has already been arranged."

"Switzerland," she whispered weakly.

"The best there is. Dr Desonay has had marvellous results," Smythe added. "You're a very lucky girl."

She packed her few things quietly, almost fearful of the excitement that pounded within her. Everything she possessed went into a small battered suitcase. Her few clothes, the little pot-pourri, the small bottle of blue-coloured scent that she had used so sparingly. Finally, she was ready. She had no fear of their rich, polished ways. John had seen to that and she had hope now that someday there would be more of her life spent with him.

The two men rose from their stools. They smiled, relieved to be on their way, and Smythe took her case. "Come along then," Kinghorn said softly.

She took one last look around the room and for a second she saw it crowded and noisy with her father and brothers. She walked over to the wall and took down the photograph of her mother and clutching it to her breast she followed them out into the lane and into the sunshine.

Epilogue

The General Strike of 1926 lasted only nine days but the miners of Britain carried on their struggle for seven months. It was not until the end of November that they accepted the terms proposed by the coal owners. Hunger had weakened their resistance. The onset of a cold, gloomy winter without coal or food or the scant comforts that their paltry wages could bring forced them into submission. They returned to the pits and worked for less money, longer hours and without any agreement on a national minimum wage.

The miners and their families constituted more than ten per cent of the population of Britain and for seven long months their abject poverty was largely ignored by those not directly involved. The cost, apart from the human suffering, was great. Over twenty million tons of coal and one million tons of coke were imported. Foreign coal contracts were slow to return and some never did. The continued use of cheap mining labour made the advance of mechanisation a luxury the coal owners were not prepared to finance. And so with the year drawing to its close and Christmas just around the corner, a unique period in British history came to an end. For a while there was the real possibility of a full-blooded revolution that would have changed the life style of everyone in this country for generations to come. It is said that self-preservation is the strongest of the instincts. To preserve a way of life, let alone better it, can lead men to desperate measures. Such things happened in 1926.

And what of the miners who derailed the Flying Scotsman? Dr John Kinghorn never existed nor did the mining village of Bolam and its inhabitants but there were men driven to commit this crime. They lived and some still live. They were jailed just about as far away from the North East as possible, at Maidstone in fact. Three were released after two years; two after three years and the remaining three tasted freedom just before Christmas 1929. To the law they were criminals. To those who knew their plight they were decent men gasping to preserve what little they had against an Establishment which couldn't care less if they had anything at all.